ON THE DARKENING GREEN

Books by Jerome Charyn

ON THE DARKENING GREEN

ONCE UPON A DROSHKY

Jerome Charyn

ON THE DARKENING GREEN

McGraw-Hill Book Company

New York   Toronto   London

This book is for Crazy and Vicki.
And the boys.

There is nothing less excusable than war and the appeal to national hatreds. But once war has come, it is both cowardly and useless to try to stand on one side under the pretext that one is not responsible. It is both impossible and immoral to judge an event from outside. One keeps the right to hold this absurd misfortune in contempt only by remaining inside it.

CAMUS

"But you can't refuse to fight, Ferdinand! Only cowards and madmen refuse to fight when their country is in danger...."

"Then long live all cowards and madmen! Or rather, may it be the cowards and madmen who survive! Look, Lola, can you remember the name of any one of the soldiers who were killed in the Hundred Years' War? Have you ever tried to find out one single name among them all? No, you can't; you've never tried, have you? To you they're all anonymous, unknown and less important than the least atom in this paperweight on the table in front of you, less important than the food your bowels digested yesterday. You can see that they died for nothing. For nothing at all, the idiots! I swear that's true; you can see that it is. Only life itself is of any importance. Ten thousand years hence I bet you that this war, all-important as it seems to us now, will be completely forgotten. Possibly a dozen or so learned men may wrangle about it occasionally, and about the dates of the chief hecatombs for which it was famous. Up to the present time that is all that Humanity has ever succeeded in finding memorable about itself, after a few centuries have gone by, or a few years, or even after a few hours.... I don't believe in the future, Lola."

CÉLINE

PART ONE

1

Father Finnocchino canvassed the apartments on both sides of the court at least three times, but he did not have much success with the Catholic boys in the building. He left with only one recruit: Crazy Bemelman. Crazy was the janitor's boy, and his mother believed in witches, talismans, and all sorts of demons, and she worshiped the "black crow" with the torn cassock, even though he smoked Lucky Strikes. Even without his mother's motives, Crazy was a likely candidate for Saint Elizabeth's. Everybody knew that half the boys there were orphans, and that Father Finnocchino kept a whole battalion of hunchbacks, dwarfs, and gnomes behind the rotting walls. Crazy belonged. Father Finnocchino upbraided all his parishioners in our building. They gave him bread for the dwarfs, but they still preferred to send their sons to P.S. 187. In retaliation, Father Finnocchino deposited lumps of moldy

3

tobacco on every floor, and sought new ways for recruiting the boys in the building. He knew that he could gain an inroad on the boys at Sunday School. In the midst of explaining the Sacraments, he would hurl anathemas at the principal of the public school, and at every landlord who owned a building on Cabrini Boulevard. He would talk about the band he was going to form at Saint Elizabeth's, and even promised to bring over one of the hunchbacks whom he had taught to play the saxophone. And every Thursday night after vespers he put on a pair of ancient sneakers and played basketball with the boys at the recreation hall, and, as I am told, even passed out a few Lucky Strikes.

Father Finnocchino seemed to be winning over the other boys, but he couldn't do a thing with me. Unfortunately for both of us, I had never been baptized, and so, I wasn't around when he gave out the Lucky Strikes, and I had to hear about the hunchbacked saxophone player from secondhand sources. Most of my uncles and all of my aunts were extremely anxious about the condition of my soul. To the Lapucci clan, which practically controlled Third Avenue and was quickly closing in on all four sides of Crotona Park, my father was an outlaw who had abandoned the Bronx and now lived with bankers and brokers "on top of the hill." My uncles hated priests and politicians with equal vehemence, but my aunt Giuseppina, the *"capo-mafia"* of all the Lapuccis, forced them to conspire with Father Finnocchino. Surrounded by dwarfs and dingbats, they sat in Saint Elizabeth's rapidly sinking cellar and worked out elaborate stratagems for capturing my delinquent soul. But in spite of their secret meetings, my father won the tug-of-war, and my soul remained intact.

Even at P.S. 187 I was always exempted whenever I broke an inkwell or came to school without a tie, and I received an extra gold star every time I completed a routine assignment, but if Howie Rosenthal brought in pictures of the *Niña*, the

4

Pinta, and the *Santa Maria,* or charted Magellan's voyage on the blackboard, the most he could expect for it was a silver star with five shriveled points. My father was Chairman of the English Department at George Washington High School, and since most of the boys and girls at P.S. 187 were eventually shipped off to G.W., I suppose the principal wanted to remain on my father's good side. I did not cherish the gold stars: in fact, I tried to trade them all for one miserable top with a chipped body and a broken point, and when the deal fell through, I offered to give them away. I had no takers. Even Howie despised the gold stars, once they had been awarded to me. And so, I pasted them in crooked rows to the back of my notebook, and when the rows began to overflow, I would paste one star on top of the other.

For seven cents I could buy a peanut butter sandwich and a bowl of tomato soup, but Howie Rosenthal was always on patrol outside the lunchroom, and whenever I tried to pass, one of his lieutenants would challenge me and search my pockets. So I saved the seven cents and made my own peanut butter sandwiches. Most of the fifth and sixth graders played punch ball in the school yard, but even without the stigmata of the gold stars, I don't think that I would have been chosen for any of the games. A bout with bronchial pneumonia when I was seven had left me with a permanently scarred lung, and I'm sure that I would have collapsed on the spot had I tried to run around the bases. Also, my fist was rather puny, and I never had much luck punching the ball. I always fouled out.

Sometimes I would sit in the yard with the peanut butter sandwich balanced on one knee and imagine myself captaining a phantom punch ball team, ordering my men to defend their bases, punching balls in every direction with an iron fist—but the shouts of the fifth and sixth grade players on the field would soon scatter my phantom team, and I would fling the sandwich into one of the cans and walk out of the yard. Then

5

I would walk over to the newsstand on Fort Washington Avenue and buy the latest issue of *Dime Detective*, or if I felt particularly bold, I might walk all the way down to Broadway and stand in front of Saint Elizabeth's.

The building was six stories high and its wooden walls were pocked with enormous holes, but its narrow windows and sinking foundation gave it a curious, diminutive aspect, and it always seemed to me that this was a perfect place for dwarfs. I would keep circling the building, and pay special attention to the backyard, but I never once saw the slightest sign of a humped back or a pint-sized head. PWA workers were constructing a playground across the street, and I had been told that the workers already had their next project planned. They would simply move their sledgehammers and bulldozers across the street, demolish Saint Elizabeth's, and lay the foundation for the largest swimming pool in Washington Heights.

I suppose I should have glared at the workers and warned them that I would give up my life to defend Saint Elizabeth's, but I looked at the sledgehammers and the bulldozers longingly, almost with lust. I wanted the bulldozers to crash through the walls and locate the hunchbacks and the dwarfs. I wanted to uncover their lairs and weed them out. Then, with the PWA workers behind me, I would make them all perform for me. Perhaps the hunchbacks would shake their crooked spines and form a conga line, and the dwarfs might form tunnels with their outstretched arms and permit the hunchbacks to pass through only when I signaled to them. But, in the midst of my triumph, I would invariably recall that lunch was long over, and abandoning the hunchbacks and the dwarfs, I rushed back to P.S. 187.

Nobody could say for sure what time Father Finnocchino dismissed the boys at Saint Elizabeth's, but whenever I strayed too long in Gristede's selecting grapefruits for my father, I would usually find Crazy Bemelman waiting for me in our

6

court, his cap pistols tucked under his belt. I don't know where Crazy acquired his concepts of banditry. Maybe in his truncated mind he saw himself as Black Bart lying in wait for the Wells Fargo Express. But in whatever form I appeared to him, there was nothing fanciful about the tribute he expected from me. If I didn't hand over one of the grapefruits or a jar of Gristede's wild blackberry jam, he was prepared to fracture my skull with both of his pistol butts. And I wasn't the only one whom Crazy waylaid. Crazy was the scourge of Cabrini Boulevard. None of the courts was safe with him around. Notes were sent to Father Finnocchino, but when Crazy's tribute kept mounting, some of us began to believe that Father Finnocchino was actually egging him on.

Finally Crazy's mother took action. When she saw that paddling him and twisting his ears only hardened him and made him more of a bandit, she entered Crazy's private world for a moment, pinned a Buck Jones badge on his enormous chest, and kept telling him that all members of the Buck Jones Rangers were sworn under the most sacred oaths to uphold the law. It worked for a while. Crazy become the protector of the court, and with his pistols drawn, he would escort us to the elevator. But unfortunately, Crazy was always a whimsical ranger, and once or twice a week he would throw his handkerchief over his nose and demand tribute again. So my father's grapefruits were never really safe, and more often than not, I had the grapefruits delivered. Frannie Faye, the Gristede delivery boy, never appealed to Crazy. He had wartlike shoulders and crisp, bell-shaped ears, and even on the days that Crazy wore the handkerchief over his nose, he always let Frannie through.

And so, by staying away from Gristede's and running home right after school, I usually avoided direct contact with Crazy. But by the time I poured some Grape Nuts into a bowl and searched through the shelves for the books that my father

7

had asked me to read, I could already hear Crazy romping in the court. When I turned aside one of the blinds, I could see his knickers hitched over his knees and his Buck Jones badge socking against his chest. No matter how expertly I maneuvered the blinds, Crazy could make out the tip of my nose or one of my eyes, and he would shout up, "Nick, Nick the Prick," and I would immediately retreat behind the stove.

Don't think I tortured myself over Crazy's badge. I would not have joined the Buck Jones Rangers, even had my life depended on it. Crazy was over twelve, and running back and forth between the walls of the court for hours at a time, with a tin badge for a companion and a pair of cap pistols that never worked, was far from my ideal. And yet, coming back from school day after day, knowing that my father's instructions would invariably be tacked to the bulletin board—"Nicky, when you have the time, go over the first three chapters of *The Turn of the Screw*"—and that I would be tested on what I had read as soon as my father came home, how can anyone blame me if, at times, I wanted to share some of Crazy's abandon, and be free to run between the crooked poles of the awning, waylay friends and escort enemies to the elevator, collect pounds of tribute, jeer at Aldo the doorman, and shout obscene names at little freaks on the fourth floor?

There were no tortures in store for me if the assignments were incomplete or the chapters were shoddily read. In fact, there was usually a charlotte russe waiting for me inside my father's book bag, and not as an enticement or a reward. But somehow, I could always see the disappointment etched on my father's narrow face if I misinterpreted one of Pindar's odes or missed any of the shenanigans in the *Golden Ass*, and the charlotte russe could never quite manage to cancel out that look.

I always felt a little overpowered the minute I came near the living room or my father's den. I'm sure now that his pipe racks and book cases and other paraphernalia were never really plagued by demons, as I believed for years and years, but even at the age of eleven I felt that his rows of pipes resented my intrusion and were ready to conspire against me; so I avoided the living room and the den, especially when my father wasn't around. I felt much safer in the kitchen. I had stocked the shelves with jars of condiments and spices and had painted the woodwork and the window sill. I ruled the kitchen with an iron hand. I refused to let my father keep his pipe cleaners on any of my shelves, or post pictures of James Joyce and Virginia Woolf on my walls. He was rarely allowed inside the kitchen. Whenever he wanted a glass of buttermilk or some cashews, I brought them out to him. He would sit in the den with the buttermilk beside him, and as soon as he heard my footfalls and felt certain that I was within earshot, he would complain bitterly to himself. "Dispossessed," he would say. "By my own tenant. Ungrateful boy. I'll sue." Then thinking that I might have strayed back to the kitchen, he would begin to shout. "Nicky, more buttermilk. Give the prisonor his due. Next time I'll know. What else can you expect from one of Katz's brats?"

Before I was three my father had already enrolled me in Mrs. Katzenheimer's nursery school on Fort Washington Avenue, and for the next two years I spent most of my time there. My father delivered me to Mrs. Katzenheimer every morning, and picked me up after five. I don't remember very much about my first year at Mrs. Katzenheimer's. I think I built mud pies and fell in love with a brutish little girl named Nellie or Naomi who made me eat my own mud pies and who might have been Mrs. Katzenheimer's niece. By the time I was four I traveled alone to and from Mrs. Katzenheimer's and even picked out an occasional grapefruit for my father at Gristede's. I had my own key, and looped through a leather thong, it hung boldly from my neck. I was always in mortal

9

fear that the thong would break and I would lose the key and be locked out forever and ever until my father came home and saw me cowering near the door. So I constantly kept one hand inside my shirt, clutching the key. But there were worse terrors waiting for me inside the door. I was convinced that horrible little creatures who belched freely and farted and pinched little boys' behinds had invaded our living room and were lurking behind the sofa and the bookshelves and inside the cavernous bowls of my father's prize pipes. I could hear the bookshelves rattle and the pipe stems cough. The little bastards never attacked when my father was around, only when I was alone. I called them "beezlebugs." At first I tried barricading myself in the bathroom, but they crawled under the door and surrounded the toilet seat. The beezlebugs stayed clear of the kitchen. They might have been allergic to kitchen odors, or perhaps they considered the kitchen some sort of sacred grounds. Whatever the reason, they never attacked. Once inside the kitchen, I taunted them constantly: squeezing my buttocks brazenly, I would offer them either cheek. After peeing in the sink, I would post several metal soldiers near the door. I knew even then that in actual combat my soldiers would have been no match for the beezlebugs, who, after all, fought without rules and conventions. But standing near the door, they still provided some feeling of safety, and besides, they made excellent bowling pins. When I first found out that the beezlebugs had besieged the living room, I ordered my father to move my toy chest into the kitchen, and after rummaging through my immy bag for five or six steelies, I would squat near the window and try to bowl over all my guards. Those that landed outside the kitchen I abandoned forever.

My father often claimed that I had been "kitchen-trained" at Mrs. Katzenheimer's. It's true that most of Mrs. Katzenheimer's charges were girls, and that I learned how to make mud pies, paper dolls, and doilies along with them, but I don't

10

recall ever doing any work in Mrs. Katzenheimer's kitchen. Somewhere along the way I grew tired of bumping off my own guards. After putting them to rest permanently at the bottom of my toy chest, I must have begun doing some active exploring under the sink and inside the cabinets. By the time I was six, I was already frying eggs for my father and experimenting with tapioca pudding and lentil soup. Perhaps my puddings and soups were able to exorcise the beezlebugs, because soon after that, they began to retreat. Boys of six aren't supposed to believe in phantoms, not even diminutive ones that are fond of belching, farting, and pinching behinds. Using some extra special will power I was able to convince myself that the beezlebugs couldn't really exist. Yet the pipe racks and the bookshelves still seemed in some way haunted, as if the beezlebugs, once invoked and called into being, could never be permanently grounded. And so, eight, nine, or ten, the kitchen was the place for me.

My father and I did very little entertaining, but we were not completely stranded. Crazy Bemelman had a way of showing up quite often around suppertime. He was always on some sort of official mission for Father Finnocchino, and it usually involved collecting money for the orphans at Saint Elizabeth's. After surrendering a few pennies, my father would invite him in. Crazy was on his best behavior during his visits. He even offered to rent out his Buck Jones badge at the reasonable rate of a penny a day, and was very gracious about the whole thing when I declined his offer.

Crazy's mother worshiped her own peculiar trinity: Father Finnocchino, Father Coughlin, and FDR. She tolerated her husband, Bemelman the janitor, a kindly man with an enormous paunch, but she never allowed him to get in the way of her three gods. As much as she adored the President and her parish priest, her gospel came from Father Coughlin. She was an active member of Father Coughlin's Radio League of the Little Flower and listened religiously to all his broadcasts. While Crazy broke his ass collecting an occasional penny for Saint Elizabeth's, his mother badgered the entire neighborhood and brought in nickels and dimes for the Shrine of the Little Flower. She kept collection boxes in every store.

Crazy's mother could talk for hours about the evils of the gold standard, and she convinced most of us, right from the start, that the world, under gold, was coming to an end. Of course, when she began talking about international Jewish conspiracies and claimed that the Elders of Zion were keeping the world on a diet of gold, she lost quite a few followers, but she was never politic in that way, and ignoring the dwindling numbers, she kept denouncing the Jews. She told us all that Roosevelt, guided by the Holy Ghost, was forcing the Elders underground and would soon load the world with silver. "The New Deal," she would say, her eyes alive with visions of freely floating silver, "is Christ's Deal," and even I would drop a nickel inside her collection box. But when Father Coughlin's feelings towards FDR began to cool, and Mrs. Bemelman began seeing for herself that the President was doing nothing to help the silver supporters, she withdrew for a week, and then came out cursing Roosevelt as a false messiah, a stooge for the Elders of Zion. The New Deal was now the "Black Deal."

Crazy's mother tried to enlist Father Finnocchino, but he had never cared for Father Coughlin or concerned himself with the battle over silver and gold. Besides, he had troubles of his own. The fire inspectors were ready to condemn Saint Elizabeth's, and the PWA workers, their bulldozers poised, were quickly closing in. Complaints had also been made that the food served in the refectory was tainted, that one of the dwarfs had died from botulism, and that hordes of rats had been seen in the backyard. Crazy's mother put one collection box aside for Saint Elizabeth's, but when Father Finnocchino refused to let her establish headquarters for her newly formed

12

Followers of the Little Flower in his tiny, beetle-laden auditorium, she slowly began to abandon all his causes, and in protest, she withdrew Crazy from Saint Elizabeth's and enrolled him at P.S. 187. But Crazy never showed up. I don't think she ever suspected that Crazy, once his satchel was packed, headed straight for Saint Elizabeth's. And when Father Finnocchino, trying desperately to raise money for Saint Elizabeth's upkeep, decided to hold a dance for boys and girls under twelve and rented the gymnasium at P.S. 187 for the occasion, it was Crazy who folded back the basketball nets and put up most of the decorations, all behind his mother's back.

If it had been just for the dance, I never would have bothered inviting Sharon Lipsky, the prettiest girl in my class. I hated dances, but Father Finnocchino had promised that his hunchbacks and dwarfs would be performing there. They were the main attraction. Everybody wanted to see Father Finnocchino's army of hunchbacks and dwarfs wielding saxophones and clarinets. I wasn't terribly annoyed when Howie Rosenthal told me, two days before the dance, that *he* was taking Sharon Lipsky, not me, and that if I tried to squawk, he would puncture both my balls. So I left Sharon to Howie, and told my father that I would take him. I risked meeting Howie and his lieutenants after three, and standing outside the gymnasium, I watched Crazy hoist the streamers and the Chinese lanterns. I could already envision the dwarfs, dressed in scarlet and gray, tuning up their clarinets. Father Finnocchino's Ragtime Band. I didn't know a thing about clarinets, but I would have gladly given my left arm or maybe even my right, had I been allowed to play along with the dwarfs on the night of the dance.

Only Crazy's mother was disenchanted. She began picketing our school. At first she was able to muster a fair audience, but when she began shouting over and over that Roosevelt's

Jew Dealers were sponsoring the dance and that Father's dwarfs were really agents of the Elders of Zion, most of us took off.

Our school was in an uproar the day before the dance. Howie Rosenthal kept snatching Chinese lanterns from the gymnasium and telling everybody that he and his two appointed captains, Dennis Moody and Michael Fink, were forming a welcoming committee for the hunchbacks and the dwarfs. "I'm gonna dance with all the dwarfs," Howie boasted, hugging his captured lanterns. Sharon Lipsky left a note inside my desk. It was a very bitter note. She claimed that she had been compromised and betrayed. "Nicholas, I never knew before what kind of boy you are. After I tell everybody that you are taking me it turns out that I can't go unless I go with Howard. What will people think? Everybody knows Howard is a sex maniac." Sharon offered to give me another chance. She would go with me, if I asked her again. Now, I sympathized with Sharon and wanted to help her out, but I knew if I assed out Howie, I would end up the loser in every way. Even if Howie and his lieutenants couldn't put their hands on me, they would simply sabotage the dance, and I would never get to see the dwarfs. So I took the easy way out and ignored Sharon's note. Sharon Lipsky was the only girl at P.S. 187 who had worn a brassiere since the fourth grade. But if it was going to be a contest between Father's dwarfs and Sharon's brassiere, then the brassiere would have to go!

I played cassino with my father after supper, but he kept commandeering all the aces and the good ten, so we switched to Steal the Old Man's Bundle, and I finally won a game. I think he let me steal his bundle on purpose once or twice. My father had papers to mark, and so, after victimizing his bundles, he excused himself and went inside his den. I brought him a glass of buttermilk and went to bed. I had always been afraid of the dark, and for a long time I slept with my father.

14

Of course, by the time I was nine I had a bed of my own, but even then, when it thundered or when the night was unusually dark, I often invaded my father's bed. I might have solved my problems by keeping a light on, but I never liked giving in to any of my fears. I did compromise a little and kept a pocket flashlight and a spare battery under my pillow. I mention all this because on that night, the night before the dance, I felt particularly uncomfortable about being alone in the dark, and yet, in a very short while I managed to fall asleep.

When my father woke me next morning and told me everything, I swore to him that I had heard the fire engines clatter during the night, that I had seen the swollen red glare outside my window, and had heard the dwarfs and the hunchbacks wail and scream, but no matter what my father believed, I failed to convince myself. The fact is that I had slept soundly all the way through the conflagration. My father left a little early. I don't remember crying, but my fingers shook so that I could hardly lace my shoes. I didn't bother taking any books with me. Even on Cabrini Boulevard the air was still clogged with smoke. I watched the boys and girls assemble phantom-like in the yard. I talked to no one. I tried to run down to Broadway, but the police had blocked off all the streets below Fort Washington Avenue. I ducked under one or two of the barriers, but a policeman saw me right away, and after jabbing my behind softly with his billy, he told me to take off. I couldn't see anything from Fort Washington Avenue, the smoke was so thick, except a huge black form that might have been the remains of Saint Elizabeth's roof. My eyes began to smart, and rubbing them fiercely, I went back to school. I came in twenty minutes late, my shirt already covered with black streaks, but Mrs. Krapperman, my fifth grade teacher, didn't say a word. Nobody even noticed me. It was Howie's day.

Howie had seen the fire. He made sure the class didn't forget that he had stayed up all night. I don't really blame him for exploiting the situation. Everybody else in the class would have probably done the same thing. "Yeah," he said, "I saw everything." He was ready to cash in on his exalted position as purveyor of the fire, and he wouldn't continue until we pleaded with him and shouted, "Tell us, Howie, tell us." And then he told us.

"Wow!" Howie said, eyeing us shrewdly. "*Wow!* Smoke was coming outa every window and the whole place looked like it was gonna choke. Pop put his scarf around my head in case the sparks started flying. The firemen couldn't get inside the building it was so filled up with fire and one of the walls crumbled and I heard the boom boom and everybody had to step back. The fire chiefs kept looking for Father Finnocchino, but nobody could find him. All we saw was the rats running out from the cellar and the bottom floor. There musta been a million of them. No wonder the walls came down so fast. There was this woman next to us and I think she was Cath'lic because she was making signs all over her chest and saying something about Jesus and Joseph. Maybe she was a nun I don't know...." I immediately thought of Mrs. Bemelman. " 'Father,' she said, 'you shoulda never, never tried to put the dwarfs on display. Oh God,' she said. Just like that. She was crying too. Well, I started choking from all the smoke so Pop took me over to Bickford's and we had some cocoa and a bun and later we went back to the fire. Only it was all calmed down now and the firemen were already charging into the cellar with axes. And there was a whole row of blankets on the sidewalk across the street with something under every blanket. They was all humped up near the middle. Pop thought it was the hunchbacks but he didn't know for sure. I kept watching the blankets but they never moved, not even one. That's it. That's what I saw." He looked at us dully for a moment. He had probably expected more of a triumph. Then he drew something out of his pocket. It was a biretta with crushed sides and a blackened pompon. He held the biretta like a captured head. His eyes gleamed. "It musta belonged to one of the dwarfs." A few of the girls said, "Wow!"

When the barriers were removed two days later, Saint Elizabeth's was already a great curio. I had to stand in line in order to see its gutted shell: only the cellar was intact. After two days, it was still smoldering. The PWA workers had already moved in. Their bulldozers rode over the foundation and cleared the debris.

No one was able to find Father Finnocchino. Had he died in the fire or escaped with a handful of dwarfs? Had he been committed to an asylum for mad priests, as Howie believed, or was he roaming the streets, even now, singing bawdy songs and bumming Lucky Strikes? I promised myself that if Father Finnocchino ever showed up, I would offer myself to him. I would meet with him inside the ruins of the cellar, and after several secret incantations he would baptize me, and I would become his acolyte for life.

In two months' time Father Finnocchino and all his hunchbacks and dwarfs were forgotten. Everybody talked about the swimming pool that was going to be erected on Saint Elizabeth's former site. The PWA workers had dug out the cellar and packed the marshy ground underneath with tons of crushed limestone mixed with gravel. The foundation was put up in less than a year and the pool opened a few months later. At first everybody called me "The Finless Wonder" because I wouldn't go near the pool. Then they all remembered my damaged lung and they left me alone.

⊰ CHAPTER ⊱

Crazy was in my official class at G.W. He was already fifteen, and should have been a sophomore, at least, but he couldn't understand two words of algebra, and we all knew that he would never earn an academic diploma, not even in two million years. I coached him every day, but it didn't help much. Mrs. Bemelman offered to pay me, but I couldn't see taking her money, especially when I knew what the results would be. I marveled at her transformation. She had stopped pestering the storekeepers with her collection boxes long ago. She had given up Father Coughlin and his Shrine of the Little Flower. And if anyone asked her about Roosevelt's second term, she would grunt mildly and say something about "the Lord's will." Nobody could get her to mention Father Finnocchino or the fire. She concentrated solely on Crazy. She was convinced that, somehow, she could turn him into a scholar.

18

She ignored his constant zeros in algebra and refused to let anything come between Crazy and her own splendid visions. But all this didn't prevent her from knocking his head against the wall. I witnessed practically every knock, as I was almost always with the Bemelmans now, hopelessly trying to help Crazy solve quadratic equations. "Listen to Nick," she would say, "you want to end up like your father? Thank you, one janitor in the family is enough! *Irwin*." That was Crazy's real name. I'm sure she had even envisioned Crazy, someday, taking holy vows. I know for a fact that she dragged Crazy over to all the neighboring parishes, but after one interview, every priest she had seen advised her that Crazy did not have "the calling." Crazy, of course, claimed that he himself had sabotaged all the interviews. He swore to me that he had extra played the fool, because he didn't want anything to do with saying mass and administering extreme unction and "crap like that." He much preferred bumping into Sharon Lipsky's tits on the sly in one of the darkened halls of G.W. or raiding the Fort Washington Y.M.H.A.

I have to claim some complicity in Crazy's actions. After all, I did join Crazy's band. I suppose it had a lot to do with things at G.W. I was even worse off there than I had been at P.S. 187. My teachers practically salaamed every time I came into the room. The word went around that I was some sort of wonder. I think my name was written over every urinal at G.W. Howie Rosenthal was already vice president of the freshman council and he used his influence to blackball me from every club and activity at G.W. And so, with no place else to turn, I hid under Crazy's aegis, and in the winter of my freshman year I joined his band.

Frannie Faye was the other member of Crazy's band. At nineteen he had still not graduated from his job as the Gristede delivery boy, and I don't think it's too unkind calling him a moron. It took him years to memorize the layouts of the courts on Cabrini Boulevard, and I'm sure he would have been lost anywhere below Fort Washington Avenue. However, we did have one thing in common: we both worshiped Crazy. "Cr-cr-crazy," Frannie would say, wiggling his enormous bell-shaped ears, "when are we gonna take over the Y?" This was the one ambition of Crazy's life. He was always talking about bombarding the "Yids" and banishing them all to Canarsie. He also knew that Sharon Lipsky played ping-pong there three nights a week, and I'm sure he wanted to capture the Y for her. Sharon Lipsky was no Dulcinea who only came to life in Crazy's mind: her tits were for real! She was surrounded by boy friends on every side, but when Howie Rosenthal was voted vice president of the council, he gained the upper hand. He went around telling everybody that Sharon had given him one of her brassieres, and when he was really roused, he would boast about the size and shape of Sharon's nipples. I think Crazy hated Howie as much as I did, but with his own demonic logic he must have figured that pulverizing Howie would only hurt his chances with Sharon. So Crazy condescended a little and let Howie live.

Don't think that the diminutive size of our band made it any less formidable. We could have frightened whole armies with Crazy on our side. And I have to admit that Frannie Faye, in spite of his moronic behavior, had marvelous faculties. His claim that he could both smell and sight Yids a mile away was no idle boast. He could read off from any rooftop on the south side of Cabrini Boulevard all the letters—except "w" which he could never pronounce—on the signboards over the shops on Fort Washington Avenue, and if only he could have grouped the letters into some appreciable form, he would have made an absolutely perfect lookout man. Obviously, planning the raids was left to me. It was great fun at first, as long as I suspected that my wholly impractical plans would never be carried out. I kept elaborate diagrams of the Y in

2 0

every drawer and even figured out a few invasions algebraically. "See," I would explain to them, pointing to one of my carefully unrolled diagrams, "we'll attack from both sides. But we'll need a cherry bomb to create some diversion. That's a must. This plan won't work without a cherry bomb." Frannie invariably socked his head; even his ears would droop. Turning to his chief, he would say, "Cr-cr-crazy, where are we gonna get a ch-cherry bomb, huh? Where?" Crazy, thinking to himself all this time, would shout, "Quiet, quiet. We'll make the cherry bomb. We'll need a mold and some powder. We can use the flint from matches. . . ." Of course, the cherry bomb was never made and I went on to newer and even bolder plans.

One night in midwinter Crazy called up to me from the court. Frannie was with him; even his scarf couldn't hide Frannie's enormous ears. I dressed warmly, and after telling my father that I would be back early, I went down to Crazy. Frannie kept shuffling his feet, trying to keep himself warm. Crazy's eyes gleamed queerly and his eyebrows drew together. I knew what he was up to: he was going to raid the Y. I thought I might get him to back down if I stalled him for a day, so I tried to tell him that it was too cold for a raid, but he waved me off. "Tonight's the night." He took out three black skullcaps from his pocket; they all had hunched sides and flattened tops. He ordered us to put them on. Crazy had obviously done some planning of his own, and I was struck with the frightening realization that Crazy's plans, unlike my own, would work. "If we wear the Jew caps," he said, "they'll think we're all Yids and they'll let us in. Then we can take over." Frannie toyed with his skullcap; my fingers trembled as I fitted mine on my head. Crazy wore his over one eye. He would have made a perfect Angel of Death.

It began to snow as we approached the Y. We watched the individual flakes kiss the rims of the huge bronze Star-of-

David that was fastened to the wall above the entrance. Frannie crossed himself. In one of the front windows I watched my lips shape an ironic smile. The skullcap on my head seemed a little ridiculous. "Shit," Crazy said, pushing us both towards the door. Crazy entered first, then Frannie. And then me. A man was sitting behind a large desk facing the door. Several older boys stood near him; none of them wore skullcaps. The man behind the desk stared at Crazy for a moment and then smiled. "*Shimshon*," he said, "*Shimshon*," and waving his arms he caught the attention of the other boys. "Look, they brought us a Samson!" They must have thought we were members of another Y. The man kept marveling at Crazy. He winked to us conspiratorially. "Tell me, where do they grow such Jewish boys?" His eyes creased kindly, though unevenly. I heard someone whistle "God Bless America." It was Howie Rosenthal. He was coming down the steps behind the desk. His brows jiggled when he saw the three of us with our skullcaps. Holding up three fingers, he told the man behind the desk, "*Drai goyim.*" Then he ran up the steps. The older boys assembled in front of the desk. The man behind the desk pointed to Crazy and me. He was no longer smiling. "Boys," he said, "please, go home. You don't belong here. Please."

Frannie Faye hunched his shoulders like a startled cat; I thought he was going to spit. Crazy approached the desk. "I'm taking over," he said, "*move.*" The boys scattered and then regrouped near the steps. The man behind the desk mumbled to himself. "*Der shtarke ... a golem, a golem ...*"

"Frannie," Crazy barked, "run upstairs and tell all the Yids to come down." God, I thought, he's really going to take over the Y. I could already envision our band, now the enemies of all propriety, storming George Washington next, my father trying to intercede for the principal and failing. Then I heard Howie Rosenthal's war chant.

He charged down the stairs, leading a battalion of six

men who wore pullovers with a Star-of-David emblazened across their chests. Their enormous shoulders and bullish necks were unmistakable: they were all weightlifters. One of them was almost as big as Crazy; he had gnarled hands and a missing eyebrow. "Hey," he said, glancing over Crazy's head scornfully while he worked his one eyebrow, "where's the *clutz?*" Howie pointed to Crazy. The six weightlifters converged around Crazy, their heavily muscled backs already hiding his shoulders and part of his head. Frannie Faye put his left elbow over his eyes; he was crying. "We didn't mean nothin'." I could see Crazy's skullcap hugging his head. "Come on, you bastards," he said, "I'll take you all with my left hand. Come on. *Kikes.*"

The weightlifters charged Crazy and clung to him, three at each arm. Crazy moved his shoulders furiously, and two of the weightlifters fell to the floor. I think Frannie Faye peed in his pants; both his shoes were wet. The weightlifters finally pinned Crazy's arms. The man behind the desk gave them a tremendous hank of rope, and they began tying Crazy's arms and legs. I watched the rope uncoil. The weightlifters tied Crazy's arms under his knees. Howie plucked the skullcap from Crazy's head, crushed it in his hand, and thrust it into his pocket. Then he redeemed Frannie's and mine. He kicked me in the ass twice; Frannie he left alone. "Come here making trouble, huh? You think it's a joke walking around wearing *yarmulkes?*" Crazy sat quietly on the floor; his eyes gazed absently.

"Where does that *schmuck* live?" the weightlifter with the missing eyebrow asked.

"Don't tell 'em, Frannie," I said.

"Shut up," the weightlifter said, "nobody's talking to you."

Frannie tried to fathom Crazy's eyes for some signal or command. Crazy offered him nothing.

23

"He lives on Cabrini Boulevard," Frannie said, looking down with one eye and watching me with the other.

The man behind the desk pleaded with the weightlifters in Crazy's behalf. "Arnold, don't hurt him. After all, what did he do? Just make sure the *banditen* never come back again." They picked up Crazy and hauled him over to the door; his buttocks kept touching the floor. One of the weightlifters lit a cigarette, cupping the match in his free hand. Then they carried Crazy outside. It was still snowing.

Frannie led the way, Howie overseeing all his directions. The snow clung to Crazy's shoulders and hair and formed narrow patches all over his face. I remember wiping his chin and forehead several times; his head kept bouncing up and down. They deposited Crazy in front of our court, his nose near the ground, and after warning the three of us they took off, Howie now in the lead. One of the weightlifters offered him a cigarette. I watched the smoke plume crookedly over the back of his head. Frannie and I stooped and started untying Crazy. "Lea' me 'lone," Crazy said, resisting us.

"You can't stay out in the court like this. Crazy, you'll freeze."

He stared balefully at Frannie and me. His teeth were already beginning to chatter.

"I ain't arguing with the ch-chief," Frannie said. "Nicky, I'll see ya tomorra." He walked away from the court; he turned around once, raising his narrow shoulders apologetically, and then crossed the street. The snow fell thickly and I could no longer see him.

"Crazy?"

"You deaf? *Lea' me 'lone.*"

I walked the length of the court, the soles of my shoes leaving blurred tracks in the snow that was beginning to accumulate, and without looking back, I went upstairs. I could hear my Aunt Giuseppina's bawling voice from the hall. Ordinar-

24

ily I would have approached our door with an appropriate show of dread, and might even have run up to the roof until my father signaled to me that she had gone, but the disaster at the Y had numbed my brain, and so, I knocked twice.

I suppose what I really wanted to do was find a way to share some of Crazy's punishment. I didn't have to wait very long. I was already thirteen and, I believed, well past the pandying age, but Aunt Giuseppina still thought it appropriate to grip my left ear and drag me halfway across the living room. "*Niccolo*" she said. "Stays out late like the biggest bum! And in the snow! You think I have the whole night to wait?" She had huge, mobile cheeks that actually roamed up and down the sides of her face; one cheek became so excited, it seemed about to burrow through her cracked skin.

"*Alfredo*," she said, turning on my father, "whose fault is it, *huh? Testa dura!* What do they teach him in the public school?" Aunt Giuseppina was still out to trap my errant soul by hook or by crook. My father might let her get away with mauling my ear, but actually he was far more stubborn and willful than she was, and in those things that really mattered to him, he never conceded an inch. "*Gesu, Giuseppe e Maria,*" Aunt Giuseppina said, pronouncing her favorite invocation, which always served as a preface to one of her wild incantations, accusations, or taunts. "What kind of boy?" She looked suspiciously at the two of us. "He cook for you, he clean for you. ..." She watched my father's face harden, and after twinkling her eyebrows mischievously, she attacked him from another front.

Aunt Giuseppina was the dispenser of all Lapucci patronage, and she was always seeking favors for my uncles, aunts, and cousins. My father was prepared for this and was usually able to counter her protestations. "Without a heart! Come to the Bronx and see for yourself. The stores empty,

2 5

not like here. Here is like the fairy tales. Every day a feast day! You come to Third Avenue. You see. *Bambini e ragazzi* with twisted bellies. Not strangers, *paesani*. And your cousins? Paulo, Giuseppe, Giacomo, the three Benitos. All on relief." She would not have dared mention my uncles, all of whom worked for Figueroa the seltzer baron, whose fleet of seltzer trucks ranged the five boroughs and who was already acquiring rights to dispatch a portion of his fleet to Hoboken and West Orange. Good times, bad times, everybody drank seltzer! "'*Fredo*, maybe they need a janitor in the high school? Or a carpenter? Somebody to fix the boiler? Giacomo has his own tools. First class!" When she saw that she wouldn't be able to place Giacomo, she shifted her attack again.

Aunt Giuseppina didn't give a rap for Roosevelt, La Guardia, or Harry Hopkins. She had room for only one hero in her heavily armored heart: Mussolini. In deference to *Il Duce*, who had brought the enlightenment to Sicily in the form of grammar books and bars of yellow soup, she named a whole tribe of her nephews *Benito*, and had I been christened properly, I'm sure I would have been blessed in the same way. If it had been up to Aunt Giuseppina, every priest in the East Bronx would have been offering endless novenas to Mussolini and his band of Black Shirts. When the *duce*, preparing to invade Ethiopia, cried for gold, Aunt Giuseppina responded immediately, and with exhortations, threats, and actual plunder, she collected hundreds of wedding rings, watch chains, and bracelets for the cause. After she heard that Haile Selassie's "black bandits" were mutilating Sicilian boys, she promised to send a small contingent of Lapuccis to join General Frusci's Italian-American volunteer regiment, and she expected my father to share some of the costs of the expedition. "Alfredo," she said, "at least for cigarette money. Marshal Balbo himself. . . ."

26

My father began his counterattack. He called Mussolini an "addlebrained idiot," who should have been a puppet maker rather than a politician. He jutted out his chin, Mussolini-like, and stormed across the room. "Let him finance Italy's destiny out of his own pocket. And if you want to send your legionnaires to die for that bastard, leave me out of it. I'm sick and tired of causes, and slogans, and calls to honor. They're all calls to madness in one form or another. If I want to get involved with crackpots, I can find all I need right on this block." My father was beginning to crack through her defenses; even her cheeks stopped roaming.

I went into the kitchen, and standing near the window, I peered between the slats of the blind. Outside, the snow whirled frantically, but I could still see Crazy's humped form near the entrance of the court. I heard Aunt Giuseppina mention my mother's name, and I knew right away that she had regained the initiative. I stayed in the kitchen. "*Troiazza*," she said, and she spat ceremoniously three times. "She was a pig, your Andrea, a pig." I moved closer to the door. I watched my father's back contract crookedly; his hands were trembling.

"Who cared about you, but the boy? Leave an infant and run off with a picture postcard painter, what kind of woman? *Troiazza!* Garbage, junk! *Cantarana!* That's what kind of woman!" Here she spat three times again. "You think we worried about the wedding, hah? You could marry her in Hell and it wouldn't bother me. But I told them, I told them, a Catholic girl who doesn't even want to be married by a priest has to turn out to be shit." And now, her eyes blazing, both cheeks performing expertly for her, she spat for the last time. "And what did she want with you?" She pointed to all the bookshelves. "Always with books, books. A hen, not a man! But the boy...."

27

Triumphant, she collected her hat, and left. Why hadn't my father defended himself? Was it because of me? It never seemed that he kept any secrets. Other boys had mothers, yes, who fed them and sang to them and washed their underwear, but that had never bothered me. My father always seemed quite adequate. I never questioned the order of things, even at Mrs. Katzenheimer's. Some children were tall, and some were short, some had snotty handkerchiefs and chapped hands and gingerbread dolls and a mommy who picked them up after school. I'm sure that between the hours of nine and five, Mrs. Katzenheimer was supposed to be some sort of deputy mother for all of us, but I never felt particularly warm towards her, and I didn't envy any of the little girls. Their mommies always seemed like cranky giants with enormous bellies and hairy faces, and there was nothing remarkable about them. I knew that I must have had a mother once, but I didn't remember anything about her. I couldn't even recall her face. And so, there was no "Mommy" for me to kiss or cry for. My father locked himself inside his den. I went down to Crazy.

The lantern cases over the main door were already clogged with snow. I wasn't wearing any galoshes, and my feet kept sinking deeper and deeper. I shielded my face with my forearm and plodded towards the entrance of the court. "Crazy?" I called, "Crazy?" Crazy wasn't there. Had he gone down to the cellar? Or had he decided to attack the Y again? I leaned against the wall, hoping that Crazy might rise up somewhere out of the snow. I don't know why, but I called out my mother's name. Andrea. Andrea. The snow seemed to mute my voice, and my own call sounded strange and distant, as if I had blasphemed by invoking my mother's name. I plodded back across the court. The lantern cases glared down at me. I stood in the hall for a little while and then went upstairs.

28

Crazy dissolved his band. Frannie Faye was so broken up that he quit his job and followed Crazy around all day. The custodians had to chase him out of the halls at G.W., but it didn't do any good. Frannie kept coming back. "Crazy, Crazy," he would implore, "talk to me." Frannie asked me to intercede for him. He just couldn't understand that Crazy was through with both of us. Was it because he was ashamed to face us after his defeat? Or had he merely discovered that Frannie and I were worthless when it came to any kind of crisis? I never found out. He wouldn't even let me help him with his algebra, in spite of his mother's threats and all the knocks on the head. After a while, he stopped showing up at school. Mrs. Bemelman was in the principal's office every other week. Even my father couldn't help her out. Crazy ran away twice. Once he went to Chicago and stoked furnaces for a few weeks. He came back with blistered hands and a sooty face, miserable, without a dime to his name.

When he was seventeen, Crazy decided to join the Army. His mother balked right away. After all, the Army was a great letdown for her. From a priest to a "soljer bum." Then, after she refused to let Crazy go, Mr. Bemelman performed the first heroic act in his life. Bucking Mrs. Bemelman, *he* signed Crazy's papers. We all knew what would happen next. She stationed him near the dumbwaiter and made him haul in the garbage pails twenty times a day. She brought out a lumpy, rat-infested mattress from the storage room and told him to sleep near the furnace. And she refused to feed him. Though the injustice was apparent, most of the people in our court sided with Mrs. Bemelman. They knew who ran the house, and they didn't want any trouble with leaky radiators and fouled-up dumbwaiters. Actually, my father and I were the only ones who befriended Mr. Bemelman. On a bad night, when the rats plagued him, we let him sleep in the living room, and I kept bringing down bologna sandwiches to him. Mr.

29

Bemelman never complained. I suppose he understood that his wife's ways were inscrutable. In the end, he become accustomed to his banishment. Perhaps I give him too little credit. Sensing that his situation was hopeless, he might have been willing to suffer through a few more fusillades, if it meant helping Crazy get away. Who am I to say?

My father began having dizzy spells shortly after Crazy left for Fort Bliss. I suppose there's no real connection between both occurrences, but in my mind, they are linked in some inexplicable way. My father wasn't the only one who suffered after Crazy abandoned our court. Mr. Dalrymple, the botanist on the second floor, fell from his window mysteriously and fractured one hip. Both of the Siamese cats in our building went into heat simultaneously and howled for weeks at a time. A few wire terriers in Mrs. Schmuckler's dog hospital on Fort Washington Avenue staged a massive revolt. After escaping from their own pound, they freed every terrier in the hospital, and then, banding together, the terriers invaded our court, broke several windows on the ground floor, and left Mrs. Bemelman's neatly kept lanes in a bad way. It seems that no one escaped the affliction. All the toilets on the left side of the court suddenly refused to flush; Mrs. Essegian's ceiling caved in; I jammed my thumb; and Mrs. Bemelman came down with a bad case of boils. I know Crazy can't possibly be blamed for everything, but I'm pretty sure that had he been around to protect the court, Crazy would have warded off most of the calamities.

My father's dizzy spells came more and more frequently. On the days he stayed home, I met with the members of his department in the English office before classes began, and after listening to all their gripes, I handed out the office assignments to Miss Pistachio, the cross-eyed student teacher, collected lesson plans, and issued my father's orders for the day. Later I telephoned my father from the principal's office. "Papa," I would say, "Mrs. Shumpater says she has a board eraser problem." "Tell her," my father would say, "that she can sit on the pot and manufacture all the board erasers she wants." Then I would cup both hands over the receiver. "Papa, not so loud. Everybody can hear. . . ." Of course, when the other kids saw how I was handling all my father's teachers, they began storing up their brickbats. My name was celebrated, not only inside the shithouses, but inside the clothing closets, on the walls of the locker room, on the taped handles of the softball bats, and on the tables, chairs, and walls of the student cafeteria. I was now "Nick, the Universal Suck," and there was nothing I could do about it.

One day, in the middle of my sophomore year, a monitor came into my class, and I was called over to the English office. Several teachers stood outside the door. Their rigid, solemnly lined faces baffled me at first. Then I stared through the door. My father was lying on top of his desk. He had just had a stroke. His lips were ashen and his eyes seemed slightly vacant. A harsh woolen blanket hugged his body and was drawn up over his chin. The school nurse hovered over him. The shades were down and her hard, hawklike face looked surprizingly macabre in the dimmed, dust-clogged light.

I rode with my father in the ambulance. The nurse wanted to come with us, but the intern insisted that we could get along without her. I sided with him. I'm sure most of her grimness was my own invention, but I wasn't taking any chances. I wasn't in the mood to wrestle with Death in the back of a bouncing ambulance, though I was confident that I would have won the match. I held my father's hand most of the way. He wanted to say something, but the intern told him not to talk. "Papa," I said, "everything will be all right." He closed his eyes and relaxed his grip. I released his hand.

Mrs. Bemelman had boycotted me and my father after we aided and abetted her husband, but when she found out

3 1

that my father was in the hospital, she removed the boycott temporarily and invited me down to her basement apartment. I would have declined her invitation, but she seemed genuinely concerned about my father's condition, and anyway, she wanted to talk to me about Crazy.

Crazy's room was small and oppressive, with a low, lumpy ceiling that seemed to press down, and three crooked walls. I suppose the room was meant to be somewhat triangular, but it seemed quite shapeless to me; the corners were particularly dark. The room was without a window or even a vent. It was directly below the entrance of the court, and Crazy's ceiling recorded every step. From the booming sounds and the steady bombardment of falling plaster chips, anyone with only half a brain would have suspected that giants walked over Crazy's head. The first time I was inside Crazy's room, when I began helping him with his algebra, I understood why Crazy, at eleven and twelve, had terrorized the court. I don't think he was really trying to get even with us for all the plaster chips. Crazy never worked that way. One of the reasons he behaved like a wildman in the court, I'm sure, is that he wanted to celebrate his temporary liberation from his confinement underground. And if he waylaid some of us, maybe he was only mimicking the actions of those malicious giants who kept trampling on his head? Crazy always had a motive, but you usually had to discover it in the most roundabout way.

We sat on Crazy's bed, Mrs. Bemelman and I. Its wooden posts were splintered and chipped and probably catered to whole armies of ants, bugs, and lice; the springs creaked and the mattress was beginning to peel; but the bed was the one impressive thing in the tiny room. It could have belonged to no one but Crazy. The huge crowns that decorated the tops of each post and the ghoulish masks that were carved into the headboard seemed part and parcel of Crazy's visionary world. I could easily imagine Crazy blessing the crowns and warring with the masks. The bed occupied almost the entire room and seemed to defy the ceiling and keep back the three crooked walls. There was no room for a bureau, so most of Crazy's belongings were kept under the bed. Despite the unsteady glare of the tiny bulb that was suspended from the ceiling I managed to make out Crazy's ancient, battered cap pistols near the foot of the bed. His mother reached under the bed and pulled out a stack of letters. I think she was crying. Sitting in her corner, her face was practically hidden. She waved some of the letters, their edges flashing dully as they came under the glare of the bulb. I recognized Crazy's handwriting immediately. He always wrote with huge, crookedly shaped capital letters. Mrs. Bemelman began complaining. "I told him," she said, "I told him the Army was for perverts and bums. They ruin boys there. Ruin them. They keep Irwin caged in a barrack. How do they expect him to sleep in a room with other men? Nick," she said, softly, only her nose showing, "you would eat out your heart if you read one of his letters. Do you know he cries almost every night. My Irwin! In the latrine where no one can see. Those bastards!" Here her fingers darted across her chest, and I think she crossed herself. "I know the kind of habits he'll end up with. Whoring and card playing. He won't be fit for anything. I already wrote to his chaplain but Irwin won't see him. He hasn't attended Mass once. And what can you expect? The kikes use the same chapel! Call this an Army! Nick, the Bolsheviks are in control. Even the President can't do a thing. That aid of his, *Rosenberg*, he runs the whole show. He'd go after Our Lord if he had half the chance. I wish Roosevelt would wise up and drown that devil or ship him to Palestine. . . ." She gripped my hand. "Nick, will you write to him? To Irwin? I know he'd like to hear from you. He's in Missouri now. Fort Leonard Wood." I don't know whether she was trying to put some pressure on me or just being enthusiastic, or maybe she was going out of her mind, because she almost crushed my fingers. God, I would have agreed to anything.

"Sure," I said, "I'll write to him," and right away she released my hand. We left Crazy's room.

I wrote to Crazy that night. It was not a very long letter. What could I say? Crazy, when you come home, we'll put some of your infantry training to good use and really smash the Y? Instead, I asked how he was, told him about a few of the calamities that had befallen the court, and then, lying a little, I said that Frannie Faye had sent him his regards. Actually, no one knew what had happened to Frannie. He never went back to his job at Gristede's, and after Crazy joined the Army, Frannie just disappeared. I wrote Crazy again two weeks later, and then once more, each time having less and less to say. Crazy never answered any of my letters.

My father was in the hospital for two months. Mrs. Bemelman said a rosary for him every night. The faculty at G.W. sent him stacks of Get Well cards in all sizes and shapes, some with hand-painted covers and others with obscene notes written inside. The sisters who cared for my father were very kind to him, and wearing their starched wimples, they washed him and fed him and changed his linen. Aunt Giuseppina visited my father almost every day. Each time she brought a priest with her who was ready to anoint my father at a moment's notice. After her second or third visit, my father had the sisters keep Aunt Giuseppina and the priest out of his room. Once I was there when Aunt Giuseppina and her priest arrived, and leaning his notebook on my back, his hand trembling all the time, he wrote, "Nick, tell her: if she wants, the *pretu* can anoint my ass." I did not relay his message.

The left side of my father's body was partially paralyzed, and it was painful watching him glare at his body as if it were some sort of betrayer and hearing him try to speak. His eyes would cloud as he searched for his words, and when they

3 4

finally came, his lips would rebel and he could hardly get them out; he could not bear hearing himself stutter and grope for words, and so, he began using his notebook. Often he would draw pictures and diagrams instead of writing out whole sentences and words. Soon my father systemized all his drawings. When they become more and more abstract, the sisters had great trouble interpreting them. I became his official cryptographer. After one or two strokes, I could often tell whether my father wanted his bedpan or some French toast.

After I brought my father home a nurse stayed with him while I was at school. Her name was Mrs. Rumplemeyer. She seemed extraordinarily beneficent to me, but my father never got along with her. She could do nothing with his diagrams, and he claimed that she burned his French toast. Perhaps his resentment for her came partly from his own disgust at his helplessness which she witnessed and constantly catered to. After a while, he would not let her wash him or empty his bed pan. That became my job. I understood my father's squeamishness. I'm sure I never would have been able to let Mrs. Rumplemeyer rub me down or remove my crap. I would have felt completely exposed.

Mrs. Rumplemeyer shopped for us, and even made sandwiches for me occasionally. Had my father sanctioned it, I'm sure she would have moved right in with us. My father was always relieved when he saw me come back from school and knew that Mrs. Rumplemeyer would soon be dismissed for the day. Sometimes I brought the *Times* with me from my civics class at G.W., and when I offered to read him about Hitler's moves in the Rhineland or about the latest peace march at Foley Square, he would shake his head fiercely and scratch out on the back of his notebook a crooked M, which always stood for *Merde*.

"Papa, Papa, there's going to be another war for sure, and you don't want to hear anything about it? Everybody thinks the Maginot line will hold forever, but Mr. Garfinkel says Hitler will trap the French underground and ride right over their fortifications." I flipped one wrist for emphasis and let my hand dive over my father's bed. "Like this, Papa, like this."

"*Merde*," he pronounced crisply, without a fault. Then he wrote out for me: "Let all the generals in the world get together and frig themselves."

"Papa," I said, "Papa," and after crossing out his sentence, I tore the page from the notebook.

I kept avoiding Mrs. Bemelman. I didn't want her to know that I had given up writing Crazy, but one day she trapped me in the hall and told me that Crazy was coming home soon on furlough. I knew that Crazy wouldn't come up to see me, but I tried to look pleased, anyway. "That's wonderful, Mrs. Bemelman." And then, continuing down the stairs, I said, "Give him my regards."

My father never cared for Mandrake the Magician or Smilin' Jack, but he loved the madcap adventures of Krazy Kat, and so, every Sunday morning I brought up the funnies for him. He never bothered with the rest of the paper, and I usually left it on the bin near the newsstand. I never begrudged reading Krazy's balloons for my father, but somehow the Kat's one-sided love affair with Ignatz Mouse always seemed a little clammy to me. The Sunday after I spoke to Mrs. Bemelman, I decided to rebel. I didn't want to ruin my father's pleasure, so I glanced at the panels with him, and with Spartanlike discipline, I read off Krazy's lines—"Werra, werra intrisking"—and then I attacked him and the Kat. "Papa," I said, "people are probably dying all over the world, *right now*, and you spend your time with Krazy Kat! I mean, at least Orphan Annie accomplishes something, and Terry fights the Japs in Indo-China. But Krazy Kat!" My attack was interrupted. Someone rang our bell. "Who is it!" I said, scowling, and then marched over to the door.

It was Crazy Bemelman. He was wearing his Army uniform and his sharply peaked campaign hat grazed the top of the door. His face was tanned and looked a little leathery, and his teeth were tobacco-stained. His belt buckle shone, and his leggings hugged his calves. He was holding an enormous heart-shaped candy box with an embroidered lid. I must have looked like a dope, because I kept staring at him. "Crazy," I said, "Crazy." I corrected myself. "*Irwin.* Come in."

One of his eyebrows rose. "I came to see your father," he said coldly, the peak of his campaign hat dipping slightly. I brought him over to my father. He put the candy box on the bed. "For you, *sir*," he said, taking off his hat. My father's lips twitched involuntarily, but his eyes seemed to smile. He reached for his notebook. I intervened. "My father wants to thank you, Irwin. He can't talk too well yet...." My father frowned at me, then, saluting Crazy jovially, he braced his lips and said, "Ir-win, o-pen the box." Crazy undid the embroidered lid. He smiled for the first time. He selected a candy for my father and then handed me the box, the blunted point of the heart jabbing my chest. Crazy told us about recruit drill, and about the men in his company, and then he told us about the stockades at Fort Leonard Wood. He had been to St. Louis and had seen the Cardinals play the Giants at Busch Stadium. He had also been to Arlington. He stood stiffly near the bed all the time he talked, the toes of his immaculately polished shoes pointing outward. He removed a tobacco pouch from his coat pocket and asked my father if he wanted a cigarette. My father wasn't supposed to smoke, but lowering his jaw defiantly, he nodded yes. Crazy rolled two cigarettes, licking the edges of the firmly packed yellow paper and sealing them, without spilling any tobacco. I sat near the bed and watched them smoke, unable to penetrate their private communion. Finally Crazy announced that he had to go. He hoped that my father would be fully recovered the next time he came home. He put on his hat, adjusting the boardlike brim.

"*Crazy?*" I said, wagging my head. "Would...would you like to take a walk?"

I could see his cheek muscles flex. "Sure," he said, after a pause.

I followed Crazy down to the basement. He wanted to stop off for a minute. Mrs. Bemelman welcomed both of us. She actually hugged me. Crazy went into his room and changed his shirt. He didn't invite me inside. He kept the door partly open and I could see a pair of boots standing like sentries near his pillow. My nostrils caught the unmistakable odor of brilliantine. Crazy was pomading his hair. Mrs. Bemelman whispered to me.

"Nick, what do you think?"

What did she want me to say? I was going to tell her that Crazy looked fine, but she didn't give me the chance. She moved closer to me and I felt that we were already conspirators. "Nick, I want him to become an officer. That's his only hope. Officers live like kings in the Army. Enlisted men are only slaves. But Irwin doesn't have a diploma. They'll let him take a correspondence course, but Irwin won't listen to me. He doesn't want anything to do with school. Nick...."

Crazy came out. I think he heard the whispering. I moved a step away from Mrs. Bemelman. Glaring at both of us, he finished looping his olive drab tie. He showed me some cartridges and his garrison belt and a dried lizard's tail that he had found one day while on maneuvers. The tobacco pouch bulged in his pocket. He gripped the brim of his campaign hat and it rode down his forehead, hiding one eye. He said goodbye to his mother, and we left. I imagined myself wearing my own uniform, a full-fledged member of Crazy's infantry. The vision passed.

We crossed Cabrini Boulevard. A little girl and her mother walked towards us. "Mama," the little girl said, jumping wildly, "look, a cowboy!" The girl's mother chuckled to herself. Crazy ignored them, his one visible eye staring straight ahead. We walked towards Broadway. A few storekeepers pointed at us. Crazy was probably the first soldier they had seen around Cabrini Boulevard in fifteen years. A boy sitting on one of the stoops aimed his peashooter at Crazy's hat. His missile struck the peak of Crazy's hat with an ugly smack. I heard a man say that the circus must be coming to town. I cursed them all.

"Crazy," I said, a little guiltily, "do you want to go over to the Y?" I figured that he might want to show off his uniform. "They'll have to let you in if you're a soldier. Sharon Lipsky still hangs out there and. . . ."

Crazy scowled. "I don't need any kike ass. Anyway, I can't sniff around. I caught a dose. . . ."

"Dose?" I said, my eyebrows knitting.

"The *clap*," he said, "the *clap*. I'm taking the treatment. You think I wanna walk around with half my pecker off? Next time I'm getting myself a first-class shackjob. No more of them Navahos for me. They all got pimply cunts." He took something out of his pocket. "Here," he said, "maybe you can use 'em."

I took the tiny packet he offered me. I tried to read the label.

He stared at me, his eyes widening in disbelief. I could feel my cheeks begin to flush.

"What's the matter," he said, "you never seen rubbers before? Forget it; fill 'em with water and use 'em for balloons."

I put the packet inside my pocket. As we approached Broadway I could see the large gate that surrounded the Washington Heights swimming pool. It was only March and the pool was still deserted. I thought I heard someone knock behind the gate. Had Father Finnocchino's dwarfs come back to haunt the pool? An enormous rat burrowed its swollen head between the bars of the gate. Crazy challenged the rat. His lips creased near the corners of his mouth, and I couldn't tell whether Crazy was smiling or not. "My job," he said. "Father used to let me chase the rats." He removed his tobacco pouch and a slip of yellow paper.

"Crazy, can I have one too?"

He rolled a cigarette for himself and then handed me the pouch. I tried to copy Crazy, but the tobacco spilled on my shoe and the cigarette refused to roll. I clacked my tongue wearily.

"Gimme," Crazy said, and shaping the paper with two fingers, he rolled the cigarette for me. He struck a match against the back pocket of his breeches and dipped his head so swiftly that the cigarette seemed to light before the match had had a chance to flare. Then, cupping one hand over the match, he helped me light my cigarette.

"Puff," he said. "Puff."

The tobacco tasted bitter, and I tried to keep myself from coughing. I inhaled accidentally, and began to choke. Crazy smacked my back several times. My eyes were already tearing, but I felt a little better. I tried the cigarette again. He started to put away the tobacco pouch, but then he reconsidered, and after tightening the strings, he offered me the pouch and all his cigarette paper. "Here, take it." He raised his hat brim, exposing both his eyes. "I gotta go," he said.

I wanted to hold him for a few more moments, so I said, "Crazy, Crazy, what are you going to do when you get out of the Army?"

"Me?" Crazy said, his eyebrows almost meeting, "I'm RA, Nick. A thirty-year man."

40

He crossed the street defiantly, halting several cars, and walked towards the IRT. A man in one of the cars asked me if Crazy was supposed to be a Texas Ranger. "Where's his six shooters, hey?" I ignored him and waved to Crazy. Crazy touched the peak of his hat, but he didn't wave back. I put the tobacco pouch in my pocket and walked along Broadway for a little while.

The Germans happened to overrun Poland at an inconvenient time: our school was planning a massive pilgrimage to the World's Fair, and now the lower termers were beginning to panic. They thought La Guardia might close the Fair and disembowel the Trylon and the Parachute Tower. Most of the seniors scoffed at the French and the Germans, but it wasn't because of the Fair. We stood opposite the row of porcelain urinals inside the second floor john and bemoaned our individual fates. Howie Rosenthal was sure that there was going to be a peacetime draft. "Nick," he said, smoking and peeing at the same time, "we're all gonna be screwed. You'll see." I watched Howie's words register on the gloom-ridden faces crowding the urinals. "*Screwed.*" I wondered if his urinal were actually some sort of oracle. My relationship with Howie had changed drastically after I was appointed editor of the literary magazine. He besieged me with whole

42

folios of poems which recorded, in veiled terms, every stage in his protracted romance with Sharon Lipsky. And in order to hold him off, I agreed to accept for the magazine one harmless little poem which described a ping-pong match between Sharon and himself, and which I privately enjoyed because I could always visualize Sharon's bouncing nipples as she retrieved the ping-pong balls. When the poem appeared, Howie immediately made me vice president and treasurer of the chess and checkers club, and invited me to attend the select after-lunch sessions inside the second floor john.

Moskowitz, the assistant principal, often patrolled the halls during the fourth and fifth periods, so Howie stationed one of his stooges near the water fountain outside the john. "We don't wanna get into trouble with Uncle Nate," Howie would say, winking malignantly. "No, not Uncle Nate." Everybody at G.W. knew that Moskowitz's uncle ran a reform school somewhere upstate, and during the senior assemblies, Moskowitz would invariably warn us that we were all prospective candidates for *Uncle Nate's.* "Shape up," he would say, "before you all get shipped out." Of course, Howie had his own theories about Uncle Nate. "It's a fraud, the whole reform school bit. There ain't no Uncle Nate." But he still kept his stooge outside the john. And on this particular day, Howie had hardly finished peeing when the stooge happened to knock. "The fuzz," he said, "the fuzz," and after flinging his cigarette behind the radiator, he and Archie Finkleberg, the captain of the football team, locked themselves inside the nearest stall. I never had much luck when it came to capturing a stall for myself and I usually ended up inside the one with the missing door and the broken toilet seat. And so, with Moskowitz jumping around, I had to pull down my pants, lean my elbows reflectively on my knees, and pretend that I was crapping, while my ass almost froze kissing the porcelain rim of the pot.

4 3

The minute Moskowitz came through the door he saw me squatting on my pot. I could feel my buttocks harden. The corners of his eyes crinkled noticeably. "Nick," he said softly, as if he didn't want to interrupt the rhythm of my bowel movements. "How's Dad?"

"Fine," I said, "fine. He should be walking around soon, and we're hoping that he'll be back at school before the end of the year." My father still had some trouble speaking, and in the midst of the most random conversations he would often stammer confusedly; but he was able to move both his legs, and Mrs. Rumplemeyer, who was still with us in spite of my father's constant protestations, was teaching him how to walk with a cane.

After he inspected every urinal, Moskowitz lingered outside my stall, and then left. We waited for the stooge's signal. When he knocked rapidly three times, we came out of our stalls. Howie congratulated me. Everybody agreed that I knew how to handle "the fuzz."

I stopped off at the bake shop near school and bought a baked Alaska for my father and an apple turnover for Mrs. Rumplemeyer, hoping that the pastry would mellow both of them and establish a temporary truce. When I came home I found Mrs. Rumplemeyer outside the door. Dark blotches streaked the sides of her dress, resembling enormous ink blots. Gripping my hand sturdily, she told me that my father had had another stroke and had been taken to the hospital. I'm sure her pinched smile was neither forced nor practiced, but I could hardly condemn her for having become slightly accustomed to grief. She must have spent half her life washing the wasted, hairless legs of dying men. I gave her the turnover and the baked Alaska.

My father was in a coma for two days and died without regaining consciousness. The sisters who watched him constantly told me that he never even opened his eyes. I knew

44

that if Aunt Giuseppina got her hands on him now she would have her embalmers paint his face and put him through one of her marathon wakes surrounded by hysterical, breast-beating women. Then there would have been the inevitable Requiem and the elaborate burial, all of which, I was sure, my father would have protested, dead or alive. I didn't want to see my father's flesh devoured piecemeal by her neatly pack-aged rituals and rites. And so, without telling a soul, I arranged for my father's burial. I contacted a Jewish undertaker, who, after hearing my plight, must have convinced himself that my father was a fallen bootlegger, because he offered to bury him at a reduced rate, "no questions asked." My father would have loved all the intrigue.

I stayed away from school and went to the movies prac-tically every day, sometimes riding all the way over to Pine-apple Street in order to track down Boston Blackie or Charlie Chan. I fell in love with Eric Von Stroheim, and hissed incess-antly at Kenny Baker and Bobby Breen. I even managed to avoid Aunt Giuseppina. Whenever I saw her approach the court, I ran up to the roof or hid out at the RKO Coliseum. Once, after barely escaping Aunt Giuseppina and spending the whole afternoon at the Coliseum watching Hitler's troops monopolize the News of the Week, I came home and sat tri-umphantly in the kitchen, playing with the tobacco pouch that Crazy had given me two years before, which I refilled every now and then with the thick tobacco from one of my father's bins. I rolled a cigarette for myself, the paper bulging unevenly at both ends. I moved into the living room and sat down near my father's pipe racks. With the smoke rising dreamily from my lumpy cigarette, I felt like some great clairvoyant who actually had the power to commune with the dead. I did not need any visions or supernatural signs: my father, I was absolutely certain, approved all my moves.

The next morning I woke with a terrible cough. I thought

that my father's tobacco might have clogged my throat, and I put away the pouch for three days. But the cough persisted. Envisioning huge, purple lesions on both my lungs, I went to the chest clinic at Saint Joseph's. After demonstrating my cough to the doctor at the clinic, and telling him that one of my lungs had collapsed when I was seven, he began tapping my knees with a little metal hammer. I asked him if I would have to give up smoking. "No," he said, feeling my scrimpy calves. Then he asked me what kind of work I did. I told him that I was still attending high school, that my father had just died, and that he had owned two houses on Manhatten Avenue and had left me an annuity, and that if I didn't want to, I wouldn't have to work for the next five or six years. "I suppose I'll do some kind of writing eventually," I said. "But what about my chest?" He gave me a large bottle filled with a blebby pink syrup, and told me to take five or six spoonfuls every day, and that any druggist would refill the bottle for me as many times as I wanted. I didn't have much faith in the syrup, but I drank three bottles anyway, and after a while the cough went away.

I became fed up hiding out at the RKO Coliseum, and so, one day, about three weeks after my father died, I got up early and went back to school. Moskowitz had caught Howie squeezing Sharon Lipsky's tits in the hall and had suspended him for three weeks. Howie was hardly nonplused by Moskowitz's edicts: instead of waiting out his three week exile at home, he spent all his mornings inside the second floor john. But Howie lost Sharon while he was still in exile. She came to school in November wearing a heart-shaped diamond ring: she was engaged to a balding, thirty-seven-year-old accountant who had a roadster with a rumble seat and a big nose. She had been seeing him on the sly for about three months. Howie told everybody that the accountant could bang her in the rumble seat for all he cared: he didn't give "two shits for Sharon." Two shits or not, Sharon left school in midwinter and married her accountant. I suppose she already had a hunch that the coming war would remove most of the available men, and she wasn't taking any chances. "Two months," Howie said. "I give her two months with that bum, and then she'll come running. Any *schmuck* can buy a roadster."

"Two months," we said, playing our parts determinedly, but we knew that it was a lost cause.

The same month Sharon was married I received a card from Crazy Bemelman. He said that he was sorry to hear about my father's death. My father had been dead almost four months, but I figured that it must take a pretty long time for news to travel from New York to Missouri, and anyway, I was glad to hear from Crazy; I saved his card.

Crazy had been in the Army for over two years and was still a private, and when his mother saw that they would never make him an officer, she began to fume at Roosevelt, the Army, and the Jews. She even began to suspect the Church. She claimed that Archbishop Spellman had made a pact with Rabbi Wise and the War Department: from now on the kikes would control all the NCO Schools and the Officer Training Schools in the Infantry, the Cavalry, and the Air Corps. She joined the German-American Bund, and told everybody that in the German Army every soldier had an equal chance. She threw away her beads and hailed Hitler as the new Messiah. It was frightening hearing her *heil Hitlers* in the halls, and she even taught a few of the young boys in the neighboring courts the goose step and the Nazi salute. When she began making arm bands for the boys with gold swastikas embroidered on them, the mothers in our building rebelled and broke up her little army. She retreated to the basement and rode her husband mercilessly. She called him a kike and a stooge for

"King Roosevelt." Mr. Bemelman only hunched his shoulders deeper and shoveled coal. I still made him an occasional bologna sandwich.

I'm sure Mrs. Bemelman rejoiced when the Germans flew over Belgium in gliders and captured bridges and forts, but Howie Rosenthal became more and more morose: he expected the gliders to land on his roof any day. "Sure," he told me and Archie Finkelberg, "fifty gliders could take New York, easy! They could cross over the Atlantic in five days, and with a few smoke bombs, no one would see a thing."

The Fink and I didn't bother arguing with him; we were grateful that the gliders were taking his mind off Sharon. Howie watched the skies for a few days with high power binoculars, and when the gliders still didn't show up, he calmed down a little. "Can I help it if Hitler ain't as smart as I thought he was? If he wants to miss a perfect chance, that's up to him." But he was still worried about Roosevelt. "Roosey's gonna suck us into the war, you'll see."

Even though G.W. had lost every game last year, Finkelberg made All City and the coaches secured a football scholarship for him at Penn State. Howie lashed at him. "I mean, the guy's so dumb it takes him an hour to spell out his name, and now all he has to do is join the ROTC at Penn State, and he has it made. He'll sit out the whole war. And what about me? You think I can get into any college? I'm on Moskowitz's shit list."

The Fink complained bitterly. "Everybody blames me!" I thought he was going to throw Howie across the room. "You think I didn't put my ass on the line for that scholarship?" He showed Howie his chipped teeth and his broken eyebrows. "And who failed four subjects, you or me?"

Howie stormed over to the Fink. "You expect me to pass when the fuzz suspended me for three weeks?"

Finkelberg relented a little. "What do you want from

48

my life? Why don't you put a little of the blame on Nick? He's Moskowitz's golden boy, ain't he?"

"Nick's all right," Howie said. "And if the fuzz likes him, that ain't his fault. And he don't have to worry about getting shoved into the Army. He's got a dead lung. Show him, Nick." I wheezed for the Fink a couple of times. I felt a little guilty about my constricted chest, and I said, "maybe it will heal in a year or two."

When Moskowitz found out that I hadn't applied to any college, he called me down to his office. He had me sit down, then leaning over his desk, his jowls wagging over my head, he began to shout. "Do you want to end up behind the counter at Gimbel's? A rag collector, a nobody? Nick, with your talent and potential?" His hairy knuckles bunched angrily and I drew my head back. "I know, it's that imp, that little Hitler, Rosenthal, he's behind everything. He told you not to apply, just to irk me. I should have shipped him out to Uncle Nate years ago."

Keeping my head at a comfortable distance from his knuckles, I told him flatly that Howie Rosenthal was my only friend at G.W., but that he had absolutely nothing to do with my decision to stay away from colleges. I know I should have also told him that I was tired of being George Washington's wonder boy, of winning spelling bees and essay contests, of hearing about his Uncle Nate, and of having to look at his bloated, pimply face for four years and listen to his own brand of carbonated bullcrap, but, of course, I didn't want to spur his hairy knuckles into action. I just told him that I wanted to take a rest for a year or two. He recalled his knuckles and crumpled the corners of his eyes. "I know," he said, "I know." He told me that my father had been a wonderful man and a faithful colleague—actually, it was my father who had first dubbed Moskowitz the warden of the shithouses—but that I was taking his death too hard, that I should consider him my pal, and that he would take me golfing if I wanted. I thanked him and left the office.

One evening in May Howie captured me and whisked me over to the IRT: he was going to raid a fraternity party at Columbia, and he wanted me to go with him. Howie coached me while we waited for the train. "Remember, we're from Alpha Alpha Gamma." We rode down to 116th Street. Howie lit a cigarette and inhaled cautiously. "Let's go," he said, "let's go." We paused in front of a brownstone on 115th Street. There was a shield over the door with an enormous omega emblazoned on it; a handpainted eye loomed between the curled ends of the omega.

"Hot stuff," Howie said, sucking his cigarette sourly.

"Well, why did you want to come?" I said, unable to stare back at the eye.

"You kidding? They got a harem inside."

Two boys wearing identical tweed coats with wide lapels approached the brownstone; they looked about fourteen years old; they were both smoking pipes with deep, furrowed bowls.

"Is Sonia Dubinsky coming?" the first one asked. "I hear she puts out for whole battalions at a time." Howie winked secretly.

"I know," the second one said. He was carrying a book under his arm: it was *War and Peace*. "Braverman says it's no fun inviting her more than once. He warned me to come prepared."

Howie trampled his cigarette and we followed them up the stairs. We walked through a creaky, uncarpeted hallway and entered a large unfurnished room. Howie whispered to me. "Don't worry, the couches must be upstairs. Remember, Alpha Alpha Gamma." No one challenged us. Howie seemed a little disappointed. There were about twenty boys in the room; they all wore coats with wide lapels, and they had very clean faces. Most of the boys were crowded around a girl with

50

painted eyes who stood against the wall, her breasts raised defiantly. "Wow," Howie said. "I bet you can walk right up and kiss her nipples." He wagged his head—"Sonia, Sonia"—and joined the boys.

There was only one other girl in the room; standing alone near the window, she wore a dark, shapeless sweater. Her face seemed kind and unassuming; her jaw was quite large and her hair was plaited over her ears like thickly stranded rope. She had hazel-colored eyes. I could tell right away that she was totally titless. Every time she sucked in air her nipples would cling hungrily to her sweater. I smiled and she didn't turn her head away. "Sonia Dubinsky," I told myself infallibly, walking over to the window.

She asked me point-blank if I went to Columbia. Even if I hadn't already forgotten Howie's magic formula of alphas and gammas, I still wouldn't have been able to lie: her hazel eyes seemed ready to pierce through any equivocation. I told her that I was a senior at G.W., and that I didn't even intend to go to college.

"Good," she said, "I hate these Columbia queers."

Her name, she said, was Sonia Rubinsky. "Dubinsky, Rubinsky," I argued reasonably with myself, "what difference does it make? As long as the Sonia is the same!" She was a sophomore at City College, and was majoring in political science. Gorky was her favorite writer. And after she told me three or four times that all fraternity parties were for drippy little mama's boys who liked to keep rearranging wooden blocks with the letters S-E-X painted on them, but couldn't really do anything else, I asked her if she wanted to leave. I was amazed at my own boldness. "Yes," she said, flexing her marvelous jaw, and she led me over to the door. I felt a little guilty about abandoning Howie, but he had already broken through the ring of boys and was nuzzling the girl with the defiant breasts, and I knew that he could take care of himself.

When I told her that I lived alone, Sonia offered to come over to my place. She didn't waste any time on preliminaries once we arrived there. Sitting on my bed, her tongue flicking in my throat, she began taking off my shirt. I had some trouble with her brassiere. It refused to unhook. Actually, the brassiere was slightly superfluous. Her nipples seemed stranded on her vacant chest like two useless buttons. I suckled them greedily, but even then, her breasts refused to rise. Sonia apologized. "Sorry," she said, "the toy department is on the fifth floor," and then, reaching over, she removed a packet from her pocketbook. "Free love is fine," she said quizzically, "but I'm still a little old-fashioned. There's nothing wrong with planned parenthood." It was the same kind of packet that Crazy had shown me two years ago.

"Well? Do you want me to put it on for you?"

I walked over to the bathroom. Sonia became suspicious after I closed the door. "God," she said, peeking in, "haven't you ever used a pro?" Her nipples wagged all the while she laughed.

In the morning Sonia announced that she was moving in with me. "I like the setup here."

I was a little taken aback. Not because I believed in any sort of propriety; it's just that she seemed so unbelievably bold.

"Won't your mother and father say something?"

Her jaw sagged sullenly for the first time, and even her hazel eyes seemed to cloud. "My mother's a first-class bitch. My father would move out too, if he only had half the chance. It's already settled. You'll help me pack in the afternoon."

As soon as Sonia moved in, I became a minor celebrity at G.W. It seems that I was the only senior in the whole school who had his own shackjob. Howie was furious. His status at school rapidly declined. He called Sonia "the titless wonder," but nobody listened to him. A shackjob's a shackjob, titless or not: it was as simple as that. He would stand outside one of the johns and badger whoever happened to pass. "You think I couldn'ta grabbed Titless myself? And who told him about Alpha Alpha Gamma in the first place? And how do you know she's really shacking up with him? I'm telling you, Nick's cherry. Ask him yourself."

Half the senior class congregated around my lunch table while I publicly unwrapped the sandwiches that Sonia prepared for me. Howie sat abandoned at his corner of the table, but even he bugged out one eye when he saw me display my own plastic salt shaker and the neatly pared celery stalks and carrot heads which I placed side by side in the middle of the table. "Nick," the Fink would say, ignoring Howie, "what's it like getting it every night?" And after tipping the salt shaker gently over the celery stalks, I would screw up one eye expertly and say, "Come over and I'll give you a demonstration." But in spite of all the publicity, having a shackjob turned out to be a real pain in the ass.

I had trouble with Sonia from the start. She dragged me down to Union Square every other day, and surrounded by asthmatic cats and pokey-faced stumble bums, she talked for hours about Stalin and the Popular Front. If one of the five cent philosophers from the other end of the Square happened to heckle her, she would shout, "Shitface," "Fascist," and "Stooge," while the asthmatic cats purred brokenly, and I collected Eskimo Pie sticks and built magnificent forts behind the benches with the missing slats. After the ordeal at Union Square, we invariably ended up at the Stanley, and sucking whole mouthfuls of jujubes, I had to sit through one Soviet film after the other.

Sonia had been a member of the Young Communist League for years, and she told me about her meetings and her rallies. "I never did any Jimmy Higgins work," she would say, her jaw jutting proudly, "I was strictly agit-prop. We

5 3

made Robin Hood and his Merry Men look like pansies with zoot suits." Then she would tell me about all the exploits of her marvelous band. She had raided the headquarters of the Young Socialist League and held its leaders hostage for three days; she had forced the local newsdealers to distribute the *Daily Worker;* she had fought the bloodsucking landlords on her block and helped the dispossessed tenants bring up their furniture from the street; and when her local A & P failed to hire any Negroes, she spearheaded a sneak attack during which she broke three coffee grinders and scattered Grape Nuts across every aisle. "Match that," she said, "match that."

When I told her that I had done nothing more exceptional than raid the Fort Washington Y once, she began to accuse me. "You know, Nick," she said, "the trouble with you is that you haven't seen anything or done anything. You're blind to everything that's around you. My God, didn't your father ever take you any place, or talk to you about anything? I wouldn't even mind if you were a Fascist. Then at least I could expose you. But you're nothing, you haven't got an idea in your head. You're just a case of arrested development." And after telling me that she was going to crack open my shell and show me a little bit of the world, she took me on a tour of the Bronx.

We boarded the Boston Road trolley and rode past row after row of identically cramped houses with narrow windows and sunken stoops. Men with battered hats and dark, sullen faces sat on the stoops, beer bottles bunched near their toes. Huge mounds of garbage were heaped regularly on both sides of the tracks, with broken crib posts peering over cartons with collapsed sides, mattress springs with distended coils, maimed lamp shades, and headless dolls. A crippled boy with an Indian hat and a moronic smile stood on one of the mounds and threw balls of dried horse shit at Sonia and me. I waved to him. Sonia began lecturing me. "This," she said, pointing to the mound, "this is what we're fighting for. So landlords won't be able to dump their garbage in the street." Then she began talking about the playgrounds and the garbage disposal units in Moscow, and how Stalin had declared war on all the rats and lice in Russia. I kept thinking of the crippled boy. I wanted to stand on the mound with him and challenge the passing trolley cars. I know I would have wound up a creditable shit flinger.

After the first few weeks Sonia stopped packing my lunches. Instead of pared celery stalks and carrots, I came to school with lumpy peanut butter sandwiches. Even the Fink could sense my disappointment. "You ain't wetting your pecker every night, huh Nicky boy?" Howie didn't bother gloating: he had his own troubles. Moskowitz wasn't going to let him graduate. "Screw the academics. The fuzz won't even throw me a general diploma." He stared darkly at me and the Fink. "Everybody's got it knocked, but I always end up with the *dreck*."

Howie disappeared the first week in June. Moskowitz sent the truant officers after him, but nobody could find him. The Fink watched the pool rooms on Broadway, but Howie stayed away from all his old hangouts. There had been reports that someone wearing a blue cap kept feeling up twelve-year-old girls at the RKO Coliseum during the Saturday matinees, and even though I knew that the twelve-year-old girls were only trying to get some attention for themselves, I still wanted to inspect the Coliseum. Maybe Howie was hiding out in the balcony, living on old candy bars? But Sonia kept tabs on my time, and she wouldn't even allow me a free hour. She was still out to educate me.

Howie showed up outside my door on the Sunday before graduation. Sonia was still sleeping. "Shh," I told him, "shh." His shirt was torn, his elbows were black, and his cheeks were sucked in. I sneaked him into the kitchen and made him seven peanut butter sandwiches. "Wake the bitch up," he demanded mildly, "I want some celery stalks."

"She'll kill us," I said. "You'll have to settle for the peanut butter."

He wanted me to roll him a bundle of cigarettes. "A week's supply," he said. I showed him my empty tobacco pouch. "Sonia's allergic to smoke."

"Jesus Christ," he said, finishing his fifth sandwich, "what kind of broad did you line yourself up with? Do you have to have her permission to take a crap too?"

I turned the pouch inside out. "Where the hell have you been? I thought maybe you were hiding out at the Coliseum?"

"You kidding? I ain't no lousy werewolf. I can't live all the time in the dark. I been hanging around this carnival at Pelham."

"Where do you sleep?"

"Under the ferris wheel," he said, flexing his elbows proudly. He talked about "shills" and "aces" and "monkey pie," and told me that he was a "bona fide carnival bum." He was already a "vet."

"One thing," he said, poising one eyebrow slowly, "you gotta know how to handle the queers. The guys who run the stands are all half queer." He removed from his pocket a wooden block that was wound with chicken wire. "Better than a blackjack," he said, gripping the block. "It keeps off the swishes." I noticed a bruise on his neck. He jabbed the air fiercely, smashing imaginary noses and gouging out imaginary eyes. "Don't think I'm looking for any sympathy, Nick. I appreciate the sandwiches, but that's not what I came for. I need some jack. The carnival's moving to Philly on Thursday, and I'm moving with it. Once we get there I know they'll need an extra shill."

The rent money was sitting in a dish on the shelf over Howie's head. I looked at Howie quizzingly before I decided

5 6

to take down the dish and offer him the money. Niggardly Nick, I called myself, Niggardly Nick. Howie counted the crisp ten dollar bills. "You sure you can afford it, Nick? I don't want no money you can't afford."

"I'm sure," I said, staring at his black elbows and cursing myself now for having offered the money reluctantly. "Wait, I can get you some more." I walked quietly into the bedroom. Sonia was snoring. I removed an old stocking half filled with quarters that I had stored behind my dresser: emergency money, quarters that I had saved religiously since I was five.

Howie had known about the stocking. He didn't want to take the money. "Go 'head," I said, "what the hell am I going to do with a sack of quarters?" Howie tied a knot at the end of the stocking, and then threw the stocking into his pocket, together with the wooden block. He began to walk a little lopsided. "Thanks, Nick," he said, "thanks. Don't worry. I'll pay you back. Howie Rosenthal don't forget the people who hurt him and the people who help him. The fuzz gets paid back too. With a mouthful of chicken wire." Then he started talking about the carnival again. "No Army's gonna get me, Nick. I'm changing my name when I get to Philly. So if you get a letter from Flash Gordon or Phil Fu Manchu, you'll know who it's from." His left elbow began to shake; he steadied the elbow with his other hand. His eyebrows worked unevenly. He wanted me to come with him to Philadelphia. "You can take Titless too! Sure, we can work up some kind of juggling act, or take over one of the concessions. What do you say, Nick?"

I shrugged one shoulder unconvincingly. "I don't think so, Howie. I never liked carnivals." His elbow began shaking again. "Howie, why don't you stick around? You can always find another carnival. Maybe we can get Moskowitz to give you some kind of diploma? You don't have to go home. I can put you up here. I'll talk to Sonia when she gets up."

57

"Forget it," he said, "I ain't sucking around no fuzz. I'm going to Philly with the troupe. You don't gotta worry about me, Nick. The kid can take care of himself." He tapped the stocking and the wooden block; the quarters in his pocket jingled hollowly. "See you, Nick."

I walked him over to the door. "Howie, lemme make you a few more sandwiches."

"Na," he said, "I ain't got the time. They need me back at the carnival. Take care, Nick, and show your bitch who's the boss."

I suppose nobody in the court really believed that Sonia was "Mrs. Lapucci," but we did have all the outward signs of propriety: I emptied the garbage regularly, and Sonia shopped at Gristede's and wore the twenty-five-cent band that I had picked out for her at Woolworth's, the band having originally come with a packet of confetti and a paper bridal veil. Mrs. Bemelman glared at us when we passed her in the hall, and she no longer told me anything about Crazy, but there was still no talk about having us dispossessed. She was much too busy to bother with us. She attended all the rallies of the German-American Bund, and played her recordings of Hitler's Reichstag speeches through the night. More than once I was woken by frenized shouts of "*Sig heil, sig heil, sig heil.*"

After Hitler captured Paris and began to talk of walking over the English Channel, Mrs. Bemelman denounced Churchill and his Jewish Parliament, and warned that Roosevelt had better come to terms with her Führer, or there would soon be a day of reckoning for all Americans. She would often stand in the middle of the court and rant for hours. There was some talk about having her committed or at least thrown out of the court, but no one followed through. She was still the dispenser of steam and hot water, and most of us knew that the proper functioning of our toilets and dumbwaiters depended directly on Mrs. Bemelman's good will. But in November, just a month before the outbreak of the war, Mrs. Bemelman began painting enormous swastikas in the halls, most of the kids in our building mistaking them for the mark of Zorro. Then, after she transferred her swastikas to the windows of the shops on Fort Washington Avenue and added the words "*Juden Verboten*" over the swastikas, and even smashed a few of the windows, she was arrested and later taken to Bellevue for observation. She never returned to the court. Mr. Bemelman visited her practically every day, but now his shoulders seemed unburdened, and he began tending the bushes in the court. I would have invited him upstairs, but Sonia had never cared for Mr. Bemelman. She called him "The Nazi" and claimed that he was the one who had inspired Mrs. Bemelman's swastikas.

Soldiers began to appear regularly now on Cabrini Boulevard. Some came with cameras and ranged Fort Tryon Park. Even Nellie Wasserman, whose father was the chancellor of the Washington Heights Merchants' Association, was hanging around with a private from Fort Dix. The peacetime draft had made the Army somewhat respectable. All the kids in the neighborhood made up their own selective service numbers and boasted of having their own draft cards. The storekeepers waved to the soldiers and the kids saluted them. None of the soldiers I saw wore campaign hats; most of them wore caps with gold shields and shiny leather bills. I had meant all along to ask Mr. Bemelman how Crazy was making out, and then, during the last week in November, there was a small notice in the *Post:* SERVICEMAN FROM NEW YORK AREA DIES IN FREAK ACCIDENT. Crazy had been killed by a runaway tank during maneuvers at Fort Riley in Kansas. The tank had been manned by a rookie crew. The *Post* claimed that there would be some sort of investigation. I suppose, in a way, Crazy was the first casualty of the war. I showed the notice to Sonia. She said that this would never have happened in the Red Army. She thought that the individual members of the tank crew should be crucified or shot.

Mr. Bemelman came up to see me a few days after the accident. He stood outside the door holding Crazy's old campaign hat. The peak was caved in, and the brim was crusted with soot and dust. Mr. Bemelman's hand shook. His whole face seemed shrunken.

"Please, Mr. Bemelman, come in."

He saw Sonia sitting in the kitchen. She was leaning against the window sill, both knees showing.

"No," he said, looking down. "Thanks, Nick. The dumbwaiter broke, and I have to fix the cables." I noticed for the first time that his left ear was larger than the right. He gave me Crazy's hat. "I was going through Irwin's belongings, and I thought you might want to have it. The last time he was in he told me you liked his hat." He left then before I could thank him, the banister already hiding his narrow back. I tried on the hat without reshaping the peak or dusting the brim. It rode unhampered down to my chin. I raised the left side of the hat, exposing one eye, an ear, and part of my nose. Sonia saw me from the kitchen. She gripped her knees and began to cackle. "What an awful, silly hat," she said finally, "what an awful, silly hat." I walked downstairs without closing the door. Even from the court I could hear her cackling. The hat kept sinking lower and lower, and I had to maneuver the brim. The kids who were playing slapball in the court held up their game when I crossed over their chalked bases. They all wanted to try on the hat. I almost bumped into a woman who had just come out of Gristede's hugging a sack of grapefruits, and she called me a lousy show-off and a bum. I walked down to Fort Washington Avenue. I convinced myself that Crazy's hat had all sorts of magical properties, that while wearing it I could commune with Crazy's ghost, and maybe with Howie in Philadelphia, or even with Father Finnocchino's hunchbacks and dwarfs. A sailor came out of the bar near the corner and broke my reverie: he wanted to trade hats. I glared at him and kept walking.

About a month after the bombing of Pearl Harbor, Sonia's father moved in with us. He arrived one night with two shopping bags and a suitcase and told us that his wife had kicked him out. He promptly took out his handkerchief and started to cry. "I told you my mother's a bitch," Sonia said, but she didn't seem particularly pleased to see her father. He pleaded with Sonia to allow him to stay. "Just for a little while," he said, still holding the handkerchief, "until I can get settled." And for the first time since we had been living together, Sonia deferred to me. "You'll have to ask Nick," she said. "It's his place." He wiggled his ears for me and blew his nose weakly, and I helped him bring in the shopping bags. But within a week I began to realize that Sonia's mother was probably my only ally.

Mr. Rubinsky was a pot-bellied little man who talked incessantly about the Spanish Civil War and the Lincoln Brigade. "If it hadn't have been for my damn leg," he would always end up saying, "I would have gone over with the Lincolns in '36. Ask anybody. It was the leg." Then he limped for us and called Franco a *puta* and a *maricón* and told us about the John Brown Battery and the Garibaldi Battalion and the P.O.U.M. and Tarragona, where, he said, the Lincoln Brigade had trained. "I knew all their moves. I always had an official report." And he would offer to give us a battle by battle description of the Civil War. Even Sonia grew tired of his commentaries and she would often halt him in the middle of a battle. "Can it," she would say. He would shrug one shoulder awkwardly, sit on his suitcase, and promise to keep his mouth shut during his entire tenure at my place, which, I was beginning to see, was likely to be lifelong.

I suffered through the summer and most of the fall with Sonia and her father. I often wondered to myself why I didn't throw them both out on their butts which had already been buttered and fattened at my expense. And even though I planned magnificent schemes, I was paralyzed in some way and couldn't act. Maybe I just didn't want to live alone. After a while Sonia took her father with her on her excursions to Union Square, and she left me pretty much alone. I would read in the mornings and play slapball later with the kids in the court, and maybe hike over to the zoo and draw the lions, or feed the zebras and the alpacas. Without Sonia around to plague me, I usually had something to do. It was in the evenings that Sonia made most of the trouble. If she had already seen the films at the Stanley, or was too lazy to attend the lectures at the Seaman's Institute or the 92nd Street Y, she would sit home and begin to probe me. "You're a freak, Nick," she would say, "and I'm going to find out why." And when I told her about my father, and that I couldn't remember anything about my mother, she would draw in her chin excitedly, and say, "There's something fishy about the whole thing. I'll bet your father was a secret lech, or maybe a queer. Did he ever bring up any of his students?" And then her father would help her rummage through my father's belongings. "We'll have the story soon. Don't worry. Just one letter or a snapshot, or an inscription in a book, that's all it takes." But all they ever uncovered was Crazy's campaign hat which I had hid in one of my father's drawers.

One evening, late in 1942, while Sonia and her father were at the Stanley, I decided to eat Chinese food at the Shanghai Palace on Broadway. While I walked towards Fort Washington Avenue, I heard the air-raid sirens wail torturously overhead. I figured I'd sit out the alert at the Shanghai, but an air-raid warden reprimanded me immediately. "This is no picnic," he said. "The shelter's over there." The chin straps of his helmet were loose and kept slapping his chest. His jowls wagged continuously. It was Moskowitz. "Nick," he said, "Nick," recognizing me. And he followed me over to the shelter, which happened to be a tiny cellar under Fort Washington Avenue. Several bicycles without fenders were pressed against one wall. I could hear the rats shuttle between the wheels of the bicycles. Moskowitz poked around the room with his flashlight. The rats ignored his beam and kept jumping through the spokes. "It wouldn't be such a bad idea," he said, "if the Nazis bombed this place." He turned off the flashlight and we stood in the dark. The sirens kept wailing. A woman and a little boy came into the room. The boy was wearing a pint-sized helmet and combat boots. He saluted Moskowitz and stuck his tongue out at me. I wondered how he would have reacted had I worn Crazy's hat. "He's a little soldier," the woman said. "His father's in the Pacific." He charged the bicycles and chased after the rats. "We'll need all the soldiers we can find," Moskowitz said; I don't think he meant to slight me.

More out of spite than anything else, I asked him: "How is Uncle Nate?"

"Fine, fine," he said, and proceeded to catalog Uncle Nate's methods for controlling delinquent boys. "He's got all Jewish kids up there. Some of them are orphans, most of them come from the Bronx. Troublemakers, but Nate keeps them in line." He dipped his head slightly and the rim of his helmet hid his nose. "You know, Nick," he said, "Uncle Nate could use somebody with your talents up there. Nick, you'd be a natural. You wouldn't even need a teaching certificate. Where can you find teachers today?" We heard several loud thuds: the little boy was bombarding the rats with his helmet. The woman called to him, "Rudy, Rudy, you'll soil your boots." I told Moskowitz that I didn't feel like moving upstate, but that I would let him know if I changed my mind. I could imagine myself telling Howie I was working for Uncle Nate! The

63

sirens had stopped wailing, and I moved towards the entrance of the cellar. Moskowitz rolled up his arm band hurriedly and blocked my way. "The alert isn't over yet. We have to wait for the all clear." His chin straps had tangled under his jowls.

When I came home later I found Mr. Rubinsky trying on my father's suits. He had rolled up all the cuffs and the sleeves for the occasion. "Not bad," he said. "With a little alteration I'll have a complete outfit." Sonia was with him: she was wearing Crazy's hat. "Nick," she said, saluting me, "we're organizing the Cabrini Boulevard Patrol. Captain Nick's Army." I sat in the kitchen. There were some empty beer bottles under the sink. "Nick," she said, "Nick, don't you want to inspect your patrol. Nick. . . ."

Sonia and her father slept on the sofa in the living room. They had covered each other with my father's suits. Sonia snored doggedly through one nostril, and her father kept chewing his gums. I stuffed three shirts and a suit into my father's battered grip, together with some underwear, my tobacco pouch, and Crazy's hat. I said goodbye to the kitchen, listened to Sonia snore for a minute and gathered some additional courage, then I went downstairs, found a drug store that was still open, and called Moskowitz. "Who?" he said. "What? Who's calling so late?"

"Nick," I told him, "Nick. Does your Uncle Nate still need a teacher?"

"Nick," he said parochially, "hasty decisions only brew trouble. Call me back tomorrow. Then I'll talk to Uncle Nate."

"No," I said. "Tomorrow is no good." I knew I would never be able to screw up enough courage if I waited until the morning, and I would be stuck with Sonia and her father for life. "It has to be now," I said, frantically. "Now."

"Okay, Mr. Impatience, it's settled. I do all the recruiting for Uncle Nate. You are now officially the latest addition to

6 4

the Blattenburg Home and School for Wayward Jewish Boys. Nick, you're a fortunate young man. Hasty or not, this is one decision that will turn out in your favor. Uncle Nate—"

"No snow jobs, Mr. Moskowitz, please. I've already bought the product. Just tell me how to get up there."

I was going to wear Crazy's hat in the telephone booth, but I didn't want any of the countermen to become suspicious, so I decided to take out the tobacco pouch instead. My jock-strap spilled out of the grip. I leaned over and tried to pick it up, but my head bumped against the wall of the booth.

"Blattenburg," I said, "Blattenburg." I couldn't locate the pouch.

CHAPTER

The train had remained in the station for almost an hour, and when a woman at the other end of the car complained to the conductor, he gave her vague answers about troop movements and wartime conditions. She wasn't satisfied until he told her that there had also been some talk of sabotage, and that there might be a bomb on the train. She immediately looked under her seat. Then, glancing systematically at all the passengers and property in the car, her eyes finally settled on my grip, which I was carrying on my knees, one of the handles having already broken off. I didn't want to become part of her little drama, and so, trying to look as inconspicuous as possible, I molded the bumps on the grip with one knee, knowing that if I shaped my eyebrows in the wrong way or juggled the grip, she would have had me thrown off the train. Her glances must have become infectious, because most of

66

the civilians on board began talking about bombs and sabo-teurs, and about the Yellow Peril that was paralyzing the entire Pacific and might even capture California. Now, it's true that the Japs had overrun the Solomons and the Philip-pines, and there had even been rumors that a pack of Japanese "secret weapon" subs was sitting under San Francisco Bay, but the soldiers who were sitting next to me didn't seem very concerned about the war. They were having an impassioned argument about who had bigger tits: Betty Grable or Linda Darnell? And when they finally agreed that Linda Darnell had the biggest "knockers" on the Coast, the one soldier who had backed Betty Grable tried to redeem himself. "Who needs knockers?" he said. "I'll bet Betty gives a better lay any day of the week!" A new argument now erupted. When a civilian tried to intervene, the soldiers cut him short. "Butt out, buddy, this is strictly RA." Then, for some reason, the soldiers de-ferred to me. "Let him settle it." I told them politely that I didn't know. They seemed somewhat offended, and halted the argument. I hid behind my grip. The conductor announced with an air of condescension that no bombs had been found under the caboose or in any of the freight cars, and after sev-eral noisy huffs, the train took off.

I was never much of a traveler. Even the occasional bouncing of the car irritated me. The soldiers pulled their garrison hats over their eyes and slept peacefully: they seemed immune to all the sights. As my mind jogged drowsily I began to suspect that we were passing and repassing the same towns and marshes and junkyards; but after recalling Sonia and her father, I assured myself that I would be able to sit out the ride, no matter how many times the same marshes and junkyards reappeared. Then, as if I had just been jostled out of a dream, I heard the conductor drawl, *"Blatt'nburg,"* and hugging the one good handle of my grip, I scrambled towards the entrance of the car. Bending both knees awkwardly, I disembarked.

67

The platform wasn't much of an improvement; it hardly seemed navigable. The planks were warped and crookedly spaced and pitted with sand and hoarfrost. There was, however, one consolation. The sun, which must have been out at least three or four hours, hadn't been able to disturb the frost, but it had already baked the planks, and I had no trouble warming my feet. A station house stood behind the platform, but its windows were boarded and its entrance was barred. The shingles on the roof had begun to peel; even its lone chimney sagged. There were no other houses around.

Huge mounds of dirt surrounded the platform on both sides of the track. A tiny, sandbagged fort was stationed between two of the mounds; the dusty snout of an ack-ack gun leaned over one edge of the fort. The gun was unmanned. I stood tentatively on two of the planks and began to chide myself. "Even Sonia was better than this." Then, almost magically, a car with a dented roof and two makeshift fenders appeared and bounced across the track; its one headlight blazed blindingly. The car halted abruptly near the platform. The driver called to me. I hopped over the planks. "Nick," the driver said, "I rushed like a demon, but with this machine you can never tell what will happen." He banged the dashboard disapprovingly. The glove compartment opened, revealing a leaky flashlight battery and two hard-boiled eggs. "They call this a car!"

Something about the driver seemed slightly incongruous, as if a vital part of him had been shorn off, and he was a little lost now without the missing piece. He was wearing a black frock coat and a rumpled blue cap with the Seabee insignia sewn on raggedly. His head reached the roof of the car, and his hanging jaw loomed behind the windshield. Weblike lines were bunched under his eyes, and both his sleeves were patched. "Uncle Nate?" I asked uneasily.

"God forbid," he said. "I'm Rosencrantz, the chauffeur."

And then he dipped his cap. "I was worried when I heard the train. It never stops here any more unless somebody flags it down." He stared at me suspiciously, his jaw now blocking half the window. "Did you pay off the conductor?"

"No," I said. "The train just stopped."

"You're lucky. It's the first time." I'm sure he didn't believe me. I pointed to the sandbagged fort and the station house. "What happened here?"

"The Army took over. They leveled the whole town. They're going to build a fort or an air strip. With the Army you can never tell. Don't worry about the cannon. It couldn't even fire pebbles. It's just there for show. They wanted to take over the Home too, but Nathanson knows too many big shots in the legislature."

"Nathanson?" I said.

"*Uncle Nate.* It was touch and go for a while. The steam shovels were already outside the gate, but Nathanson won in the end. The Republicans control the county, but he warned them that the President owed him special favors. Who figured they would listen? The Republicans are his private bugbear. He calls them *The Japs.*" He stepped out of the car. "You'll have to come in through my side," he said. "Only one door works." His shoulders rose over the dented roof.

It was only after we were both seated that I dared ask him about the headlight. "How come you leave it on all the time?"

"Do I have a choice?" he said slyly. "I can't shut it off. The wires tangled somewhere, and now the light shines day and night. Like an ark."

"Won't the battery burn out?"

"Let it burn. I'll say a prayer over the electrodes!"

We rode along a narrow, unpaved road, the front fenders knocking relentlessly and the exhaust pipe leaving a green fog in our wake, a favorite trick of the Green Hornet. But here, on the unpaved road, the fog seemed out of place. It didn't take me very long to discover that Rosencrantz was an absolutely insane driver. The car zigged and zagged across the road, slapping back overhanging branches and scraping broken mailboxes and abandoned gates.

"It's the tires," Rosencrantz claimed. "They retread them now with string. Where can you find a good tire? Even Uncle Nate can't do a thing. And he has connections with the black market." We both heard a heavy bang and Rosencrantz halted the car: a fender had fallen off. He stepped out and refitted the fender, the tails of his coat flapping against his knees. This time he drove more cautiously, encountering difficulty only with an occasional branch. "Who wants to disturb the fender?" Then, as if he were merely switching gears, he began talking about Robespierre and Diderot and the notorious Dr. Destouches. "You've heard of the Doctor, eh Nick? Sometimes he goes under another name. But in the dispensaries near Paris he is simply Dr. Destouches. A known collaborationist, and an anti-Semite to the bargain. They say he's Petain's personal physician. But who can believe all the stories they tell? I'm sure the Underground would like to blow off his head and send it flying through the sewers of Paris, but they probably have more important targets. Just mention his name to Uncle Nate! He calls Destouches *The Golem!* You know, a lost case, one without a soul. But he interests me, my Destouches. He was a hero in the other war. With ribbons and the whole regalia. And also, a wounded head to go with it, and a bad case of shell-shock. He hears the knocking in his ears all the time and he can't sleep. So they call him names now. Pig! Fascist! But there's another story behind his Fascism. What does he want with war again? With the Germans in power, he's a Fascist. Let the Russians take over tomorrow, he'll be a Communist. And if Willkie wins next time and the Marines jump over Paris and capture the

70

Eiffel Tower, my Destouches will be a Republican in a week. My sympathies are with him: the man wants to stay alive. I'm told he suffers from hallucinations. He keeps dreaming that he's sitting on a pile of shit. He knows the condition of the world, Destouches, believe me."

I watched him warily, holding my grip with both hands. I cautioned myself: "If Uncle Nate hires philosophical chauffeurs, what will he expect of me?" Rosencrantz seemed to sense my dismay. "I know," he said simply, "I know." He opened the glove compartment and handed me a hard-boiled egg. "Eat," he ordered me. "Eggs are good for the bladder." The egg was coated with oil and rusty battery leakage, but I ate it anyway. Then he told me:

"Nick, I'm only a chauffeur part-time. Officially I'm the rabbi for the Home. I could tell you whole histories, but I'll make it short. My congregation threw me out and I ended up here!" He touched his jaw with one hand. "You are looking at a rabbi in exile. And to commemorate my disgrace, I shaved off my beard. Where could you find a rabbi on Simpson Street with a naked chin? Now I walk around with a freak's face. But I can't complain. Uncle Nate leaves me alone. I bless the bread for him, teach my Bible class, deliver a cockeyed sermon on occasions, and drive him around. He knows my sermons are harmless, so what does he have to fear? Believe me, Nick, the boys here aren't the only lost souls. I mention myself as a classic example. And don't think the driving puts me off. I enjoy being a chauffeur. And if I refused to drive him, would it do me any good? He would put me in charge of the laundry or the kennels. Everybody here has two functions at least. Even the boys. They're all part-time soldiers. Sure, Nathanson has manufactured his own hysteria. He's told them that an attack is imminent. What attack? It's wartime, and Uncle Nate holds all the reins. His word is the law. Nick, do you want another egg?"

"No," I told him. "No."

"Soon you'll meet the whole crew. You'll find a rigid hierarchy here. Uncle Nate keeps us all in boxes, but even the boxes are graded: some are roomier than the rest. After all, Uncle Nate can't terrorize the boys all by himself. He needs his henchmen. First on the list is Mama, the social worker, with all her theories and case studies still the number one bitch and a whore in her heart. But you'll find it out for yourself. Next comes Rubin, Uncle's head screw, himself a graduate of the Home, which makes him even more of a fink than he would be under ordinary circumstances. Uncle Nate leaves all the dirty work to Rubin. And Rubin has for himself two assistants, Murdock and Billingsgate, the Jailers. Two Gentiles that Uncle Nate recruited from this area. He says that their job isn't for Jews. But believe me, I could have found him plenty Jewish candidates. The Jailers are bad birds, this is true, but it has nothing to do with their religion. There's more on the list, Nick. Rubin's band of bulldogs who back up the Jailers' every move, then Dobrilubov, the Cossack cook, who is also the shop teacher. And Pebbleby, the janitor, a walking scarecrow. And on the bottom of the list you will find Rosencrantz, the chauffeur-rabbi, whose box is the narrowest of all. But there is still something on bottom of the bottom: the boys. Uncle Nate keeps them ten in a box. The boys are too numerous to list, but I'll give you a sample. Matches, who burned his mother alive. An accident, of course. And Bullets Bucharevsky, who is a specialist in tortures. He likes to carve his initials on other people's chests. Lovely boys, but I prefer them all, even Bullets, to Uncle Nate and his associates, one of which I myself unfortunately am, and you will soon be in the same position. But enough, I'll leave the briefing to Uncle Nate. I'm sure he'll have a few surprises for you."

Rosencrantz halted the car near a wooden fence with

a number of missing ties. "We'll have to walk from here, Nick. Nathanson doesn't like me to keep the car inside his property. I always leave it near the road."

We stepped out of the car, Rosencrantz offering to carry my grip. I thanked him and told him that it was very light and that I could manage it. He saw me staring at the fence.

"Nick," he said, "the fence is nothing. It's no more than a marker." He pointed to the kennels that were placed in strategic positions all along the fence. The kennels had white-washed walls and neatly shingled roofs. "There is Uncle Nate's protection." A bulldog with an enormous snout lounged inside the kennel nearest us, eyeing us disdainfully. "That's Shadrach, Rubin's general, the lead dog. I could ram the car into the fence and it wouldn't make any difference to him. He never growls when I'm around. He knows I'm harmless. If you came alone, Nick, he would have you pinned on the ground by now with half your head in his jaws. An intruder would not get very far here, believe me. But as soon as he sees you're with me, then Shadrach will have nothing to do with you."

We both scrambled under the fence. There were several sheds behind the kennels. Most of them had makeshift roofs, and their chimneys generally sagged. Each shed had only one window. "The barracks," Rosencrantz said. "The boys live there. Uncle Nate is trying to simulate a military arrangement. So he has his own little army. And the boys don't mind. They enjoy drilling with wooden rifles."

We walked past the kennels and the sheds, and approached a large house with a gabled roof. "The home of the general staff," Rosencrantz said mockingly. "They say it used to be one of Harriman's estates, but I think that's just a rumor that Uncle Nate himself has propagated. He enjoys creating his own histories. Folklore is his favorite subject. If you listen to him, the Jews invented the world and will have

7 3

a hand in destroying it. He is a great believer in all sorts of messianic claptrap. Every time he hears the thunder crackle he convinces himself that his deliverer will come and free him and the Home and all the Jews throughout the world. And the President too. He wouldn't want to have a world without Roosevelt." He pointed to one of the gables. "Nick, you see that window, with the boards over it, that's where Nathanson keeps his little dungeon. If you're a nuisance, you get a warning, and then maybe one of the Jailers works you over, but with a major offense you get three to seven days upstairs. Ask one of the boys to tell you about the Dungeon. Bullets is in there now. Uncle Nate gave him the maximum." We heard a repeated thud coming from the cellar of the house. I stopped and tried to peek through one of the tiny cellar windows, but the glass was backed with wire, and all I could make out was a few gray forms. Then I heard a prolonged shout. "Ahhhiii."

"God," I said, stepping back.

Rosencrantz gripped my arm. "It's nothing," he said. "The boys are drilling in the gym. Murdock is teaching them some Japanese bayonet charges. He used to be a Marine."

A man came out of the house and stood on the porch. He had a short, thin body and an unusually large head. He was wearing a black skullcap. Rosencrantz turned towards him and dipped his cap knowingly. "*Shalom*, Rubin, *Shalom*." His shoulders drew together under his black coat.

"Rabbi," Rubin said. "Mama wants to see you. *Now*."

"Nick," Rosencrantz said, shaking my hand; his palm felt moist. "We'll talk later. Goodbye." He boarded the porch and opened the screened door. He was at least two heads taller than Rubin. "Later, Nick," he said again, and ducking his head, he disappeared behind the screen. Rubin walked towards the edge of the porch. He was wearing thick-soled work shoes. He placed both thumbs in his mouth and whistled. I noticed a stir in one of the kennels. Then the bulldog that

74

we had seen before bounded past the row of sheds, leaving a ragged curtain of dust behind him, and before I had the chance to turn around, the dog was already on the porch nuzzling Rubin's knee with his armor-plated head. "Salute Nick," Rubin commanded him. "Come on, Shad." Shadrach raised one forepaw grudgingly.

"Come on up," Rubin said, smiling. I was a little alarmed: his smile seemed extraordinarily kind. He began rubbing the bulldog's back. "Did the Rabbi give you his usual spiel?" he asked me, but there was no indication of a threat in his voice. "We ought to hire him as a guide."

I shifted the grip to my left hand.

"Here," Rubin said, "let Shad carry your bundle for you." Before I could protest, Shadrach gripped the handle in his mouth, and with his bountiful jowls wagging, he carried the grip across the porch, leaving a track of saliva.

Rubin touched my shoulder and then twirled his skullcap teasingly. "Come on," he said, opening the door. "I'll take you in to see Uncle Nate. He's expecting you. Uncle don't have an easy time here. I should know. I gave him plenty trouble myself when I was a kid. He had me in the Dungeon once for thirteen days. That's still the record. Did the Rabbi tell you about the Dungeon?"

"Yes," I said demurely. "That must have been quite an ordeal."

"You said it. These little punks can't go more than five. They have a picnic here. In the old days Uncle never let up."

I felt a bony tail sweep past my leg. Shadrach had followed us into the house.

← CHAPTER ⊅

5

The hall was exceedingly narrow, and whenever I tried to keep abreast of Rubin, my shoulder would bang against the wall. Even Shadrach had some difficulty; he held the grip loosely, but it still hindered his pace. A dim, unshaded bulb hung from the ceiling by a twisted cord. I had to duck my head in order to avoid the bulb. Both walls were lined with posters that had probably been salvaged from a recent War Bond drive. In one poster, a grim looking minuteman, surrounded by a halo of stars, was taking pot shots at Hitler and Hirohito, who were dressed as ducks. In another, Hitler, Mussolini, and Tojo, their cheeks glowing obscenely, were being used as kindling for a huge bonfire. Rubin stopped in front of a door at the end of the hall. Shadrach's crumpled ears perked slightly as he approached the door. He dropped the grip and seemed to be standing at attention, his buttocks

76

stiffening instantly. Rubin knocked on the door with one knuckle. "Uncle?" All three of us heard the gruff reply. *"Come in."*

"Shad," Rubin said, "wait here." Then he turned from the dog to me. "Uncle don't like him messing up his carpets." Shadrach retrieved the grip and backed away from the door with a calculated gait, like a faultless, mechanical sentry, only his left ear, which had uncrumpled itself and now flopped freely, showing any real signs of life. Rubin and I entered the inner sanctum.

I was hardly disappointed. Uncle Nate was a shorter, fatter version of Moskowitz, with the same wagging jowls and crinkling eyes. He was sitting behind a mahogany desk with short, firm legs. On the desk there was a penknife in the shape of a torpedo, a Bible and a stamp album with equally frayed covers, and a miniature U-boat with a cracked hull, together with a leather bound folio containing the inevitable photographed portraits of Missy Le Hand, of Fala, the President's Scottish terrier, and of FDR himself wearing his Navy cape aboard the *U.S.S. Missouri.* An orderly row of photographs was also displayed on the wall behind the desk. I recognized many of the faces on the wall: Al Jolson, Sigmund Freud, Eddie Cantor, Benny Leonard, Leon Trotsky, Hank Greenberg, John Garfield, and Bernard Baruch. A forked sconce with two tiny candle-shaped bulbs was dug into the wall on either side of the desk; most of the room remained in partial shadow. A lumpy carpet covered part of the floor. Rubin ushered me cautiously towards the desk. He stood between the sconces, his ears glowing fiercely. Uncle Nate was wearing a Bundles for Britain badge on his lapel. He rose and greeted us. Then he sat down again. There were no other chairs in the room.

"How was your ride from the station?" he asked me, his eyes crinkling steadily. I'm sure he noticed my discomfort.

7 7

"I hope Rosencrantz wasn't discourteous. You must think it odd having a member of the rabbinate serve as a chauffeur. But we are very pressed for manpower in these times. I'm sure you are already aware of that, as it is one of the reasons you are here now. Of course, you come highly recommended. My nephew rarely makes a mistake. But, in regard to the Rabbi. I assure you, Nick, I'm not trying to be disrespectful, or to undermine his station here."

"Don't worry, Uncle," Rubin said assuringly. "The Rabbi took advantage of the ride. I watched him from the porch. He didn't waste a minute. The Rabbi's always peddling his wares."

One of Uncle Nate's eyes closed: the eye seemed to admonish Rubin. "Yes," he said, turning to me, "the Rabbi has his views. And God knows he's welcome to them. Of course, the Rabbi is concerned mainly with spiritual alignments. Quite a different thing from running an institution of correction. Do you know, Nick, that not one of our graduates has ever returned to the world of crime. Occasionally we hear of an arrest, but nothing serious. Misdemeanors, but no felonies. We have a spotless record here. Oh, there was one exception. Only one." He arched his thumb and began snapping his fingers. "Rubin, what was his name? . . . that one."

"Meyer Schneck," Rubin said automatically.

"Yes, Schneck. A psychopath. There was nothing we could do. His mind was already decayed. Delusions," he said, waving his hand. "He killed a bank guard on Southern Boulevard. For no reason. He wasn't even trying to rob the bank. No, there was nothing we could have done for Schneck. Our record is spotless. But the Rabbi doesn't seem to understand. He doesn't really know the boys. They respect force. They would pounce on any opening, any sign of weakness on our part. I know. We provide a core of stability for them. They have had enough chaos. I know. Order is what they want.

You will find no shabbiness here, Nick. No indirection. We provide a way of life for the boys. We civilize them." Then, his jowls wagging rhythmically, he jutted his chin in Rubin's direction. "Rubin," he said softly, "Rubin is our prize. He is one of our graduates, you know. Rubin, how many times were you arrested before the court sent you here? Do you remember, Rubin?"

"Seven times, Uncle. Seven times."

"Nick, you would never have believed that a fourteen year old boy could have had such a record. Our Rubin was a master with an ice pick or a zip gun. And he could make out fine with a book of matches. None of the vegetable stands on Jennings Street was safe with Rubin around. And it wasn't only vegetables that Rubin went after. The merchants had to pin down their pants. Rubin caused a holocaust wherever he went. The court didn't know what to do with him. He had already broken out of three different reform schools. They were going to hold him in a detention home on Welfare Island until he was ripe for Sing Sing. But then they decided to put him in my personal care. And don't think there was a miraculous transformation when Rubin arrived. On his first day here he robbed my watch. My keepers wanted to send him back to the court. But I tamed him." He pointed slyly to the ceiling. "We have our little dungeon upstairs. Rubin was a regular customer. Rubin, tell him what the boys thought of me in your time. Don't be shy. *Tell him.*"

"Uncle," Rubin said impishly, "we thought you was the biggest bastard in the world."

"*Precisely,*" Uncle Nate said. "And the boys here today have a similar reaction. But I get results, Nick, I get results." He opened the top drawer of his desk. I noticed a pile of Victory letters inside the drawer. He began sifting through the pile. The soiled corners of several War Ration books showed under the letters. "Here," he said, "I get letters from

79

our boys every day. Ninety-seven of our graduates are now on active duty. I keep a careful record. Nick, we are represented in practically every branch of the service. Rangers, Seabees, Air Corps. We even have a lieutenant. Rubin, do you remember Shweikopf?"

"No, Uncle."

"He must have been before your time. An extraordinary boy. Under different circumstances he would have been a whiz kid. I'm sure of it. He was with MacArthur in the Philippines and he's now training with the British Commandos. I don't know the whole story yet. It's top secret. And," he said, clamping his jaws solemnly, "two of our boys have already given their lives for the United Nations. One in Luzon and the other was caught in a Nip raid somewhere in the jungles of Sumatra. His body was never found. There was even some talk of cannibalism. Shapiro. Lennie Shapiro. Both boys have been placed on our Honor Roll. I know it's small thanks for giving up one's life, but we have to find some little way to signify our appreciation and respect. No, Nick, we don't cater to shirkers here. The boys learn their responsibilities, and in record time."

Someone began scratching the door.

"It's Shad," Rubin said, raising one shoulder awkwardly. "He can't wait outside doors too long. Don't worry, Uncle, I'll teach him a lesson." Rubin opened the door. Shadrach, both ears drooping guiltily, peeked into the room.

"Rubin," Uncle Nate said, "forget about that mutt for a minute. I'm expecting a little trouble tonight. Look out for Benny and the Indian. And Matches." I thought I saw Uncle Nate wink.

"Uncle," Rubin said, "everything is under control." Then he left the room and closed the door behind him. I heard him kick Shadrach's flanks. "You gotta go, Shad, if you can't behave." The dog whined miserably.

8 0

"Rubin," Uncle Nate called, "cut the racket."

"Okay, Uncle."

I heard them both pad slowly down the hall. Uncle Nate saw me glance at the faces on the wall.

"My collection," he said, turning his neck slightly, so that he might watch me and the wall at the same time. "Nick, I hope you are not offended by my little show of pride. I assure you that I am not offering my walls to celebrities just because they happen to be Jewish. These men on the wall have all had a share in changing our way of life. After all, Eddie Cantor and the Goldwyn Girls were American institutions while you were still in grade school. And Garfield. Wait until after the war. He will make Raft and all the rest look like small timers. Nick," he said secretively, "do you know that Garfield was once here at the Home for two weeks. Honest. He was in transit from one reform school to another. He wasn't Garfield then. Just Garfinkel. Julie Garfinkel. He had his own reputation. Not in Hollywood circles, or with the women, but with the bums and the boxcar Bennies from all the jungles this side of Chicago. I won't say that his short stay here made a man of him. After all, he didn't even have the time to see my attic upstairs. But I told him to his face: 'Julie, you have the look of one who will go far in this world. Shape up. Say goodbye to the boxcars and try another field.' And Nick, two years later he was already on Broadway." Then he slapped his thigh depreciatively, and seemed about to scold himself. "But I'm not only talking about show business people. Entertainers are all of the same breed: scamps and good-for-nothings. Nick, look at the world today. Our whole century has been shaped by Jewish thinking. Trotsky, Einstein, Freud," he said, marking off the names on his crooked fingers. "Nick, in two, three hundred years philosophers and historians will undoubtedly say that *this* was the Jewish century. Undoubtedly. What about the President?

81

How could he get along without his three musketeers? Morgenthau, Baruch, and Sam Rosenman." He drew his head halfway over the desk and screwed up one eye shrewdly. "And George Washington? After all, we have had a tradition of Jewish Secretaries of the Treasury. Now Morgenthau, and then Levine."

"Levine?"

"*Alexander Levine.* Of course, the history books refer to him as Hamilton. That is the name he picked out for himself. It's difficult enough being a Jew now. Can you imagine what it must have been like in the eighteenth century? He tried to deny the actual origins of his birth, and he threw around himself a cloak of illegitimacy. It was very fashionable in his time. And posing as the bastard son of the Scotsman Hamilton was for him much more acceptable and legitimate than being the son of the merchant Levine. Especially since his mother Rachel, who was a tart in her own right, abandoned the merchant and later lived with the Scotsman. Let the history books tell their stories. The merchant was his father! Nick, you didn't know anything about this?" he said, obviously trying to look a little baffled.

"No, Sir." My ankles were already aching, and I leaned one knee against his desk.

"Nick, are you trying to set a precedent? I have one name here. *Uncle.*" He sneezed once or twice and his nostrils began to wrinkle. "I'm afflicted with all sorts of allergies. Dust or coal or pollen. It's all the same for me. And I have to keep away from fresh fruit. The chemicals they spray them with do more damage to me than to the bugs and the flies. Nick, I should have stayed in the Bronx. The country is not for me." He removed a handkerchief from his pocket and dabbed his nose; the end of the handkerchief trailed along the desk and brushed the hull of the crippled U-boat. "Nick, what were we talking about? Before my nose went out of commission."

"Uncle," I said uncomfortably, "we were talking about Levine."

"Yes," he said, folding the handkerchief. "Levine. He was a political realist. He understood the demands of the world. Washington would have been lost without him. Do you know that our man led the expedition that broke the Whisky Rebellion? First he appointed himself the Secretary of War. He was at heart a soldier. He understood that any organization if it wants to survive has to be backed up by force. I agree. The President would choke on his Four Freedoms without his bombers and his Navy. And the same situation prevails here. We have our own little army at the Home. Of course, I have had to twist the truth around a little to make it serve my own purpose. I won't deny it. The boys are almost completely unaware of what is going on outside the Home. We have a radio here, but I select the boys' programs beforehand. I allow them their quota of comic books, that's all. They only know what I tell them. And I've told them repeatedly that the Nazis have invaded Canada and are already building tunnels under Niagara Falls. And so we're on a constant alert. I could mobilize the boys in a minute. And Nick, a German invasion is not so fantastic. U-boats have already been spotted off the Sound. And who is to say that it would be impossible for them to send over a small expeditionary force? Nazi Commandos. And what about an attack from the air? I've already requested the War Department to send me an antiaircraft gun. I expect to hear from the President in a few weeks. Yes, Nick, I'm guilty of enforcing my own little fantasies. But where's the crime? The boys are kept on their toes, and if anything should ever happen, we'll all be ready."

I heard the doorknob click behind me. A short, fat man

with a bald head and huge, hanging ears entered the room. "Uncle," he said, "I'm sorry. I thought you were alone."

"No, no, Eugene, it's all right. Nick, this is our chef, Eugene Dobrilubov. We are extraordinarily lucky to have him. His grandfather prepared caviar for half the kings of Europe."

Dobrilubov saluted me with his earlaps; they waggled obediently. "Uncle," he said cryptically, "it's on. Maybe tomorrow. Maybe tonight. But it's on."

Uncle Nate stood up and strode across the room. I noticed his enormous behind. His Bundles for Britain badge dropped on the carpet. I stooped and picked up the badge. Uncle Nate huddled with Dobrilubov near the door. "Fine," I heard Uncle Nate say. "Just make sure Bucharevsky stays in the brig." Dobrilubov left.

"I'm sorry for the interruption, Nick. But a few of the boys are planning a little party for me. And I want to come prepared." He sat down again, his jowls touching his chest. I handed him the badge. He couldn't manipulate the clasp, and leaning over the desk, I helped him pin on the badge. "I'm a great admirer of the British," he said, pointing to the miniature British and American flags that were engraved on the badge, their poles forming a tipped cross. "Churchill is an army in himself. They say he is coming to Washington next month. The Senators are afraid of him. Only Mrs. Roosevelt can tame him. She helped support Churchill's canteens long before we entered the war. Fala himself is a lifelong member of Bundles for Britain. Nick, the dog has his own badge. And I do whatever I can. Today even the pennies count. The boys pitch in. We help support a crippleage outside London."

"A crippleage?" I said.

"Absolutely. A home for crippled girls. Girls without legs, or arms. Some were maimed by the bombings, and some were crippled before. They would be waifs without the home, begging in the street. They are trained at the home to make

84

flowers and baskets and wax fruit. Where would they be without the crippleage? The boys understand. They know what it means to walk the streets without a penny and with no place to go. The girls send us baskets every Christmas filled with mountains of wax fruit. The director calls us a godsend. For him the boys are saints." His thick lips formed a brittle smile. Then he tugged his sleeves officially. "Nick, I'm sorry, but I don't have too much time to talk. Why should I keep anything from you? I'm expecting a little trouble. Nothing serious. I would be disappointed if the boys didn't try to pull a stunt occasionally. But if it gets out of hand the results would be unfortunate. Nick, I'm embroidering a simple story. Forgive me. It's a bad habit with me. I've put one of the boys from A Company in the attic. He's been there almost a week. Arnold Bucharevsky is his name. The boys call him Bullets. He comes from Rubin's old neighborhood. Actually, their cases are quite similar. That's one of the reasons why I've taken a special interest in him. If I can curb some of his spleen and get him to cooperate, all my Companies will be under control. Rubin has already cowed the rest of A Company. They wouldn't lift a finger for Bullets. It's your Company, D Company that I'm worried about. Two or three of the boys are organizing a little insurrection. They are going to make an attempt to free Bullets. It's futile. They know it. I know it. It's like a game with them. War maneuvers. They've been learning Commando tactics, and it's gone to their heads. They expect to get caught and be punished. It's part of the game. And I've assigned D Company to you, because I don't want the boys to suspect anything. With a new Company Commander around they think they will be able to confound us, and they will probably strike tonight." He tried to assure me. "Nick, understand, it's nothing. The boys know they have a good deal. The Rabbi can tell you a hundred stories. It isn't Shadrach or any of the other bulls that are keeping the boys here. This is the only home they have. It's

85

a game, Nick. Everything is under control." He reached over and removed from the bottom drawer a black skullcap and a noisemaker with a wooden handle. "Nick," he said, "I don't want to make you part of any conspiracy. But it would help for now if the boys thought that you were Jewish. You know, having an Italian name and with Mussolini in the war, the boys might become a little confused. But, of course, you have a perfect right to object. It would make things simpler for us, but it's up to you, Nick."

"I don't mind, Uncle. Whatever you say." I reached for the skullcap even before he offered it.

"Good, Nick. I'm sure we'll get along fine." I tried on the skullcap. It sat on my head like a crumpled parachute. "All our Jewish personnel wear skullcaps, Nick. I hope you won't mind. It provides a certain identity for the Home. We are not exactly a religious organization, but we are supported for the most part by various Jewish agencies. And don't worry. You won't be out of place. All the boys here wear skullcaps. It's part of their uniform." He picked up the noisemaker. "Nick, Mrs. Hirschhorn, our social worker, will explain most of the procedures to you. She is in charge of our academic program." He cranked the handle suddenly, and the noise-maker began to sputter like a slightly disabled machine gun. "Pebbleby," he called. "Pebbleby." He cranked the handle again. "It's impossible to get help in these times. You have to hire loafers or cripples. *Pebbleby!*"

The door opened partway and a man wearing a watch cap that was beginning to unravel stuck his head tentatively into the room and then pulled it out again. He seemed to have a retractable neck.

"Come in, Pebbles, come in."

Pebbleby opened the door a little further and eased his way into the room, his ragged chin entering first. The soiled bib of his overalls kept slipping off his stooped shoulders. He

8 6

wore a pajama top with a faded design under the bib, and a pair of brogans with lopsided heels; he limped slightly and seemed to favor his left leg. He waited near the door.

"Uncle," I said, already assuming a confidential tone, "my name? What's my Jewish name?"

"Oh, yes," Uncle Nate said. "I almost forgot. Lipshitz. Mr. Lipshitz." Then he turned his head abruptly. "Pebbles, take Mr. Lipshitz to Mama."

Pebbleby kept the door open for me. "Lipshitz," I said, trying to find some measure of familiarity. "Lipshitz." Uncle Nate seemed slightly distracted. He stared blankly at the noise-maker, the sconces on either side of him casting irregular shadows on the desk. We left the room.

"Lipshitz."

⁅ CHAPTER ⁆

We climbed a staircase near the porch; the steps were seamed with metal strips that were beginning to buckle, and I almost tripped twice. The railing was loose and the whole staircase creaked. "Hold on," Pebbleby cautioned. "Mama's on the third floor." He, however, climbed recklessly, his brogans smacking the metal strips.

We met the Rabbi on the second floor. He saw me wearing the skullcap. And after smiling owlishly to himself, he said, "So he's baptized you already. Uncle Nate doesn't waste much time."

"I'm Lipshitz now," I said dourly. "Lipshitz."

"Not bad. It's a close fit."

"The hat?"

"No, the name. From Lapucci to Lipshitz. Leave it to Uncle Nate. Believe me, Uncle has his points. Pebbles, where are you taking him?"

88

"To Mama."

"Pebbles, I'm relieving you. I'll show the gentlemen how to get to Mama. You're dismissed. *Go.*"

Pebbleby thanked the Rabbi, and immediately began hopping down the stairs. The Rabbi ignored the rumbling staircase. "Nick, watch out for Mama. She's Uncle Nate's personal property. They both were made from the same pattern. She's poison."

"Rabbi," I said, behind a cracked smile. "The skullcap will protect me." I don't really know why I should have wanted to devil him, but I did. He started to laugh, but then he changed his mind and pouted instead. "Nick, it's no joke. You'll see for yourself. Mama's door is near the stairs. You can't miss it. I would walk up with you, but I have to prepare a sermon."

"Thanks, Rabbi," I said, and I walked up to the third floor. I stood on the landing and peered through the stairwell. The Rabbi's blue cap kept appearing between the balusters. I found a door near the landing; it was open. I peeked in. Two huge cabinets guarded the rear wall; their drawers bulged and their lopsided roofs scraped the ceiling. A woman stood on a chair between the cabinets and dusted the bulging drawers. She was wearing a black cardigan and a corduroy skirt. Her buttocks swelled under her skirt.

"Mama?" I said. "It's me. Mr. Lipshitz."

Mama turned around. The top of her cardigan was unbuttoned, and I could see part of her brassiere. Her chest was enormous, and the individual cups of the brassiere squeezed her breasts together and hugged the cardigan like two impenetrable shields. She stepped off the chair and her breasts jumped and almost flipped out of their cups. Mama saw me staring at her bosom, but she didn't seem the least bit embarrassed. I tried to look away once, but it didn't do much good. Finally, sensing my embarrassment, she buttoned the cardigan.

"Lipshitz," I said again.

8 9

Mama began to laugh; her bosom heaved slightly. "Oh, Nick, you don't have to pretend with me. I know all of Uncle's tactics. You don't have to wear the cap here, really."

"I don't mind, Mama."

"Anyway, the boys will find out in a week or two. They have their own spy network." She was holding a rag in her hand; it seemed to be the dislocated sleeve of an old pajama top. She stood between the cabinets and touched their dented sides. "I know I'm indulging them," she said. "But I keep all my files here, and I've become quite intimate with them, really. My twins. They hold the record cards of every boy at the Home, and Nate makes me keep them here in this silly room. We're having an austerity program, you know." She pointed to a folded cot with a sagging bottom that was leaning against one of the cabinets. "Nate makes me sleep on that dreadful thing. It's a demonic contraption, really. I'm sure its plagued with all sort of devils. You should hear it rock at night. I'll give you a demonstration some time. Actually, it's my fault. I could never keep a regular bed here with my cabinets. I tried it once. It was like traveling through an obstacle course. I couldn't get from one end of the room to the other. It was a gruesome decision to have to make, but the bed had to go. Oh, I'm sorry," she said. "I shouldn't be so impolite. But I so seldom have visitors that I'm becoming a semibarbarian." And after searching through the bottom drawers of both cabinets, she found a folding chair. "Please sit down, Nick." The chair had a very low seat, and my behind almost touched the floor.

"Nick," she said, "I suppose Nate wants me to tell you about our program."

"I think so," I said.

"Well, as you can probably see for yourself our entire program has been curtailed because of the war. We can't even fill our quotas. Nate has been able to do very little recruiting."

"Recruiting?"

"Yes," she said, "you might say that our boys have been handpicked. You see, we have a rather peculiar status here. The boys have to be sent here by special request. And before the war, Nate was able to attend most of the sessions of the Bronx children's court. He had to work with lawyers and investigators, but he could get almost any boy he wanted. Of course, Nate was shrewd about the whole thing. He picked out mostly waifs from the East Bronx, and the court was only too glad to palm them off on him. So we have our collection of little Arabs. But with the gasoline rationing and the restrictions on cars today, Nate is stranded here, especially when he has to depend on Rosencrantz to chauffeur him around. And our numbers keep dwindling. We're down to thirty-seven boys. A skeleton corps. And only God knows how long we'll be able to survive. The Army has already excavated the town." She watched me fidget in my chair. "Did Nate tell you how the boys are billeted here?"

"You mean, the different Companies?"

"Yes. Nate devised the plan himself. There are four Companies now. We used to have six. Each Company has its own barrack, and unfortunately they're all down to half strength. There are only six boys in your Company. It's the smallest. Of course, we've been terribly understaffed, and D Company has had a rotating Company Commander since June. I've been with your boys the past three weeks. Actually, before the war, the boys were billeted according to their intelligence quotients. Nate and I would administer the tests immediately after the boys arrived. A Company, of course, was reserved for the brightest boys. Nate would usually pick his trustees from this group. The boys in B and C weren't nearly as bright, but they were still close to average. It was in D that the trouble started, and then in F Company, we bunched all the morons. The other boys helped watch over them. Now things have become quite scrambled. You'll even find a moron or two in A Company. But we've tried to herd all the misfits into your Company. Their IQs are generally lower than the rest, but some of the boys sabotage their own scores out of spite, so you can never really tell. Also, the two youngest boys at the Home are in D. Larry Farbovich and Little Notte."

I heard someone walking over my head. "Big Notte," she said, ignoring the footsteps, "is in A Company. Nate is making him a trustee soon. He's the oldest boy here."

The ceiling began to bulge in several places.

"Mama," I said, "who's upstairs?"

"It's nothing," she said, "only the Dungeon. It's Bullets Bucharevsky's home now. But don't worry, he's in A Company."

"Who brings him his food?"

"Rubin. Rubin takes care of all his wants."

"I'll bet," I said, "I'll bet." I wanted to ask Mama if Rubin brought Shadrach up with him, but I didn't want her to think that I was taking Bullets' side.

"Why was he put up there, Mama?"

"I don't know, Nick. It was a whole series of offenses. I think he tried to poison Shadrach. Come, I'll show you your Company folder." She stood on her chair and removed a large manila envelope from the top drawer of the cabinet on her left side. The envelope was marked "D Company: 1942." I could hear Bullets through the ceiling rapping out a tune. It sounded very much like the Army Air Corps Hymn. "Mama," I said, "is he trying to signal to us?"

Mama moved her chair next to mine. "He keeps himself busy that way, Nick. It's nothing." She opened the envelope. "All your boys are in here." Then she took out the record cards. A snapshot was stapled to the upper left-hand corner of each card. "I work with all the boys, Nick. Of course, we can only provide the most primitive kind of therapy. But I do the best I can under the prevailing conditions. Nate is thinking of making you my assistant. We'll talk about that some other time. You'll notice that I've made detailed notations on the back of every card. I summarize each individual session with the boys, even our casual conversations, whenever I can." She handed me the top card. "Eliot Wagshal. The boys here call him Matches."

"*Matches*," I said. "Rabbi Rosencrantz told me about him. Didn't he burn his mother alive? Or was that somebody else?"

She frowned for the first time. "I wish Rosencrantz would stick to his sermons. It was Matches, Nick. But it's not as simple as that. Eliot had a very strong attachment to his mother. His father abandoned them both when the boy was four or five, and left a few articles of clothing: a hat with a felt band, a plaid tie, and some kind of robe. Eliot is very vague about the robe. His mother would tell him that all men are *liars* and *fucks*. Those are the words that Eliot remembers. Liars and fucks. I have it written here, Nick. And Eliot began to blame himself for his father's disappearance: somehow he had driven his father away and made his mother unhappy. He thought that he could rectify his own misdeeds by pretending to be his father. But wearing the robe and the hat only compounded his guilt, so he hid them behind his mother's washtub. Yet he couldn't resist touching the felt band of the hat. I don't want to go into all the erotic associations that the hat provided for him, but I'm sure he had his first ejaculation while touching the felt. Though Eliot would certainly deny this. But when his shame and guilt became too overpowering, he brought the hat down to the basement and threw it into the furnace: he must have hoped that he would be able to rid himself of his sins, just as he had rid himself of the hat. But, of course, it didn't work. Destroying the hat had simply

9 3

jarred him into realizing the enormity of his own crime: his father couldn't possibly come back because Eliot himself had killed him. Oh, Nick, it's a classic case, I know. Boys have had the same realization thousands and thousands of times. But you cannot imagine how Eliot must have suffered. And in order for him to bear his crime, he needed to find an accomplice, someone who could take over the major portion of his guilt. He convinced himself that it was his mother who had made him burn the hat. He had done everything to please her and protect her. She would dote on him and call him her own little man, but the more attention she gave him the more he began to feel that she was bribing him for having murdered his father. And the final atonement for him now would be to destroy both his mother and himself. And one night, just before he was twelve, he dressed himself in the robe while his mother slept, and then set fire to his mother's curtains and the closet where she kept most of her clothes, but the fire began to frighten him, and he ran downstairs. And," Mama said, "his mother was trapped in the fire." The snapshot showed a boy with pointy ears and a wide mouth; he had obviously blinked while the photograph had been taken, but there was nothing else about him that would have distinguished him as a pyromaniac, though it's also true that I had no real conception of what a pyromaniac should have looked like. "Eliot will be thirteen in a few weeks. He still refuses to take any blame for his mother's death: he only blames himself for not having died with her. Of course, it's far more complicated than I'm making it seem. I've simplified things for you and have shown you only the basic patterns. Actually, Eliot has told me very little about himself. I've had to piece everything together from a few random shreds. But, in any event, Rosencrantz has no right to talk about him in that way."

"I'm sorry," I said. "I didn't know. . . ."

94

Mama shuffled the cards and showed me the other boys: Boris Potash was the oldest boy in the Company. His record card vouched that he was only sixteen, but Mama thought that he was twenty or maybe even twenty-five. It didn't seem to make much difference, because Boris had the mind of a six year old. Uncle Nate had caught him masturbating several times, and put him in the Dungeon for a day. Boris howled during his entire stay and defecated all over the floor. He was never put in the Dungeon again. Boris had a very hairy body and the boys often called him "Wolfman." Most of the Company ignored him, but Little Notte teased him occasionally; Little Notte was only eleven, but he was one of the leaders of the Company. He was already taller than his brother, Big Notte, who was seventeen and was being groomed for Rubin's job; Larry Farbovich was also eleven, but he still wet his bed and cried during electrical storms. His mother had given birth to him in an insane asylum. The Company allowed him to be the Wolfman's keeper; Amado Benveniste was known at the Home only by one name: Benny. He was a Sephardic Jew and knew hundreds of gypsy incantations and card tricks. According to Benny, his forebears had been chamberlains and physicians to the royal courts at Smyrna and Salonika, and his great-grandfather, Comprado Benveniste, had been a special advisor to the Sultan of Turkey and had interpreted dreams for his entire harem. Benny had lived in hobo jungles since he was eleven, and once in Montana a deputy sheriff had broken his shoulder during a boxcar raid. He was the undisputed Company champion in chess, checkers, Monopoly, and knucks. Only Little Notte could compete with him. Benny was also a chemist of sorts. Mama suspected that it was Benny who had prepared the birchbark juice that was used in the attempt to poison Shadrach; the Indian rounded out the Company. Billy Moonshine's mother was a full-fledged Mohawk who had been a waitress at the Blattenburg Inn before the town council evicted her for soliciting and for other immoral acts. The Indian, however, refused to leave. He hid out in the abandoned water tower during the day and raided the town during the night. In order to keep on good terms with the council, Uncle Nate agreed to take the Indian in. And the Indian, for some mysterious reason, surrendered himself voluntarily to Uncle Nate and became a ward of the Home. Nobody knew anything about the Indian's father. The Indian did not get along well with the other boys. He was thirteen years old.

"Mama," I said, "what about Bucharevsky's card?"

"He's not in your Company, Nick."

"I know, Mama. But I'd like to see it, anyway."

"We don't have the time, Nick." And standing on her chair, she returned the folder to its proper cabinet.

Someone knocked. It was the cook, Dobrilubov. "Mama," he said, ignoring me completely. "The boys will be up from maneuvers any minute. Uncle wants you downstairs." Then he waggled one ear and left.

Mama withdrew a furled American flag from behind one of the cabinets. She asked me to carry the flag. Its pole was only about two feet long and was capped with a silver Star of David. We walked down one flight, Mama gripping my arm and avoiding the metal strips on the stairs, and then we entered a classroom with a cracked ceiling. Uncle Nate stood near the door, warming his hands. "Hello, Elsie. How is our teacher making out?"

"Fine," Mama said, "fine."

There were only about twenty desks in the room, but they were bunched recklessly, without aisles or rows, and their seats were extremely low. Uncle Nate probed one of the desks and pulled out a peach pit, a broken pen point, and a clay scrotum that had obviously been modeled with great

9 6

care. Rabbi Rosencrantz came into the room. The Rabbi was wearing a white skullcap with a flat roof and a wiggly pompon. The bill of his Seabee cap stuck out of his pocket. He stared at the scrotum and smiled to himself.

"An interesting replica. Mama, you can add it to your collection."

"Rosencrantz," Uncle Nate said. "You're not behind the wheel now. From a chauffeur you might expect such remarks, but not from a rabbi."

The Rabbi flexed his jaw, undoubtedly for my benefit. "Nate, from this rabbi expect only the unexpected. It's a question of misplaced identities. After all, where does the chauffeur end and the rabbi begin?"

"Rabbi, spare me your philosophies. Hold them for your sermons. There they will have a better use."

The walls shook suddenly and the desks began to hop. "The Maccabees," the Rabbi said. "The Maccabees are here." First there was a mild boom, and then the unmistakable tramp of marching feet. The sound was unrelenting. I anticipated whole battalions. Then the marching stopped. A man with an enormous paunch entered the room. The Rabbi motioned to me. "*Murdoch. The Marine.*" Murdoch assembled his paunch and saluted Uncle. "All Comp'nies accounted for, Uncle. A Comp'ny won firsts again in bayoneting and body blocking. D Comp'ny still hasn't taken a point. But I'll work them into shape, Uncle. Don't you worry about that." The rounded peak of a skullcap emerged from behind the doorjamb.

"Murdoch," Uncle said. "Bring in the boys."

"Comp'nies," Murdoch bawled. "March. *Hut. Toop. Thrip. Forp.*"

The boys filed into the room. They wore identical uniforms: black skullcaps which came down to their eyebrows, indiscriminately colored sweat shirts which were invariably pocked with cigarette burns, mustard stains and decalcomanias, and fatigue pants with baggy pockets and wide cuffs. Their faces were smeared with grease. They marched past me, their skullcaps barely reaching my chin. Another man came in. His head grazed the lintel of the door. He dwarfed all of us, even the Rabbi, and especially the boys. His churlish grin defied the room. Two bulldogs followed him in; they both wore leather muzzles. The man carried a drillmaster's stick and kept poking the bulldogs' square behinds. The other Jailer. Billingsgate.

Uncle Nate prowled the room with one crinkling eye. "Bill, where's the Indian? The Indian isn't here."

"He went to the john, Uncle."

"You left him alone?"

Billingsgate smiled crookedly, upsetting his pitted cheeks, and slid his stick under one arm. "He wouldn't pull any tricks on me, Uncle. He knows better."

"Bill, I want him up here *now*."

"Okay, Uncle. I'll escort him myself." The bulldogs followed the Jailer out of the room, both of them panting under their muzzles.

The boys assembled behind the desks, their skullcaps forming irregular rows. The faces were indistinguishable under the grease, but I recognized Matches instantly; his pointy ears gave him away. Uncle Nate kept staring at me. I looked down. I had forgotten to unroll the flag. I fumbled with it and Murdoch finally took the flag away from me. He twirled the pole and the flag immediately unfurled.

"Boys," Uncle said, "the maneuvers are over. How can you pledge allegiance with dirty faces? It would be a sacrilege."

The boys wiped their faces with the hems of their sweat shirts. A band of captured gnomes. Their skullcaps and their cockamanies and their fierce, old men's faces drew me to them

98

immediately. I wanted to stand with them behind one of the desks.

The Indian turned up in the middle of the pledge. There was a welt over his left eye. One of his baggy pockets was missing, but his skullcap was still intact. Billingsgate led him into the room, the dogs arriving in their wake. The Jailer gripped both of the Indian's ears. The Indian grimaced, but he refused to howl.

"Uncle, you were right. You can never trust an Indian. He was trying to flood the latrine."

"Indian," Uncle said, "take your place."

We completed the pledge. Then Mama took over. The boys sang the national anthem for her. Mama's wagging nipples kept them in tune; none of the boys missed a single note, not even the Indian. Murdoch twirled the pole in the opposite direction and the flag furled automatically.

"Boys," Uncle said, "seat yourselves, please."

The skullcaps now formed new alignments: most of the boys sat two in a seat. Their shoulders kissed and their arms crowded the desks. Two boys with identically pinched faces sat behind the desk nearest me. One of them was slightly taller than the other, and with a black lump under each eye, he looked somewhat fiercer and wiser. The taller of the two was undoubtedly Little Notte. Behind them, but a little to the left, sat a boy with hairy knuckles who was playing distractedly with a paper doll. Even from where I stood I could see that the doll had Uncle Nate's features: thick jowls and a sagging paunch. Some spittle dribbled down the boy's chin. He actually had a few gray hairs. The Wolfman. And the boy who sat in the same seat and wiped the Wolfman's chin with the doll's left leg was obviously his keeper: Larry Farbovich, the bed-wetter. There was a pained expression on Larry's face as he jerked the doll, and I wondered whether he had just peed

99

in his pants. I searched the other faces, but I wasn't able to locate Benny. And so, D Company still seemed incomplete. Uncle Nate clasped his hands behind him. His stubby fingers moved like marionettes while he talked.

"Boys, you know the whole story. Repetitions aren't necessary. Jews are dying all over the world. In Asia. In Africa. In all the countries of Europe. Even in America. The Nazis have henchmen everywhere. Who knows. Maybe even here at the Home." Uncle Nate looked directly at the Rabbi, then at Mama and the two Jailers, and finally at me. Even the bull-dogs didn't escape his glances. "But we are not unarmed. We are not without will or courage. Let the Nazis come. We will welcome them with sticks and knives and fingers that have become claws for the occasion and we will drive them back to the sea. We will show them what it means to start up with Jewish boys. And remember. Every act of insubordination, every misspent minute, every infraction of the rules is the same thing as sabotage. Boys, boys. Do you want to help out Hitler and his henchmen?"

A stray voice here and there said, "No, Uncle, no." Uncle Nate was satisfied. His voice softened. "Boys," he said, his jowls wagging compassionately, "please, don't betray your-selves. If we join ranks and have a truly united front, nothing will be denied us. Boys, our pledge."

The boys stood up, and raising their foreams, each of them formed a V. Larry Farbovich took away the Wolfman's doll. "Wolfman, the pledge, the pledge." The Wolfman didn't respond; the spittle gleamed on his chin. Then a boy with swarthy skin and a slightly misshapen shoulder wiggled two fingers in front of the Wolfman's face. The Wolfman closed one eye, and with the thumb and forefinger of his left hand he shaped a crooked V. The boy with the swarthy skin had a peeled apple on his desk. Part of the apple had been dug away: I couldn't tell whether he was fashioning Mama's boobs or another scrotum. I tried to recall Mama's files. I was sure that the boy with the apple was Benny. Amado Benveniste, the descendant of court physicians and chamberlains; there must have also been an artisan somewhere in his background. D Company was now complete.

"Boys," Uncle said again, "the pledge."

Keeping their Vs intact, the boys pledged to uphold the laws of the Home, to pray for the President and Mr. Churchill, and for the Allied forces, and especially for all Jewish servicemen, and to harden themselves for the coming encounters, and to keep a bold and vigorous heart; even the Wolfman mouthed the words of the pledge.

"Sit, sit," Uncle said, and the skullcaps aligned themselves in twos again. "Now, boys, we must get on to other things. Most of you already know that after careful consideration our board of directors has chosen a teacher for you. He will be taking over the academic program and will also be the new Commander of D Company." He beckoned to me with his hand; his rumpled palm seemed to censure me. "Boys, Mr. Lipshitz." I heard Little Notte whisper to his brother: "*The new Screw.*" I sought out the other faces in my Company, but there were no auspicious signs. Matches stared at me with complete contempt. The Wolfman bunched his fingers and tried to frighten the doll; he was obviously unaware of my existence. Larry Farbovich contorted his face. The Indian refused to look at me, but he still held out one finger stiffly. I guessed his intentions. Benny worked on his apple with the twisted prongs of a fork. Several of the other boys simply glared at me. I felt wholly abandoned, but I refused to desert my Company. I would dazzle the boys. Make them admire me.

"Boys, I'm sure Mr. Lipshitz would like to say a few words to you." I kept my hands in my pockets and gripped my thighs. "Boys," I tried to say, "boys...." The skullcap squeezed my head and my throat jammed.

Mama rescued me. She told the boys that I would be preparing a program for them, that they were to report promptly every day after maneuvers, and that each of them would be issued a notebook. The boys ruffled their gnomelike faces.

The cook came into the room carrying a gunny sack over one shoulder. A huge carton trailed behind him: the carton was piloted by Pebbleby. Larry Farbovich signaled to the Wolfman. "*Essen,*" he said, "*essen.*" The Janitor dropped the carton in front of the desks. Then the cook took over. "Boys," he said, "today we have chopped liver, lettuce and tomato, kosher bologna, cream cheese, strawberry jam, and peanut butter. On white. Rye bread is becoming scarce. Some are toasted, some are plain. Some are garnished with mayonnaise. It's pot luck today. Whatever Pebbles gives you, eat. No trading. Pebbleby, distribute the chow." Pebbleby dove into the carton and pulled out a battalion of lumpy sandwiches. The cook himself made regular stops with the gunny sack and dropped off two apples at every desk. The apples confounded the Wolfman.

Uncle Nate raised both his arms. "Rabbi, please, a benediction. We are not barbarians here."

The Rabbi blessed the sandwiches and then said, "Maccabees, make sure you digest."

After the Janitor made his rounds, he gave out the remaining sandwiches to Mama and the rest of us: I ended up with a bologna sandwich. The bread was soggy and the bologna was bitter. I waited patiently for my apple, but there weren't enough to go around. The Rabbi was a little luckier than I: Pebbleby had saved him an apple. Billingsgate removed the dogs' muzzles and fed them each a sandwich; the bulldogs ate the sandwiches whole.

I heard a muffled bark somewhere over our heads. Then a scream. "*Jesus. Shit. Help. No more. Jesus. Shit.*" The boys

102

stopped chewing: their skullcaps jumped. The carved apple shook in Benny's hand.

"Rabbi," I said. "What happened?"

The Rabbi's chin rose towards the ceiling. "Rubin is giving Bullets a workout in the Dungeon. Nate wants to help along our appetites."

Uncle Nate looked at me. Then he sent Dobrilubov out of the room. The barking and screaming stopped in a little while.

"Rosencrantz," Uncle Nate said. "You will have to squeeze in your sermon now. The schedule is being curtailed."

"Nathanson, do you expect the boys to digest chopped liver and my teachings at the same time?"

"Rabbi, it's up to you. Let it be now, or forget about it."

The Rabbi adjusted his skullcap. "First," he said, "first we will have a little review. *Notte*. Not you, *the other one*. Notte, what did we study yesterday?"

Little Notte stood up and flexed his earlaps impishly. "The Bible, *Rebbe*, we studied the Bible."

"Notte, which book?"

"The one about the two Kings. Solomon and Saul. No, *Rebbe*, it was David. David and Saul."

"Where did we leave off, Notte?"

"*Rebbe*," Notte said, "don't rush me." His brows jiggled unevenly. "I remember now, *Rebbe*. Saul was supposed to be the King over Israel and Arabia, but the Lord wanted to pick his own King, and he picked out David. Saul wasn't gonna take lip from anybody, so he decided to kill David and stay the King. Now David was hiding out in a cave. I think it was near the border in Arabia. And Saul went looking for him, but he didn't know that David was inside the cave. The story gets a little complicated here, *Rebbe*. Saul has to take a

103

crap . . . excuse me, Mama. I mean, he had to *relieve himself*, so like a dope, he picks out David's cave and goes in. And while Saul is squatting inside, David's boys tell him: 'Pal, here is the big chance. Go and kill the King.' So David sneaks behind him, but instead of killing him, he cuts off the tail from the King's robe. And when Saul leaves the cave, David comes out and bows down in front of him. 'King,' he tells him, 'my boys advised me to slit your throat while you were on the pot, but how could I do such a thing? A King is still a King.' And David shows him the tail for proof. Okay, maybe Saul's a bastard, but he still knows the difference between right and wrong. 'David,' he says, 'you are the righteous one, not me. I came to you like the Black Jack with evil in my heart, and you paid off my evil with kindness.' And there's two morals to the story. The first one is: *never take a crap in the dark.*"
A few of the boys giggled behind their skullcaps; even Mama laughed. Uncle Nate glowered at the Rabbi. "Uncle," Little Notte said, "don't blame the *Rebbe*. I made up the moral myself. It's the other one what counts. *Rebbe* says that all the business about Goliath don't mean a bean. It's inside the cave that David proves he is the real King. Righteousness always wins out in the end. And even the Black Jack can't stand up to it. Right, *Rebbe?*"

"Right, Notte. But it isn't only a question of righteousness. There is also another side." I waited for the snickers and the cockeyed looks, but instead, the boys' gnomelike faces actually softened. I was, I must confess, aboundingly jealous. "What we call morality is sometimes a cover up for something else. Maccabees, there is often an irresistible and unbreakable tie between the pursuer and the pursued, between the keeper and the kept, between the displacer and the displaced, between the hunter and the hare. And this tie, which is nursed with fear and hate, can even develop into a kind of love. Remember. Once the hunt starts, the hare would be lost if the hunter

104

should disappear. His whole existence depends on the hunter's moves. It also works the other way around. Where would the hunter be without his hare? No, no, one depends on the other. It was the same with David and Saul. And believe me, it happens all over. On the battlefield, in the playground, in the boudoir. I could even show you a few samples here at the Home."

"Rabbi," Uncle Nate said, "the sermon is over. Boys, you are all dismissed. Murdoch, march them down to their barracks."

Murdoch saluted Uncle Nate and began marking time with his feet. The boys left their apples on the desks and marched over to the door. Billingsgate poked the Wolfman's back with his stick. "Get in line, boy, get in line." The boys filed out of the room, their skullcaps bobbing rhythmically. The Indian left last.

"Rosencrantz," Uncle Nate said, "I think we would all be better off if you did a little less rabbiing and a little more chauffeuring."

"Nathanson, that's your prerogative. But how can you expect me to teach, unless you allow me to explore—"

"Rabbi, we can get along fine without your banalities. I'm warning you. You are playing with fire. In my opinion, you are already in the doghouse. One faulty step, and Billingsgate will put your satchel on the road. Rabbi, it's a long, long way to the Bronx. And you can't afford any more trips. Am I making myself clear, Rabbi?"

The Rabbi removed his skullcap; the pompon sagged.

"Rabbi?"

"Yes, Uncle. It's all very clear." Carrying the skullcap gingerly under one arm, the Rabbi walked out of the room. Billingsgate muzzled the bulldogs. I swiped an apple from one of the desks.

The barrack did have a door, but the latch had been ripped off, and the frame itself overlapped the doorway and blocked out D Company's one tiny window. The barrack had been built without a foundation, and even a mild storm would have probably carried it off. I knocked three times and then went inside. The door kept slapping against the wall. Six cots were lined up near the doorway together with six tiny wooden lockers; none of the lockers had a door. A blistered candle stood in a tin holder on top of each locker; only four of the candles were lit. A shower stall and a dented piss trough and two wooden, box-shaped commodes faced the row of cots. There was a wooden gate near the other end of the barrack. A bed and a closet were stationed behind the gate; it was obviously the Company Commander's headquarters. I was glad to see that Uncle Nate allowed his Commanders at least one token of aristocracy: I had my own private commode. It stood unobtrusively between the closet and the bed.

The boys were sitting on the cots; their faces seemed slightly haunted in the wavering candlelight. I didn't really expect the boys to stand and salute me, but they might at least have acknowledged my right to be in the barrack. They were, after all, in my charge. Of course, the Wolfman was playing with a battalion of wooden soldiers and hadn't even heard me come in, but the other boys refused to compromise themselves. Larry Farbovich helped the Wolfman assemble his troops in battle array. The Indian sat with his knees up reading a comic book: it was a dog-eared Donald Duck. Matches and Benny were playing cards. Was it poker or rummy? I couldn't tell. Benny rolled a cigarette, but instead of paper he used a dried leaf. Only God knows what kind of tobacco he had: it was green and wiggly and produced purple smoke. He kept the tobacco in a coffee tin on his cot. Matches turned in his cards. "No stinkweeds," he said. "You can smoke all the punk and Shredded Wheat you want, but that's the limit." Benny didn't bother to appease him; he smoked solicitously, shuffling the cards. The purple smoke drew the Wolfman to Benny's cot. He held out his hands and tried to catch the smoke. "*Inky, dinky, doody.*" His chin shook excitedly. His hands resembled mittens.

"Larry," Benny said dryly, "keep him away from my bunk."

Larry led the Wolfman back to his troops.

The cracks between the floorboards were choked with weeds and strange, cuplike flowers without stems. I stooped and smelled one of the flowers.

"Boys," I said. My voice seemed to ricochet off the narrow walls; it came back sounding hollow and forced. I wanted to hide behind the gate. I removed my library card from my wallet and pretended to study it carefully. The boys watched me. I felt much bolder. "Boys, I'd like to go over the Company roster. It will be easier for me to get to know you better that way. Just raise your hand when I call off your name." Benny blew a prodigious smoke ring and thrust his fist through it.

"Little Notte?" I said, watching the ring disintegrate.

"Here," Notte said, "here I am, *Commander Shitz.*" He stared at the library card. "What kind of roster is that? Don't it have my official name? Bagelbaum. You better mark it down. I'll spell it for you, Commander. B-A-G-E-L-B-A-U-M."

"Thanks, Notte. I appreciate it. I'll try to remember. Bagelbaum."

He pursed his lips shrewdly. "But there's one catch, Mr. Shitz. You see, that ain't really my official name. The name belongs to Uncle Bernie. He lived with us for a little while. I had seventeen uncles altogether. My mother believed in the shuttle system. She kept changing off from one *uncle* to another. You want to hear the names of all my uncles?" Notte left his cot and walked over to one of the commodes; he circled the commode and then came back to the cot. I'm sure he was trying to devil me. "Huh, Mr. Shitz?"

"No, Notte. I'll manage without them. Larry. Larry Farbovich."

Larry raised his hand. I stared him down and he offered no other resistance. I knew how to handle the other boys.

"*Indian,*" I said fiercely. The Indian kept his comic book over his face.

Notte decided to intercede. "Commander, his name is Billy. Only his friends and his enemies can call him Indian. That's his rule. And you don't fit into the first category or the second. Not yet. Call him Billy."

"*Indian,*" I said again. The Indian raised the comic book an inch and spat between his knees. The edge of the comic

108

book cut his chin crookedly. "Listen, I don't know how the other Commanders dealt with you, but I'll keep you in the barrack a week. I mean it. I want some cooperation." My show of strength seemed paltry even to me. Why did they have to challenge me? Couldn't they understand that I was really on their side? "All right. Billy, Billy, Billy. Are you satisfied?"

The Indian dropped his comic book. He saluted me with both hands. Then he bugged one of his eyes. I preferred him with the comic book over his face.

"Wolfman?" I said.

Notte waved one hand. "Hey, hey, watch your language. You want me to make an official protest to Uncle? Just because he is a little slow in the head, it don't mean you gotta take advantage and call him names. He's Boris to you. Right, *Wolfman?*"

The Wolfman abandoned his troops. He smiled knowingly and said, "*Pish, pish.*"

"Keeper," Benny said. Larry led the Wolfman over to the trough, and after stooping and struggling with each button, he finally opened the Wolfman's fly. The Wolfman peed into the trough; his aim wasn't very accurate.

I went behind the gate. "Carry on your business, boys. We'll continue with the roster tomorrow." I decided to inspect the closet. I found one of Mama's nightgowns inside, and also a brassiere with black lace; the cups, as I had suspected, were enormous. My grip was under the bed. I heard the Wolfman moan. "*Benja, Benja.*" He put his hands over his eyes and stumbled towards Benny's cot. "*Benja, Benja.*"

"Shut him up," Benny said. "Light the candles, huh? You know he goes crazy when all the candles aren't lit."

Matches lit the other candles. He seemed to deliberate over the holders, and I thought that he might be saying a prayer. The Wolfman watched the candlewicks burn. He tried to shape the flames with his fists. Then he cupped one hand and caught the dripping wax.

"Keep him away from the candles," Benny said. Larry brought two Civil War soldiers over to the Wolfman. One of them had been carved with an amputated leg. Larry deployed the soldiers on the lockers, but they still couldn't entice the Wolfman away from the flames.

"Boris," Benny said sharply, "your bunk, your bunk." The Wolfman looked at the flames longingly for the last time, and then shambled back to his troops. The tufts of hair behind his ears kept touching the brim of his skullcap.

Benny rolled cigarettes for Notte and Matches; the barrack was soon clogged with purple smoke. The Indian seemed to scorn Benny's cigarettes. He removed an enormous stick of punk from his locker and lit one end. The ashes began to clutter near his knees.

I emptied my grip over the bed; Crazy's campaign hat came tumbling out. The tobacco pouch was inside the peak. I put on the hat and pulled the brim sharply over one eye. Only the Wolfman seemed to notice my hat; he probably thought it belonged to an alien army. Then I dangled the pouch, already knowing that it could never compete with the purple smoke or with the Indian's punk.

Notte smoked near the door. I saw him crumble the cigarette suddenly and start to drive off the puffs of smoke that had gathered near his head. "The Jailer, the Jailer," he said. The Indian crushed the lit end of the punk against his palm and then hid the stick behind his locker. Matches dusted the commodes with one sleeve of his sweat shirt. Larry abandoned the Wolfman and smoothed the blankets on his own cot. The Wolfman seemed to sense the general panic and tried to gather his troops. "Boogyba," he said, "Boogyba." Benny worked on the Wolfman's locker, arranging the soap dish and the bandage box and removing the lumps of wax from the candle holder.

110

He managed to blow out the Wolfman's candle before Billingsgate came in. The Jailer was carrying his drillmaster's stick. He sniffed the air. "It stinks heah," he said, expanding one nostril at a time. "Where's the junk?" The coffee tin was still sitting on Benny's cot. The Jailer smiled and twirled his stick like a magic wand over the tin. I actually expected something magnificent to happen, but when the tobacco remained in the tin I began to doubt the stick's powers. "Caught you with the goods this time, huh Benny boy?" He carried the tin across the barrack and sprinkled the shower stall and piss trough with the green tobacco. He turned over the emptied tin and fitted it on Notte's head, and then strode back to Benny's cot. I saw his stick jump twice. There was a red mark on Benny's cheek, but he hadn't flinched. "That's gonna cost you ten demerits, Benny boy. You're already next in line for the Dungeon. Just keep smoking that junk." Billingsgate saw the Wolfman's troops deployed on the floor. He kicked them towards the gate. One Confederate soldier hopped over the gate and landed between my feet. His features had been intricately carved. His face bore a pained expression. An ear was missing.

"All right, all right," Billingsgate shouted. "Line up for inspection."

The boys assembled in front of their cots. Somehow, I was sure that the Jailer's summons was also meant for me. I stiffened immediately. Was he going to inspect my quarters? I was still wearing Crazy's hat.

Notte's cot was nearest the door. He stood in front of his locker, the coffee tin riding his head. "Take off the pot," the Jailer said, and then gripped one of Notte's ears. "He been making trouble for you, Commander? He's the wise guy in your Comp'ny. Him and the Indian. But at least the Indian keeps his mouth shut. *Commander?*"

"No," I said. "No." He released Notte's ear. Then he

kicked over the cot. "Make that bunk over, boy. I want those blankets smooth." He blew out Notte's candle. "This is wartime. Don't you know what it means when Uncle says he wants you to economize?" He ordered the other boys to blow out their candles. "Matches, you can keep your candle burning. We all know you got special interests in fire, boy. We don't want to ruin the party for you." The Jailer seemed very pleased with himself.

The Wolfman began to whimper. "Boogyba." He tried to take Larry's thumb, but the Keeper shooed the Wolfman away from his cot. "Benja, Benja."

"Make that dummy cut the racket before I crack his ass." The Jailer watched Benny move towards the Wolfman's cot. "Take another step, Benny boy, and you gonna earn yourself another ten."

"Boris," Benny said, "*shah. Zai shtil.*"

"Keep it in English, Benny boy. No kike talk."

Benny flapped one arm expertly and his shadow rose across the wall like a flying cape. The Wolfman marveled at the shadow.

"Cut the magic show."

Benny dropped his arm slowly; his crooked shoulder jumped.

"Bye-bye, Draka." The shadow seemed to linger in the Wolfman's mind.

The Jailer inspected the other cots. He gave Larry two demerits: one for not folding his blankets properly, and the other for having wax on the rim of his candle holder. "Shape up, Keeper." Matches fared a little better: only one demerit. His cot was not in line with his locker. The Indian ended up with seventeen demerits. The Jailer found his stick of punk. He made the Indian chew it. I listened to him count up the Indian's demerits. "Five for the punk, Indian. If I ever catch that on you again, boy, you gonna be shipped out to the reservation. Lemme tell you. Indian, you ain't worth a dime. Then you get three demerits for having a disgraceful bunk. It ain't no fartsack, Indian. You gotta air it out by and by. And how about a bath? I don't know how you boys can tolerate him. Two demerits, Indian, two for smelling like a skunk. How much is that so far, Nohhte? I ain't so good when it comes to figures."

Notte considered the Indian's demerits. "Seven, Jailer." His face was expressionless, but his nose gave him away: it glowed mischievously. "Seven."

"Okay, Nohhte. You get another five for having stains on your blankets. I see we ain't got rid of your bad habits yet, Indian. You know how Uncle hates bunk parties. He don't go for cooper-*a*-tive activities." He smiled waspishly, and then, catching my eye, he winked twice. "You gotta watch out for that, Commander. All them mothering Indians are brought up with peculiar ways. We don't want him corrupting the other boys. And I'm tossing you another five, Indian, for being a pain in the ass, and for trying to make a fool outa me upstairs. Telling me you gotta take a hot shit, and then busting up Uncle's latrine behind mah back. And you get three for making me have to look at your ugly Indian face. How much does that make now, Nohhte?"

"Seventeen, Jailer."

"Okay, Indian. That's enough for tonight. But maybe I'm gonna make a special trip back heah tomorrow, and if I don't see some improvement, I'm gonna bust you right down to the ground. You believe it, boy. You believe it."

The Jailer seemed to be tiring: he let Benny get by with only three additional demerits. He saved the Wolfman for last.

"Don't you know what the word inspection means, Chuggerhead?" He poked the Wolfman's belly with his stick. Then he threw his blankets on the floor. "It's lucky for you, boy,

113

that Uncle got a soft spot in his head for idiots. Otherwise you'd be down on the farm in Katona with the other boobs shoveling shit for a nickel a day. That's the rates, boy. Anybody heah want to volunteer for the farm? Indian, you want me to put your name on the list? There you won't have Uncle around to look after your rights. You just don't know how damn lucky you are. Lemme tell you. I've been on all the farms. Come on, Chuggerhead, lemme see you fold the blanket." He guffawed obscenely, cracking his tongue against his teeth. He pulled the Wolfman's skullcap over his ears. I saw Benny reach over and pick up his candle holder.

"Bill-Billingsgate," I said. I had already convinced myself that Crazy's hat gave me some sort of immunity, but I still wasn't sure how the hat would fare against the Jailer's stick.

"Aw, Commander," the Jailer said. "I was only having some fun with him. If we start coddling him, he's only gonna get outa hand. He's putting on a big act, that's all. I hear him talking kike with Benny all the time. The Wolfman could match wits with Moses any day of the week. That's a fact. It wouldn't surprise me none if he was the leader of the whole shebang. I've seen all the operators. The bossman always poses like a dummy. That's the way they throw you off."

I was ready to scowl, but the hat kept sinking, and it finally reached my chin. "Awright," he said. "The inspection's over." The hat must have cowed him. I immediately raised the brim. "Just keep your asses glued to the bunks. I don't want to see a soul move. I ain't even sure I'm gonna allow you to breathe."

Billingsgate saw my pouch on the bed. He walked over to the gate. "That Duke's?"

I shrugged one shoulder. "I don't know too much about tobacco."

"How about rolling me a cig, Commander? For a sample."

"I don't have any paper."

114

"That's awright." I saw him bend over the commodes. He came back with two strips of toilet paper. "Try these, General."

I couldn't maneuver the toilet paper. "Here, lemme try," he said, and he came through the gate. He licked the edges of the paper, and pouring the tobacco expertly, he rolled two cigarettes; they were both exquisitely shaped. He removed a wooden match from his pocket and struck it against his belt buckle. The match flared instantly and lit our noses and the grooves under his eyes. We sat on the bed and smoked. "Nick," he said, "we oughta perform together." The boys were already out of earshot, but he insisted on moving closer to me; our knees touched. "I don't usually treat 'em so rough, but I wanted to make you look good. I was beginning to wonder when you was gonna start turning me off. Hey, the hat's a lulu. Where'd you pick it up? Your grandfather a Rough Rider? Uncle thinks Benny and the Indian might try something tonight. You don't gotta worry about Nohhte. He's all talk. And Matches ain't much good. They wouldn't have no use for him on a raid, unless they was intending to burn us out. It don't even pay to try and figure out these little bastards. Benny and Bullets can't stand each other, and here's Benny putting his ass on the line for him. Nick, I gotta go. Uncle's giving us all special details tonight. Here, Nick, I'll make you a hero." He stood up and started to shout. "Listen, Commander, I don't gotta take that crap from you. I take my orders from Uncle. You got any complaints about the way I handle my inspections, send them on to him."

I didn't want to become part of the Jailer's little conspiracy, but with him standing in front of me and shouting, there was nothing else I could do. And so, I followed suit. "This is my barrack, Jailer." The hat began to sink again. "You tell Uncle that from now on D Company is off limits for you. I'll do my own inspecting. Take a walk, Jailer."

115

"*Beautiful, Nick....* Yeah, Lipshitz, I'll take a walk. Right up to Uncle's office." He strode past the cots and stopped near the door. "Boys, you better take your last look at Commander there, 'cause he ain't gonna be heah very long." Then he left. The door kept banging against the wall. The boys' faces seemed grimmer than ever. I wanted to call the Jailer back. Maybe my protests hadn't been convincing enough? I began to suspect that we hadn't fooled the boys at all.

The Indian left his cot. He stuck his hand through the heart-shaped opening on top of the commode nearest the piss trough, and after probing the wooden wall, he pulled out a hunting knife with a broken handle. The blade glinted in the dim light. "I'm gonna slice him up," he said. "Jailer." He began lunging with the blade in all directions. I stood behind the bed. "First his ears and then his eyes." He smiled weirdly to himself. "I'm gonna save his balls for last."

The Wolfman began whimpering again. "Benja, Benja."

"Notte," Benny said, "light his candle for him."

"Benny, the candle ain't gonna help. You know what he wants."

"I don't care what he wants. *The candle.*"

Moving his shoulders reluctantly, Notte lit the Wolfman's candle. The Wolfman's humped shadow swept across the ceiling. He ignored the flame. "Benja, Benja."

"Christ," Benny said, and walked over to the Wolfman's cot. He scowled at the entire barrack, and then began to sing:

> *Oif'n pripetchik brent a shmipetchik*
> *Un in shtub iz hais.*
> *Un der Rebbe lerent klaine kinderlach*
> *Ver, ver vais.*

The Wolfman giggled to himself. "*Shmipetchik,*" he said.

"Boris, *shluf*."

The Wolfman pleaded with him. "Benja, Benja. *Noch amol*."

Benny sang the same song. The Indian put away his knife. The Wolfman lay down on the cot drawing his knees close to his chin. Benny took off the Wolfman's skullcap and covered him with two blankets. "*Shluf*." The blankets rode the Wolfman's knees and formed a toppled pyramid. The top of the Wolfman's head was almost completely bald.

I wanted to redeem myself in some small way. I knew that if I could get to Benny, the other boys would give in automatically. "Benny," I said, "Benny. Look, I'm not for Uncle. Believe me. I want to help. If you hold the Company together, I'll keep Uncle and the Jailer and the bulldogs off your back. And Rubin, too. Benny."

Benny stood near the Wolfman's cot. "Notte," he said, "tell the Screw that we don't need his help."

"Mr. Shitz, Benny says—"

"I heard him," I said. "I heard him. All right, under the blankets. Lights out."

"Notte, tell the Screw that he's disturbing the Wolfman's sleep. And tell him one light stays on. The Wolfman always has bad dreams in the dark."

Notte scrambled towards the gate.

"Don't bother, Notte. I already got the message. And you can tell him that if the Wolfman has bad dreams, it's his fault. He's the one who won't cooperate. Good night."

I hung my shirt and pants in the closet, near Mama's brassiere. My baggy underpants almost reached my scrimpy knees. I decided to wear Crazy's hat through the night. I didn't intend to sleep. I would keep an all-night vigil. I wasn't going to let Benny or the Indian fall into Uncle's trap. No, the boys would be safe as long as they remained in the barrack. I would patrol the barrack every half hour. One of my

117

eyes closed. I tilted the peak of the hat to show the boys that I wasn't asleep. I saw my face in the tiny closet mirror. There were deep gouges under both eyes. My cheeks had disappeared. Nick, look how you've aged in one day. No, it's just the shadows. One day. Where's Sonia? Another time. Another place. I know. I should pack my grip and run out of the barrack before I get sucked in. But how would I get past the bulldogs? Maybe I could charm them with Crazy's hat? It's just the bed. I've never slept in a strange bed before. If Papa hadn't died, I wouldn't be here. Sing me a lullaby. A onepenny, twopenny song. With a cow and a fiddle and a pocketful of rye. And a rabbi with a bald chin. Wolfman. Winnie the Pooh. Papa never sang songs. Only stories. Tell Tigger the tiger to tuck in his toes. Uncle says the Nazis are coming. Under the falls.

The Wolfman talked in his sleep. I wondered if he was having a bad dream. I wanted to sing him a twopenny song.

PART TWO

I might have slept through Uncle's reveille had it been an ordinary bugle; after all, a bugle would have been appropriate with the barracks and the rest—but a ram's horn! Its prolonged bleat seemed to pierce my skull and juggle my brains. I opened one eye at a time. The Wolfman was sitting on his cot. The other cots were empty. I cursed myself for having abandoned the vigil and fallen asleep. The boys hadn't even bothered leaving decoys. Their blankets were bunched defiantly under their cots. My campaign hat was sitting on one of the commodes; its peak had been crushed in. I didn't waste any time searching the barrack; I knew the boys weren't around. The Wolfman formed a pontoon with his wedged fingers and spanned his bald head. "*Yamka*," he said. "*Mein shaine, klaine kepele*." I retrieved his skullcap. Then he took my hand and led me out of the barrack.

The other Companies were assembled on the lawn in

front of the big house. We both waded through the frost. The lawn was flooded with dried leaves. I don't really know where the leaves came from. There were no trees around. The frost clung stubbornly to the leaves and invaded the Wolfman's shoes and mine. I stumbled several times. Rubin turned around. He was the one who held the horn. Its tapered end was slightly rumpled. Shadrach sat near Rubin's knees; his tail was buried in the leaves. I noticed Dobrilubov and Murdoch mingling with the Companies. Mama and Uncle Nate huddled behind Shadrach. Uncle Nate wisely wore galoshes and a winter coat. The Rabbi sat on the porch. He was wearing his Seabee cap again. He waved once to the Wolfman. *"Rebbe,"* the Wolfman said, but he steered me away from the porch. We both lined up near C Company.

"All right," Rubin said, "all Comp'nies present and accounted for. A Company, sound off."

The boys in A Company repeated their names in spitfire fashion. *AbelowitzApplebaumBachenrothBergerBotnick-DershkowitzFeigGenzelMandelbergNotteWinklerYuchtman-Zlatkiss.* B Company kept the same pace. *FrydaGelberGelefskyKaplanKrinskyLumishMondscheinNossek.* C Company lagged slightly. *Blumenfield ChalfinCharyn Melnick SadovnickSpitzerWinder Wohl.* Then Rubin arrived at D Company. The Wolfman bore the disgruntled looks of the other boys. He searched the rows of skullcaps. *"Benja, Benja."*

"It seems to me, Commander," Rubin said, without smiling once, "your Company ain't in full strength. Anybody hear Little Notte sound off? Or the Indian? And the other three clowns? Commander, you know the present whereabouts of the five missing boys?"

"No," I said, moving closer to the Wolfman. "No. Your horn woke me and. . . ."

Uncle Nate spoke for me. "Rubin, please. You are persecuting the wrong party. The Commander is not responsible for Benny's midnight antics. The antics are our own affair."

"I wasn't persecuting nobody, Uncle. I know Nick didn't have nothin' to do with it. I was trying to show the other Comp'nies that we didn't stage any shyster deals just to keep 'em entertained. The breakout was legit."

"Rubin, I'm sure the other Companies are aware that we are not in the habit here of conducting sideshows. Please."

"Okay, Uncle." Rubin blew three times into the mouth of the horn; the rumpled end capsized after each bleat. I could feel my stomach drop. I saw the skullcaps first. They were pressed against the screened door of the porch. Then the door opened and the boys filed past the Rabbi, forming a crooked row. Billingsgate's two bulldogs accompanied them. Both dogs were unmuzzled and kept snapping at the boys' heels. The boys hopped across the lawn. Billingsgate ambled behind them; his drillmaster's stick was broken. Notte's sweat shirt was torn; his knuckles were bruised and he tried to lick them, but the dogs kept throwing him off balance. The Indian wasn't wearing any pants. There were gashes on both his knees. One of Benny's eyes was closed. He groped behind the Indian. For some reason the dogs left him alone, but Billingsgate prodded him with the broken stick. He began walking in a circle. Matches paused and led Benny in the right direction. His sweat shirt was mottled with red blotches; the cockamanies mingled with the blotches and formed star-shaped patterns in the mild midmorning sun. Larry Farbovich's face was unmarked, but his hands kept trembling and he drew them inside the sleeves of his sweat shirt. The dogs drove the boys over to Rubin and then regrouped behind Shadrach. Shadrach licked one paw disdainfully.

Rubin began the inquisition. He walked around the boys twice. Then he paused in front of Benny. "Did you have a nice party, Benny?" Benny's crooked shoulder twitched uncomprehendingly. Matches jumped between them, the dead leaves crackling under his feet. "Leave him alone. The Jailer did enough to him." His pinched face bristled fiercely.

"*Me?*" Billingsgate said. "Hell now, why does everybody gotta go and put all the blame on ol' Billingsgate? I didn't do a thing. I just slapped him silly, that's all." He tensed the stick. "Back in line, Matches. Back, back."

Mama broke through C Company suddenly, and sweeping past me, she shielded Benny and Matches. "Nate," she said, glowering at the Jailer, "put the *golem* back in his cage. The boys have had enough."

"Uncle," Billingsgate said, "there ain't nothing about insults in mah contract. I'm only doing mah job, that's all. I don't gotta hear that talk from her. Maybe I use mah stick a little too often, but she has her own ways of scarring their hides."

Uncle Nate intervened. "Bill, please. Do we need squabbles now in front of the boys? Mama, let me vouch for him. His behavior was not excessive, I assure you. The occasion unfortunately called for extraordinary measures. Do you think I enjoy seeing bloodied faces?" I heard the porch door slam. The Rabbi had disappeared. Mama moved away from the boys.

Uncle Nate scrutinized them singly, apportioning his glances. "And what did you accomplish, my Katzenjammer kids? Is Bucharevsky out of the Dungeon?"

I watched Uncle Nate wield his glances, his eyebrows bunching sternly in his support; the boys looked at the ground guiltily. Larry Farbovich began to cry. His pants were already wet.

"Mr. Lipshitz, shall I tell you what your boys planned for us? Oh, it was no slipshod undertaking. My commandos had a three-pronged attack. Benny would have been satisfied with nothing less. That's why he needed so many accomplices

124

this time. Had they found some use for Boris, I'm sure they would have included him in the plan too. Let me give you a full report. Don't think that the Indian's misdemeanors in the latrine yesterday was merely a whim. It was part of the plan. The preliminary stage. To confuse us he let all the faucets run. But his little flood was only a diversion. Benny sent him down to weaken the seams in the main pipe. And when the plan went into operation during the night, our Indian was supposed to puncture the pipe and cause a general commotion on the ground floor. But the tactic never came off. The cook happened to be in one of the stalls when the Indian came in. But Benny knew better than to rely on the Indian for his only support. He sent Notte over to B Company with a sack of twigs, a roll of toilet paper, and two boxes of candles. Sure. The boys figured a little bonfire behind the barracks would keep us all away from the house. But leave it to Notte. His little fire kit wasn't complete. He had enough candles to start a hundred fires, but not one match. And by the time he ran back to D Company, Commander Murdoch discovered the sack of twigs, and all the matches in the world would have done Notte no good."

"Benny," Notte said. "Don't believe it. The Marine was waiting for—"

"Notte, now is not the time for excuses. Fate is sometimes a very perverse fellow. One day he is on your side and the next day he's not."

"Uncle, it had nothin' to do with fate. It was a trap. All the way."

"Notte, do you want the boys to have a false impression? It's a simple story. You bungled the job. *Notte*. No more. We have to find out what happened to the central party. When the cook reported to me after finding the Indian in the latrine, it didn't take me long to figure out what Benny was after.

125

And I sent Rubin and Bill up to the fourth floor. You know I leave Pebbleby on guard every night outside the Dungeon. The boys had already disposed of him. His hands and feet were tied, and Farbovich was sitting on his face. We foiled the plan just in time. Benny had his bomb in position against the door of the Dungeon, and Matches was ready to ignite it. They were only waiting for Notte's bonfire or the Indian's maneuvers in the latrine. After all, Benny is no amateur. He needed something to muffle the noise of the bomb. Here," he said, "here is specimen A," and he removed a paper bag from his pocket. "Don't let the bag fool you. The bomb is potent. Believe me. I spent half the night trying to analyze its contents. I know it contains some charcoal and scraps of birchbark for a binder, but even the biggest chemists would never be able to uncover Benny's formulas. Boys, it's probably the first birchbark bomb in the world. Think of it. Think what Benny could accomplish, if only he would give up his diabolic instincts and work for the right side. For Roosevelt and for the Home. The Nazis would never have a chance." Then he turned abruptly. "Rubin, bring out specimen B. Pebbles, please." Rubin didn't bother using the horn. "Pebbleby," he shouted. "Pebbleby." The Janitor came out of the house. His limp seemed aggravated. Both his cheeks were covered with bandages. "Boys, you want more proof? Here! Pebbles, tell them." The Janitor removed his watch cap and molded it nervously with his hands. "Uncle," he said, "they beat me. Beat me blue. The devils. This one was worse'n the rest." He pointed one trembling finger at Matches. I expected Matches to recoil; instead he welcomed the accusation and smiled blithely. "Oh, Uncle. He was gonna take out my eyes."

"Uncle," Matches said, "next time we won't let him off so easy. Don't worry, Bullets ain't gonna be upstairs for long."

"Matches, I give you my personal guarantee that there will be no next time."

Uncle Nate then confronted each of the five conspirators. He dealt with the Indian first. "Indian, I don't expect any gratitude. I'm not seeking rewards. But who took you in when nobody wanted you? Who clothed you and fed you? And look how you repay me! Your minor mischiefs don't bother me. But when you join plots, Indian, this I can no longer tolerate. Remember, Indian, if the Home is destroyed, you will have no place to go. You will become a scavenger again, eating garbage from the streets. Remember." He paused in front of Matches next. "I don't intend to waste my time with this one. Matches, you are a hopeless case. Completely incorrigible. As far as I am concerned, you are no longer at the Home. You have lost your official status here. Commander Lipshitz, please strike his name off your roster. We'll let him eat with the dogs." Then he moved on to Larry. "Farbovich, you know you have one function here. And that is to watch over Boris. Who gave you the right to leave him alone in the barrack and take part in Benny's expedition?"

Larry wagged his head penitently. "Uncle, I'm sorry. It won't happen again, Uncle. Never again. I didn't want to go. They made me. I wanted to stay with the Wolfman."

"Stop whining, Farbovich. Just make sure there is no repeat performance. And you, Notte, you. I expected more from you. Not because you are any better than the rest, but because you are at least a little smarter. This is the first time you let yourself get involved in one of Benny's schemes. Notte, you know your brother was supposed to be made a trustee next week. Was it worth ruining his chances for such a hollow effort?"

"Let him look out for himself, Uncle."

Uncle Nate smiled faintly, breaking the grim line of his protruding lips; I preferred his frowns. "Notte, Notte," he said, "if you are such a bandit at eleven, what can we expect from you later on? We will need an entire police force for

127

you alone. And Benny. He is the biggest disappointment of all. To waste his talents in such a feeble way. Benny?"

Benny's shoulder now shook uncontrollably. "Uncle," he said. "Uncle. Uncle. Uncle."

"Mama," Uncle Nate said, "the boy is senseless. Take him to his barrack, please. And look after his eye."

Mama walked Benny past Rubin and Uncle Nate. *"Benja,"* the Wolfman cried, trying to follow them, but Billingsgate blocked the Wolfman's way.

"Bill, let him go through."

The Wolfman shambled across the lawn, his skullcap hopping crazily on his head. He finally caught up with Mama and Benny. I saw the Wolfman grip Benny's hand and lead him over to the barrack. Benny's shoulder kept shaking.

Uncle Nate turned to the other Companies. "Boys," he said, "you are the real victims of this uprising. In order to make sure that this never happens again, I will have to suspend all privileges. No radio for the next two weeks."

Several boys in B Company mumbled to themselves.

"And Mr. Lipshitz. I'm restricting your boys to their barrack for an indefinite period. No one is to leave. Rubin, you can dismiss the Companies. Wait, wait. We haven't dealt yet with Bucharevsky. Boys, let this be a lesson for all of you. I'm keeping Bullets upstairs for another three weeks."

Rubin's brows wove unevenly. "Uncle," he said, "there ain't nobody alive who could take the treatment for three more weeks. The record is thirteen days. That's the limit. He's already sweating blood, Uncle, and he's only been in the box a week."

"Rubin, dismiss the boys. *Please.*"

Rubin turned sullenly and dismissed the Companies. I waited until the first two Companies marched towards their barracks. Then I said, "Uncle...."

"What? Louder, Lipshitz, please."

"I'd like to talk to you."

"Here? Now?"

"Yes, Uncle. Now."

"Bill, take over D Company for a little while."

"Awright, wise guys," Billingsgate said, "keep in line." I watched my diminished Company march haltingly across the lawn. I heard Dobrilubov count cadence for B Company. "One, two. One, two."

Uncle and I stood on the emptied lawn. His lips seemed to shed some of their grimness. "Nick," he said softly. "I know. It wasn't a pretty spectacle. All this. But I assure you, Nick, it had to be done. It's unfortunate that the whole affair coincided with your arrival at the Home. I would have preferred that you see our milder side. But I couldn't suspend my activities simply to accommodate you. Nick, I expect your sympathies to remain with the boys. I would be disappointed in you if this were not so. It's not my policy to hire golems and bullies. But, Nick, remember, sometimes you have to censure your own feelings for the general good. You think I enjoyed punishing them? Nick, Benny's plan was magnificent. The whole little band deserved a commendation. None of my boys here are ninnies. Believe me, I myself was on Benny's side. But I also have my official position. As the director of the Home I had no other choice. I had to retaliate, or there would have been bedlam."

"Uncle," I said, "I know the boys had to be punished. But not that way. God, what did that bastard do to Benny!"

"Nick," he said, "sometimes the Jailer gets out of hand, I know. He can be brutal. He was conducting his own little private investigation. He took Benny down to the cellar for that purpose. Nick, I was never even told. I assure you. It will not happen again. Nick, that's why it is so important to me that you are here. I need someone with your sensibilities and intelligence in my organization. After all, Rubin can only be

129

trusted so far. He's not very strong in the brain department. And Mama's right. The Jailer's a golem at times. Nick, I'm expecting Rubin to be drafted any day. Then," he said, "then I want you to take over. And Nick, I hope that what happened this morning will not leave a bad taste. Believe me, there is no trouble whatsoever in the other Companies. Bill doesn't have to lift a finger. The boys patrol themselves. Give them their radio twice a week and they're happy."

"Then why don't you just break up D Company and let A, B, and C each take two or three of my boys."

"Nick," he said, "I told myself the minute I saw you: Here, here's a man with initiative. Do you think Rubin would have been able to come up with such a scheme? He doesn't have the equipment. But Nick, there is one thing wrong. If I shift your boys into the other Companies, then I have three possible sources of insurrection. Now I only have one. No, when there is a cancer around, it's best to isolate it and keep it in closed quarters. But if we work together, I'm confident we will be able to come up with something that will be mutually amenable. Nick," he said, extending his hand, "do we have our little pact?"

"Yes," I said, finally giving him my hand. We stood together on the lawn for a moment. Then he turned his back. "Nick, I have an important appointment. We'll talk again later." He trudged towards the house, his galoshes leaving a definite track in the leaves. I noticed for the first time that Uncle Nate had a slight limp.

In the end, the boys didn't seem very bothered by their confinement. Benny put the shower stalls and the commodes to good use. The boys played slug and asses up against the walls of the stall, and the commodes became barriers for monkey in the middle. The Jailer inspected the barrack almost every day. He still cursed the Indian, but he left Benny and the Wolfman alone. The boys were a little put off by the Jailer's restraint. They were sure that Uncle was up to something.

During my teaching assignments, Murdoch or Mama stayed with my boys. Uncle generally kept the Rabbi away from the barracks. He had already suspended the Rabbi's Bible classes, and the Rabbi's religious functions at the Home came to a complete standstill. He was no longer called upon to bless Dobrilubov's sandwiches, and he was even denied the right to pray for the Jewish servicemen overseas and for the United Nations. For the most part, the Rabbi remained incommunicado.

I met with the other Companies six days a week in the classroom on the second floor. Of course, it was impossible trying to teach them anything. They didn't know the first thing about long division and short division, about commas and question marks, or about Montcalm and the French and Indian War. They had never heard of Balboa and Vasco da Gama, and when I tried to tell them about the impressment of American seamen and the War of 1812, most of them stared blankly at the ceiling or sneezed into their skullcaps. During the third day of class, I asked each of them in desperation to go back to his barrack and pick out the name of one historical figure. I anticipated hearing about Al Capone and John Garfield, but even Batman would have satisfied me. Unfortunately, I took the wrong precautions. There were no shirkers this time: the boys actually seemed eager to volunteer their names. "Zevi Hirsch Masliansky," said Aaron Zlatkiss of A Company. Barry Mondschein of B Company backed him up with "Mordecai Manuel Noah." Then came a barrage of names from C Company: "Louis Lipsky, Felix Warburg, Chaim Weizmann, Nathan Birnbaum, Menachem Ussishkin. . . ." The boys obviously enjoyed seeing me befuddled. "Ussishkin," I said to myself, trying to locate one familiar name. Big Notte finally stood up, and with his skullcap arrayed over one eye, he said confidingly, "*Zionists*, Mr. Lipshitz. Uncle coached us."

After swearing to myself that I would never again stray far from Vasco da Gama and long division, I dismissed the class.

Mama began her therapy sessions with my boys on the fourth day of their confinement. She seemed a little disap-

132

pointed when she saw me sitting on my bed reading one of the Indian's comic books. I'm sure she would have preferred not having me around. "Today," she said, "today we're all going to have a little fun." I saw Notte put his fists secretly under his sweat shirt and shape two enormous boobs. He wiggled them while Mama talked. "We're going to tell each other about our adventures before we came to the Home. Larry, would you like to start?"

Larry's buttocks shrank. "No, Mama. I ain't got nothin' to tell. No adventures. They just brought me here. I had nothin' to do with it. Nothin'. Uncle told me to watch the Wolfman. That's all I know."

"Larry," Mama said, purring. "There's nothing to be afraid of. Notte, come, break the ice. Show Larry how easy it is to tell something about yourself. You can be as creative as you want. You can even use a few of the boys as props."

Notte disengaged his fists. "An adventure, Mama?"

"Anything, Notte."

He tilted his head perspicaciously. "Anything? Then the Indian gotta help me out. He gotta stand by the toilet boxes and act like a gorilla."

The Indian refused. Mama tried to prod him. "Billy, it will be just like charades." But the Indian was adamant. "That ain't my line, Mama."

"Tough," Notte said. "I can't do a thing without a gorilla." I heard him suck his lip. "I know, Mama. The Wolfman. The Wolfman's a natural. Benny, line him up. Give him his cues. Tell him, Benny. A gorilla."

Benny glowered at all of us. "Leave Boris out of it."

"Benny," Mama said. "Please. Boris will enjoy himself. It will give him something to do. Please."

"Ah, Mama. I wouldn't know how to tell him. I don't know the kike word for gorilla. Let the Screw play the part."

133

I hid my head behind the comic book.

"Wait, wait," Notte said. "I want the Wolfman. Lemme try. Boris. Gor-ill-a. Apeman. King Kong."

The Wolfman was wonderstruck. *"Kee Konk."* His pouchlike cheeks wagged with recognition. *"Benja. Kee Konk."* He climbed on top of the commodes, hunched his shoulders and growled. Then he shielded his face with one hand and grabbed at the air with the other.

"No, no," Notte said. "He thinks it's the end of the picture." Notte ordered the Wolfman off the commodes. "It ain't the top of the Empire State Building. You're in a cage." He walked around the commodes and shaped four walls with his outstretched arms. "Cage, see. *Shpill* like you're in a cage." The Wolfman hunched his shoulders again for Notte. "That's it. Just like that." Then Notte came back to Mama.

"Mama, it was like this. Me and Biggy worked the rodeo and the circus. We practically owned Madison Square Garden. Okay, we hadda cough up fifty cents each time to get in, but Mama, it was worth it. We hit ten purses and wallets a visit, and all the cotton candy we could eat. When it was an off day for the bulls, Biggy wanted to go for fifteen, but I always held him back. 'Big Notte,' I hadda tell him, 'you know my style by now, so don't push me. *Ten*, and then we enjoy the show.' Mama, you shoulda seen my technique. I had the fastest pair of hands in the business. Even the pros couldn't compete with the *Phantoms*. That's what they called us in the *Daily Mirror*. They had it all on top of the page. RASH OF PETTY THEFTS AT RINGLING BROTHERS. THE PHANTOMS STRIKE AGAIN. They even began using fancy words. UBIQUITOUS. Mama, it took me an hour just to look it up. And I explained it to Biggy ten times, but he never caught the meaning. 'Biggy, it means the head bull at the circus thinks we can be ten places at the same time. That's all.' But don't get me wrong, Mama. The purses was only the preliminary. It didn't mean

134

nothin' to me unless I enjoyed the show. I only worked the rodeos because of Biggy. I never cared for cowboys and horses. The circus was the place for me. I didn't give two farts about the trained seals and the jugglers and the high wire guys, only the side show downstairs. After Biggy and me hauled in our quota of purses, we'd load up with cotton candy and go around to the fat lady and the giants and the dwarfs. And then we would walk over to the menagerie and talk to the baby elephants and the one gorilla. Wolfman, that's your cue. *Growl.*"

The Wolfman growled for him and dangled his hands below his knees.

"Mama, the gorilla was the main attraction. They had a big sign over his cage telling how it took Frank Buck seven weeks to capture him. *King Kong, Jr., the Killer of Borneo.* Mama, the minute I saw him walking with his ass tilted up and with his own crap piled in the corner, I fell in love with the gorilla. You know, the way they talk about Romeo and Julietta. I'm telling you, Mama, it wasn't a one way deal. The Kong went crazy over me too. Ask Biggy. He was the witness."

Notte now approached the Wolfman coyly, hiding his chin behind his left shoulder. The Wolfman responded immediately. He scrambled around the commodes, whooping wildly, and then molding his brows, he trained on Notte a goofy, shameless smile.

"Mama, watch him. That's the way. The gorilla smiled like that every time I came around. You shoulda seen that gorilla go. He woulda made the acrobats upstairs look silly. You ain't never seen a gorilla take a crap standing on his head, and without interrupting his smile. Mama, you know me. I don't like to pass off the blame on anybody, but it was the smile that ruined us. Everybody knows that a guy who's in love can't be trusted. I just couldn't take seeing the Kong

135

cooped up like a rooster, with people throwing peanuts in his face and flying balloons in front of the cage. And Mama, it wasn't only the gorilla. In my condition, I couldn't help pitying the giants and the dwarfs and the fat lady with the billy-goat's beard. And I decided to free the whole side show. I climbed right on top of the cotton candy stand and shouted, 'Dwarfs and everybody, come down from the platforms. It's time for a revolt. Help me free all the animals from the cages. I'm taking the gorilla to the Bronx.' The dwarfs didn't pay no attention to me, but the bulls started coming from all directions. I jumped off the stand and Biggy and me headed for the entrance, and we woulda made it too, but Biggy couldn't hold in the purses and the dollar bills. They kept flying outa his shirt, and people started grabbing for the bills all over the place. Then I heard one of the bulls shout, 'The Phantoms, the Phantoms,' and I knew that was the end. The Juvenile Bureau didn't know what to do with me. They couldn't ship me out to Sing Sing. I was only nine. So they sent me up here with Biggy. That's it, Mama. The whole story." Notte winked at the Wolfman. He came back to the cot and the boys made a place for him. He sat between Benny and Matches. I couldn't help it, but I had to sneeze. Mama frowned. "I'm sorry," I said. Benny's face hardened noticeably, and Notte put his fingers behind his ears and wiggled them at me. I'm sure it wasn't only the sneeze that had made me an interloper. I put down the comic book and walked towards the door.

There were no signs of life on the lawn. The bulldogs were kenneled, and the other Companies were drilling with Murdoch in the cellar. I heard their bayonet charges. I decided to seek out the Rabbi.

I met Pebbleby near the porch. He was carrying a cucumber and several radishes inside his watch cap; his cheeks were still bandaged.

"Pebbles," I said, "do you know where I can find the Rabbi?"

The Janitor kept shifting his neck. "*Commander*," he finally said. "The Rabbi's in his room."

"Fine. How do I get there?"

"It's on the third floor. The room next to Mama's." He gave me the cucumber and the radishes. "For the Rabbi. That's all I could sneak out. Uncle keeps the kitchen guarded."

I thanked Pebbleby in the Rabbi's behalf, and then I went up to the third floor. The Rabbi's door was closed.

"Rabbi, it's me. Nick."

I heard a muffled sound through the door. I went in. The Rabbi was sitting on a toilet bowl in the middle of the room. A shriveled flypaper ribbon hung over the Rabbi's head and left a ragged shadow on his nose. He sneezed once and the end of the ribbon jumped. There were several piles of books near the door. I climbed over them and approached the toilet bowl. "Rabbi?"

He looked up for the first time; after squinting for a moment, he flexed his jaw.

"Rabbi, should I come back some other time?"

He smiled and patted the bowl with both hands. "Lipshitz," he said, "I had Uncle Nate install it for me. I told him I can't function properly without my own toilet seat. Did you know that Martin Luther first met the Devil while he was on the pot? Mama says that I have an anal personality. All my problems come from poor toilet training. Who knows. Maybe she's right. I'm no rectumologist. Lipshitz. . . ."

"Rabbi, nobody's around. I'm Nick, remember?"

"Oh, I'm sorry. If I sit too long I always end up in a stupor. But it can't be helped."

"Rabbi," I said, "Pebbleby sent up a cucumber and some radishes."

137

"What would I do without Pebbles? He keeps me alive. Dobrilubov puts worms in all my sandwiches."

I looked at him suspiciously. "Rabbi, why would Uncle want to keep plaguing you for one sermon?"

"Nick, it had nothing to do with sermons. Nate thinks I inspired Benny's attack on the Dungeon."

"But that's crazy."

"No, Nick. Uncle's right. Of course, there was no direct involvement on my part. That's understood. But Nate knows that the revolt would have been impossible without me. Nick, I was a part-time rabbi even before Nate appointed me his chauffeur. I had one title then. Commander Rosencrantz. I was in charge of D Company. *Your boys.* I marched them over to the lawn every morning and then slept until the middle of the afternoon. What could be simpler? But Nick, it's not in my nature to keep away from trouble. In the Bronx they called me the Radical Rabbi, and believe me, it wasn't because of my religious zeal. My enthusiasm went in the other direction. I'm an anarchist, what can I do? It's a compulsion with me. A fever. I abandoned my congregation and preached in the streets against the Democrats and the Republicans, against the new order and the old one, against the Communists and the Socialists, against mayors and governors, against war pacts and peace conferences, against the fire department and the police department, and even against the board of directors of the synagogue. And so, I ended up here. And I promised myself, Rosencrantz, stay away from all obligations. Every involvement is a trap. Become mechanical. A machine without a heart. Keep the world between you and your toilet seat. But Nick, it never works. Could I sit idle here and watch Nathanson manipulate the boys? Nick, don't misinterpret. I'm not questioning his motives. When Uncle hoards sugar and canned goods in the cellar, it's not for himself. It's for the boys. Who can blame him? He wants to keep the Home. But

138

I cannot abide regulations and restraints. Any power over the will is poisonous for me, no matter how many sanctions it may have: God, country, the common good, survival of the species. The beetle needs his dung, and the Rabbi needs dysfunctions and disorders. And so I told the boys that no authority is sacred, that they had the right to revolt any time their individual freedom was threatened, and as a belated reward Nate has restricted me to my room. 'Rabbi, keep your bony behind on the toilet seat.' Don't worry. Uncle knows. What did I accomplish for the boys? I'm a menace to any organization. My philosophies are only good for breaking wind. The explosions are loud, but the silence comes back just the same." He clasped his knees and stared abstractedly at the flypaper.

"Rabbi," I said, breaking his reverie, "tell me something. Why don't the boys accept me? I try to be a tolerable Commander. I don't hold a stick over them or even tell them what to do. Oh, I won't say they hate me. It's not as strong as that. But they just don't seem to have any use for me. I'm on their side, Rabbi. I mean it."

Pumping his chin, the Rabbi motioned to the shelf behind the toilet bowl. A kitchen knife and a salt shaker with an impossibly dented cap were its only occupants. I brought them both over to the Rabbi. He proceeded to peel the cucumber and scrape the radishes. Then he untwisted the dented cap, stuck two fingers into the shaker, and drew out two tiny mounds of salt which he balanced delicately on his fingertips. I declined the cucumber, but I offered to try a radish. It had a dungy odor.

"Nick," the Rabbi said, munching half the cucumber, "you can't expect the boys to love you? For them you're only Uncle's latest lackey. Another screw. Why should they have any faith in your sympathies? I've taught them to be suspicious of every one of Uncle's moves. He has a habit of alternating doses of sugar and gall, of thunder and quiescence, of extreme wrath and sympathetic understanding. And believe me, Nick, it's not done in a whimsical way. He balances off Mama and the Jailer, Shadrach and me. Hot and cold, hard and soft. Like a tinhorn Jehovah."

"But Rabbi, where do I fit into the picture?"

The Rabbi bunched one eyebrow rather bizarrely. "Nick, do you think it was an accident that Nate assigned D Company to you? He wanted to give the boys an illusion of safety. He wanted to make them feel that with you around they would be their own masters, that they would be able to get away with anything. And what happened? The minute they tried something, he brought his wolves down on them and crushed their little revolt. And now Nate can afford to bring back the calm. The Jailer will retire his stick for a little while. But Uncle's practiced lulls are more oppressive than his storms, because you can feel the agitation and the rancor building up. No, Nick. Save your sympathies. That's not what the boys need. Break Uncle's quiet. Agitate. Harden yourself. Be merciless with the boys. They won't like you any better. But this way Uncle won't be able to throw them off their guard."

"Rabbi," I said, "I tried firmness with them. It didn't work. It's because of Benny. I can't find a way to reach him."

"Benny?" the Rabbi said, sucking the salt from his fingers. "Trotsky would have had a use for him. The boy would have made Stalin eat crow and pumpkin pie. Nick, he was my chief disciple in the Company. What, could I make the Indian or Matches understand Bakunin? They had enough trouble trying to pronounce his name. But Benny. The boy is a born insurrectionist. When I told the boys that men usually band together for one purpose only: to consolidate the harm that they can cause, the Indian picked his nails with his knife, but Benny understood. And don't think he just swallowed down my theories. 'Rabbi,' he said, 'what about the Maccabees?'

140

Now I watched every word. 'Benny, the only way to fight organized tyranny is to organize yourself. But what happens when the oppressed rout their oppressors? Then they, in their own turn, begin to oppress. Never mind the intentions. All organizations and institutions end up causing more harm than good.' He looked at me for a minute. How could I turn away? His eyes were like magnets. Then he said, 'Rabbi, when you're right you're right.' Nick, what can I tell you? He's an extraordinary boy. You hear the way he converses with Boris. Did he know any Yiddish when he came here? The Sephardim have their own brand of gobble talk. Only turkeys and Chinamen can understand them. 'Rabbi,' he told me, 'teach me kike.' So we sat and studied every night, just so he would be able to talk to Boris. Did the other boys care? Notte teased Boris left and right. *Wolfman.* Nick, the boy has his problems, but don't be fooled by his looks. He's no dope. Believe me. Something happened to him, yes, but his mind is not impaired. If you only understood a little Yiddish, you would know what I mean. But what can Mama do with him? Does she expect him to perform on her IQ tests? So she labels him an idiot and closes his file. And let me tell you something about Mama's tests. They're worthless. She went to Hunter College twenty years ago for two terms and she calls herself a social worker. Elsie Hirschhorn of the Crotona Y. And what did she do at the Y? She was a receptionist and an attendant in the girls' locker room. And the director sacked her when he found out that all the maintenance men were banging her after hours on the wrestling mat. What do you think Uncle picks out for his Home? Only damaged goods."

Pebbleby appeared suddenly. "Rabbi, Uncle is coming up."

The Rabbi bolted from his toilet seat. "Nick, go." The flypaper dangled in front of his nose. His jaw rumpled slightly. "If Nate finds you here, he won't even allow me the toilet

141

bowl. But remember. Be stern with the boys. No mercy. Pebbles, hide him behind the stairs. *Go*."

Pebbleby led me over to the landing; his brogans squeaked. We heard Uncle Nate resting on the second floor. He was breathing heavily. Then he began climbing the stairs. His shadow appeared first. The stairway was poorly lit, and Uncle proceeded cautiously, hugging the wall. He mumbled to himself. "Rabbis. What do they want from my life? Nate, you're sixty-three. They retire generals at your age. I should will the German Army my prostate gland. They would lose the war in a week. Nobody knows." He passed us, his shoulders tilting crookedly. Pebbleby nudged my arm. We tiptoed down the stairs. I watched my shadow walk.

ᛂ CHAPTER ᛋ

10

I tried to put the Rabbi's policies into practice. I banned monkey in the middle and denied the boys the use of the shower stall for asses up. It didn't help much; they merely wrote the word *Screw* over the door and centered their games around the commodes. And when I denied them the commodes too, Notte complained that my moves were unconstitutional: no one was allowed to take away his squatter's rights. But after that, he didn't put up much of a fight. Benny must have told him to ignore me. It wasn't worth arguing with the screw.

Two days after my interview with the Rabbi, I found a wooden replica of myself sitting under my blanket. I had been fashioned with a campaign hat bearing an unusually elongated peak, and a scrotum that almost reached my knees. I also had only one eye; it had been placed directly over my nose. Searching the doll for pin marks, I cursed the Rabbi and all his

143

policies, and then carried the doll gingerly over to Benny's cot. He was playing blackjack with Matches and Notte. Larry was helping the Wolfman build a fort for his soldiers. The Indian, as usual, was reading a comic book. This time it was Sheena, Queen of the Jungle. I decided to employ a little tact in approaching Benny. I permitted him to deal the cards, and then showed him the doll. "Benny, I don't mind the hanging balls, but did you have to make me with one eye?"

"Notte," Benny said, matter-of-factly, "tell the screw that dolls aren't my department."

"All right," I said, without bothering to confer with Notte, "then who did it?"

Notte pointed slyly to the Indian's bunk. The Indian turned the page of his comic book, then he raised one eye.

"Indian?" I said.

Notte answered for him. "Don't blame the Indian, Commander. He never knows how they're gonna come out."

"But I don't understand. I saw Benny carving an apple in the classroom. I thought he...."

"Apples is apples," Notte said judiciously. "You're on the wrong track, Commander. The Indian does all the art work in this bunk. Who do you think put together the Wolfman's sojers? He can carve on anything with his knife."

The Indian didn't say a word. He was obviously enjoying Sheena. I looked at the doll again. Aside from the one eye and the stretched scrotum, the Indian had caught my features perfectly. The prunelike expression on the doll's face was undoubtedly my own.

That afternoon, when Pebbleby brought in our supply of sandwiches and apples, and also a special treat for the day, coconut macaroons shaped like Liberty Ships, which Mama herself had baked, he told me that Rubin had received his draft notification. "He's gonna be leaving for Dix any day."

Uncle Nate had already told me about Rubin, but I was

144

still a little startled. I had thought that Uncle could afford to hold Rubin's job in pledge for me, because he knew all along that Rubin would never be drafted. But even if Uncle had miscalculated, he would undoubtedly ask one of the Jailers to take over Rubin's operations. I could hardly see myself giving orders to Shadrach, holding conferences with the Jailers, torturing Bucharevsky in the Dungeon, and mastering the ram's horn. And when a week passed without a word from Uncle, I assured myself that I would not be involved. Then, just when my calm had been restored, I found a note concealed in my bologna sandwich. It was blotched with mustard. Rubin wanted to see me. He was waiting for me in the classroom on the second floor. Pebbleby still had to deliver sandwiches to A Company, but he agreed to mind the boys for a little while. I could see that he was very unhappy about the whole thing. He didn't want to stay alone with the boys. Matches glared at him. "Commander," Pebbleby said, "please. Whatever you have to do, make it short. I wanna come out of here alive."

I called the Company to attention. "Boys, I'd like you to give Pebbles your complete cooperation. I mean that. I'll be back soon."

I moved towards the door. "*Commander,*" Matches called over my shoulder, "you don't gotta worry about the twerp. We don't bother nobody unless it's an official raid. He's safe for now." Pebbleby wasn't taking any chances. I saw him walk behind the gate.

Rubin was sitting behind a desk near the back of the room. His skullcap and his angular face startled me at first: I thought he was one of the boys. I looked between the desks, but Shadrach wasn't around. A tiny flame licked Rubin's nose. He had struck a match, but his hand trembled and the flame wavered and eluded his cigarette. I approached the desk and held the match for him. Rubin sucked in his cheeks and the

145

cigarette lit instantly. The smoke curled over his nose and hid most of his face for a moment. "Nick," he said, his face taking form again behind the broken shield of smoke, "I don't go in for intrigues, but I couldn't find no other way. FDR just sent me his greetings. I'm going in tomorra. Uncle picked you out to take over for me. I can't say why, but that's up to him." I watched Rubin maneuver the cigarette; it burned unevenly. "It ain't permanent, see. Just until I come back. Uncle's gonna try to get me into the Rangers. That way maybe I'll be able to send for Shad later. All the Rangers get their own dogs. If they lemme take Shad, I could capture Hitler for 'em. Me and Shad'd parachute right over the Reich house. So don't get any fancy ideas. The war ain't gonna last very long with me in it." He crushed the cigarette against the cracked wall of the ink-well on his desk. "Uh, uh. Rubin's coming back. And just because he ain't gonna be around for a little while, don't think you're gonna take advantage of Uncle. I left the Jailer instruc-tions. If he catches you lining up with the Rabbi and Mama, he's gonna hang you from the rafters, with your ass kissing the sky."

"Mama and the Rabbi?" I said.

"Come on, we ain't got no time for dummy shows. The Rabbi's been decking out with Mama ever since he's been up here. Why you think they got adjoining suites? Or maybe they just like to play Monopoly at night? But Mama ain't buying up Marvin Gardens with the sounds I hear her making. No. I thought the Rabbi was your boy, Nick. I bet he's got a lot to say about Uncle, but he don't believe in talking about himself. I ain't letting Uncle get shafted, lemme tell you that. Sometimes I gotta handle things in my own way, but I always look out for Uncle."

We both heard Shadrach whine.

"Damn that lousy dog. I don't even know why I bother

146

worrying about him. Shut up," he said, shouting through the wall. "Shut up. I'm gonna break one of your pipes, Shad. That's another thing, Nick. I want that dog fed. And scrubbed every night. And make sure he gets enough exercise. You're in charge until the Rangers call for him. And if I find out you ain't been watching out for his interests, I'll be back here sooner than you think."

The dog kept whining. "All right." We left the classroom and walked partway across the hall.

"Rubin," I said, "is taking care of Shadrach going to be my only duty? What about Bullets? Am I going to be in charge of the Dungeon too?"

Rubin glanced at me obliquely, his chin at full tilt. "Who said anything about the Dungeon? You keep away from there. The Dungeon can take care of itself."

We paused in front of a narrow door near the end of the hall. "Wait here a minute. I gotta break you in. Shad ain't used to visitors." He entered a tiny room with a sunken ceiling; it had probably been a closet before Rubin's occupancy. Shadrach was sitting under Rubin's cot, his jowls slumping miserably. "Shad, we got a guest today. I brought you your new boss. You better behave, Shad. You're already on Uncle's shit list. And I ain't gonna be around to keep you out of trouble. Okay, Nick, you can come in."

I entered cautiously, anticipating an early exit. I had to keep my neck locked. My head almost reached the ceiling. Shadrach growled halfheartedly. Rubin admonished him. "Shad, you ain't got no choice. Either you get along with him, or Uncle's gonna ship you out to the nearest frankfurter factory."

Shadrach complied immediately, saluting me with his bony tail. But his jaws were still in growling position.

"He ain't a bad dog, Nick. You don't have to keep him

on a leash or anything. He goes wherever you tell him. But one thing. He don't like to be alone in the dark. If you gotta pen him up, make sure there's a candle around."

There was a ditty bag and a shaving kit on Rubin's cot. He opened the bag and removed a needle holder, a battered thimble, and a spool of thread. I surveyed the lumpy walls.

"Is this going to be my new room, Rubin?"

"Na," he said, selecting a needle. "Uncle's keeping you in D Company. You can operate from there." Then he removed his shirt, and smiling sheepishly, he said, "I ain't got nobody to do my sewing for me." He raised the needle apologetically and showed me the rents in his patched sleeves. "I ain't letting 'em catch me at Dix with a torn shirt. You don't make the Rangers that way." His shoulders were unbelievably scrawny and formed two craglike points. He began patting the cot. "Hey, Shad, where's my specs? I can't do any sewing without my specs." I threaded the needle for him. He found his glasses under the ditty bag. Then, sitting on the cot, with the shirt lying in his lap and the glasses hiding half his face, he maneuvered the needle. His elbow dipped awkwardly, and his crooked stitches formed scars in the patched sleeves. He wore the thimble on his little finger. He pricked his thumb several times.

"Bastard," he said, sucking the damaged thumb. Shadrach raised one ear bewilderedly. Rubin abandoned the shirt. "Nick," he said, "one more thing. The raids. Make sure Uncle's protected at all times."

"Rubin, maybe Benny's a whiz with bombs, but I don't think he would ever try to harm Uncle? Would he?"

Rubin smiled to himself; he seemed slightly sinister in spite of the glasses, the skullcap, and the shirt in his lap. "You don't gotta worry about Benny. We got all his moves mapped out. Uncle keeps a spy in every bunk."

"What?" I said. "Spies."

148

"Forget it, Nick. Just make sure you check with the Jailer and the cook every day." He began sewing the sleeve again. His shoulders caught the rhythm of the moving needle and bobbed irregularly. Spies. The Indian in the latrine. Matches behind the barrack. Benny, Notte, and Larry upstairs. The Wolfman. They left him alone. Maybe the kike talk is just an act? Uncle trained him. No, Benny would have found out. Larry? He's too frightened. He would never be able to hide anything from the other boys. Notte. Notte is the spy. It couldn't be anybody else. No wonder he couldn't start the fire. It had nothing to do with matches. Notte. He tore his own shirt and pretended that he had scuffled with the Marine. Notte. The Phantom. And Big Notte is probably the spy in A Company. Uncle has all the boys boxed in. Benny never had a chance.

"Rubin, who's the spy in my Company?"

"I told you to forget it."

"But how can I help Uncle if you don't tell me anything?"

"Don't worry about it, Nick. The cook takes care of that end."

"Rubin, is it Notte? Is Notte the spy?"

"Na," he said, driving the needle snakelike through the sleeve. "It's Matches."

"Matches?" Shadrach dropped his jowls on my shoe. "But he's the one who stepped on Pebbles. And he defended Benny out on the lawn. Did Uncle tell him to put on a show?"

"Not Matches. Once the raid starts, he plays for keeps. That's the way he operates. Uncle don't mind. As long as he lets us in on the action."

"But how does Uncle get his spies?"

"It ain't Uncle. It's Mama. She does all the recruiting. That's why Uncle allows her all the private sessions she wants when the boys first get here. Mama's terrific when it comes to

149

sniffing out a potential spy. She softens 'em up first with all her psychology."

"She puts a little English on her therapy, doesn't she, Rubin?"

"Yeah," he said, "that's it." He was too busy sewing to notice my sour looks. "Only Mama's beginning to balk. She don't wanna do any more recruiting. But Uncle's got all the spies he needs. He even got one or two spares. The cook trains 'em after Mama does the sniffing. He's got a regular school for spies. But he works with 'em one at a time. That way the spies got nothin' to do with each other. If one of 'em turns out to be a fink, he can't louse up Uncle's organization. Uncle just works a switch. He takes the fink out of the Company, and puts in one of the spares. You have to get up pretty early in the morning if you wanna put one over on Uncle."

"Rubin, who are the spies in the other Companies?"

"Hey, hey, you already know more than you oughta. If Uncle finds out I been telling you about his organization, he's gonna pickle my ass and serve it on a silver platter. But he picked you, not me. And I ain't gonna be around to watch out for him. The Marine got his own ideas. Him and Bill wanna drive out Uncle and the boys, and turn the place into a hunting lodge. But they ain't gonna have a hunting lodge for long when I get back, and they know it. But the next time Benny pulls a fast one, I want you backing Uncle up. That's why I'm telling you all this. If something happens and Matches can't get to the cook, he can still report to you." Rubin returned the spool, the needle, and the thimble to the ditty bag. Then he took off his glasses. The glasses had left two deep marks on the sides of his nose. "Nick," he said, putting on his shirt. "Make sure Uncle never finds out that you been up here. This is a confidential meeting. Strictly between me and you." The stitches had gathered on both sleeves and

150

formed humplike ridges. "I want you to take Shad now. I ain't got the time for ceremonies."

"Rubin, are you sure he'll go with me?"

"He'll go. Shad, up." I had expected the dog to counter Rubin's command with at least a little token resistance, but instead, he ruffled his snout resignedly, and followed me over to the door. "Remember, Shad, Nick is the boss now. Whatever he says goes."

I paused near the door. Rubin was already arranging the articles in his shaving kit. "Rubin," I said. His shoulders drew together before he turned around. I knew that he would never become a Ranger.

"Rubin, what happened that time when Uncle kept you in the Dungeon for thirteen days?"

"What?" he said, his cheeks hardening grimly. "*Nothin' happened*. I sweated out my time in the box. Uncle couldn't break me, and he knew it too. Now take the mutt with you and beat it."

I wanted to wish him luck at Fort Dix, but he had turned his back again. Shadrach waited for my next move. I walked towards the landing without turning around. I could hear Shadrach bringing up his armored butt. I don't know why I should have been seized with such demonic thoughts just at that particular time, but I had an almost irresistible urge to rampage through the building with Shadrach and run out Mama, Uncle, and the Rabbi. Shadrach followed me down the steps. I had undoubtedly fallen upon a series of shifting alliances. Billingsgate had helped break the revolt, but he was also aligned with the Marine against Uncle and the Home. The Rabbi preached anarchy and the breakdown of all alignments, yet here he was cursing Mama and shacking up with her at the same time. And Mama recruited Matches for Uncle's organization, and then turned around and protected the boys

151

out on the lawn. And Matches. He spied for Uncle, and then fought like a demon for the boys. And where did Commander Lipshitz fit in? My mind did not permit me to ramble for very long; it drove me back abruptly and mercilessly to Matches. There was no way now of avoiding him. While I was with Rubin I had even had the thought of exposing Matches to the other boys. I suppose I would have been willing to do almost anything to ingratiate myself to Benny. I tried to tell myself that I had been outraged, but it wasn't so. There was no way of condemning Matches and Uncle and Mama and Rubin and the Jailers and the Rabbi without condemning myself. I was bound up with them, and even running back to Cabrini Boulevard would not have freed me or enabled me to break away.

I heard the shouts before I stepped off the porch. Shadrach raced with me over to the barrack. He waited for me near the door. The boys had trapped Pebbleby inside the shower stall. Notte was balancing himself on the rims of the piss trough. Larry and the Wolfman flanked the stall with the Wolfman's troops. Matches and the Indian were working the faucets. Benny was behind the gate; he was sitting on my commode and wearing Crazy's hat. Pebbleby clasped his hands and rocked back and forth in the stall. The entire floor was soaked. The water had uprooted Benny's stemless flowers, and they swam around the cots. The boys saw Shadrach first. Notte jumped off the piss trough. Matches and the Indian released the faucets. Benny remained on my commode.

"Commander," Pebbleby said, climbing out of the stall. The boys had stuffed his pockets with candles and salami sandwiches. "Oh, Commander." Shadrach glared implacably at the boys; both his ears were already poised. "Devils. Matches told them to throw me down the toilet."

Matches poised his skullcap cherublike and smiled. "I just wanted to hide the evidence, Commander, that's all." I'm sure he expected me to censure him. I stared at him and said nothing. He must have sensed that my stare had nothing to do with the soaked floor, because his smile shrank abruptly. Benny threw the campaign hat on my bed and came through the gate. Matches deferred to him and stood near the Indian. I didn't allow him to escape my stare; his lips trembled for a moment, and then his eyes assumed command and gleamed queerly. What was he thinking? *Screw you, Commander. Who's Benny gonna believe, me or you?* Now I was the one who backed away. Benny finally broke our little drama. I thought for a moment that he was going to talk directly to me. But he twisted his neck suddenly and said, "Notte, tell the Screw that if he wants to leave his deputies here, he has to pay the price."

"Benny," I said, "I've had enough for one day. I want everybody by his bunk." Shadrach backed me up; he kept prodding Benny's knees with his snout. The boys marched over to their cots.

"Commander," Pebbleby said, removing the candles and the salami sandwiches from his pockets, "no more trouble. I gotta go. Uncle's gonna murder me. I ain't been to A Company yet. And what am I gonna feed them with?" He dropped the soggy sandwiches one by one into the commode that was furthest from the shower stall. We all heard the repeated plops.

Notte recited to himself. "Hasten, Jason, get the basin. Plip, plop, get the mop."

"*Plip, plop,*" the Wolfman said. "*Plip, plop.*"

"All right," I said. "You've all had your fun. Now I want you to apologize to Pebbles."

Benny sat on his cot and folded his arms. The other boys followed suit; even the Wolfman, though his arms became entangled, and Larry had to free them for him and then help him fold them again.

"I gotta go," Pebbleby said, and he left the barrack hurriedly.

Shadrach went behind the gate and sat near my commode. I was still furious. "You've won this time, but there's going to be a change around here. Anybody keeps making trouble and he's going to be shipped out to another Company. I mean that."

I walked over to my bed. The boys glared at me. I was glad that Shadrach was around.

┤ CHAPTER ├

11

I suppose I began putting on airs immediately. I took to wearing Crazy's hat wherever I went. After all, I was now the head Screw. I met with my two assistants every day. Billingsgate began calling me Chief. The Marine kept saluting me. I suspected from the first that they were putting me on, but they never countermanded any of my orders. The cook wouldn't tell me anything about his school for spies, but he did make me extra sandwiches. I even inherited Rubin's thermos bottle, and the cook obliged me with hot coffee or tea as often as I wanted. My teaching duties were temporarily suspended, and I would spend most of my time making the rounds of the barracks, and charting new activities for the boys. Shadrach always accompanied me. The Home had a communal radio, and it was my job to bring it around to each Company. The chassis was shaped like a Swiss chalet, and even had carved eaves and dormer windows. The speaker, of course, was housed under the eaves. The radio was quite heavy, and I had to carry it from Company to Company on the Janitor's broken-down cart. I would often pass half the afternoon with A Company listening to the daytime serials. Shadrach growled every time Captain Midnight came on. Uncle had taken away D Company's radio privileges, but Notte kept asking me about the programs. "How did the Fat Man make out last week, Commander? Did the Hornet ditch Kato yet?"

I had actually expected the boys to despise my new position, but in some perverse way they seemed to take pride in knowing that their own Commander was Uncle's head Screw. They even became more tolerant of Shadrach. The Indian offered to feed him, but I declined his offer. I wasn't taking any chances. The boys had already tried to poison Shadrach once. Benny still kept up his ritual: "Notte, tell the Screw. . . ." But even he softened his stand a little and would often send over Notte with questions. "Head Commander Shitz, Benny wants to know when Uncle's gonna allow us to use the radio again?"

"Tell him," I would say, tilting my hat summarily and assuming a gruff tone, "tell him that I'll work on Uncle for him."

My relations with Matches also gradually improved. Once he saw that I didn't intend giving him away, he began saluting Shadrach and me, and he now cleaned my commode along with the others. And Mama no longer seemed to mind having me around during the therapy sessions. But I resisted all her overtures. When Matches faltered, whom would she wheedle next? As soon as Mama came in, I often left the barrack. If I had a little free time, I went up to the Rabbi. He still kept railing against Mama and Uncle, but I no longer paid much attention to him. I suppose I really wanted to diddle

156

him, and I had to hold myself back from asking him if he played Monopoly with Mama at night. The Rabbi, of course, was immediately suspicious of my new position. "Don't worry," he said, "it's all part of Uncle's new policy. Keep the calm. But when the explosions come, he'll tumble you over in a minute. And he'll put the cook or the man with the stick in charge. Nick, I don't like the signs. At least Rubin, in his own way, kept the peace."

"Kept the peace? What about Bucharevsky in the Dungeon?"

"*Bullets*," the Rabbi said, stroking his bald chin. He was ready to fly off his toilet seat. "Nick, now is the time for a little liberation. Test some of your power. See if you can persuade Uncle to free Bullets."

I backed off immediately. "Rabbi, I'll formulate my own policies, thank you."

"Nick, it's your obligation. The Dungeon was always Rubin's territory."

"Rabbi, don't talk to me about obligations. Bullets is all right where he is. If Uncle sends around the Jailer to pinch-hit for Rubin, then I'll act. Not before."

"Nick, one concession. One. Pay a visit to the Dungeon. Go up and see Bucharevsky for yourself."

"No," I said. "No."

I must have been out to spite the Rabbi in my own wacky way, because that afternoon I did go upstairs to the Dungeon. Pebbleby was on guard outside the door. He sat on a bench, his chin embedded in his watch cap. His neck stiffened as soon as he saw me. It didn't take him very long to glean my purpose. "Commander," he said, "you don't want to go in there, no. I'd rather have your boys for a lifetime than spend a minute with him. You don't know the artillery Rubin brought with him every time he came up. You ain't even got the hound with you?"

"Shadrach? I left him on the porch." There was a slot with a wide lip near the bottom of the door. A jar and a plate stood nearby. The jar was half filled with urine which had already turned brown. The plate was cluttered with moldy asparagus shoots. "Pebbles, I'm going in."

He looked at me once. Seeing that it was hopeless, he shrugged one shoulder and handed me a flashlight with a bulging neck. Then he became a little indignant. "Don't expect me to come in and bail you out. You're on your own, Commander." The door was bolted in three places, and I watched his shoulders swerve as he undid the bolts. I went inside. He locked the door quickly behind me and began clicking the bolts. The flashlight shook in my hand, its beam zigzagging across the wall. The Dungeon was even smaller than Rubin's room. There was a narrow pen with screened sides in the middle of the floor. I steadied my hand and trained the beam on the pen. There was no one inside. "Commissioner," someone said, "ditch the light. You want me to go blind?" Bullets was sitting behind the pen. He was smoking a cigar. "Here," he said, lighting a candle and placing it on top of the pen. I turned off the flashlight. His face seemed ogrelike behind the candle. The wavering light notched his cheeks and his chin. He wasn't wearing a skullcap.

"Bullets," I said, "how come you're not inside the pen?"

"That," he said, strumming the wire walls, "that's just for the tourists. Hey, *Kimo Sahbee*, did the Rube leave any cigars for me before he left?"

"What?" I said.

"My supply is dwindling. The Rube promised me another box. It ain't no picnic lying around here all day. Where's Shad? I got a few bones for him."

"What the hell is going on here," I said. "Is this a dungeon or a country club?"

"Don't blow your stack, Commissioner. You wanna

bring Doctor Syvana up here?" He must have seen my forehead wrinkle up, because he said, "*Uncle, Uncle.* You'll spoil
the whole setup for me." He began staring at my campaign
hat.

I sat on the edge of the pen. The wire pinched my behind. "What about all the screaming and the barking? Wasn't
Rubin supposed to work you over? I thought. . . ."

Bullets gave me a demonstration. He banged the walls of
the pen and began screaming for me; the candle rocked. "No
more, Commissioner, please. No more. I'll do anything you
say. No more. Please. Ahhhhh. Ooohhhh." Then he smiled
mischievously. "It's all an act. Rubin taught me the works. He
told me to put on a good show for Uncle and the boys."

"You mean Uncle doesn't know what's going on up
here?"

"You kidding? He thinks Rubin was giving me the treatment all the time. But me and the Rube are *landsmen.* We both
come from Charlotte Street. Rubin and my cousin Shloime
used to go bopping together." He pressed my knee confidingly. "They drowned a boogy once in Indian Lake. The aces
dragged the bottom for a week before they found him. He
came up with a blue head. Imagine. A boogy with a blue
head. I think his name was Calvin. And the boogies took their
toll on us too. Shloime only has one good eye. And they
caught my sister Frimke in Crotona Park one night and she
almost ended up with a nigger baby. No, the kikes from Charlotte Street hadda stick together or the boogies and the micks
woulda drove us into the Bronx River. So don't expect Rubin
to take it out on me. All the screaming and the hullabaloo was
just to keep Uncle happy. He thinks I'm sweating it out in
the box."

"What about Benny? Didn't you know that he tried to
storm the Dungeon?"

"Benny? Oh, the spick from D Company. He's a weirdo.

159

He's always trying to pull stunts like that. It wouldn't make no difference to him who was inside. He'd even spring Uncle if the Jailers ever locked him up. A weirdo. The Dungeon's okay. I don't need no victory party. I'll stick it out here. The guys in my Company ain't got no hair on their balls anyway. I miss the radio, Commissioner, that's all. Rubin used to give me a report every day and he even sneaked the box up here once. We listened to Jack Benny together. Rochester's okay, boogy or not, but I still say Dennis Day's a first class quiff. Hey, Commissioner, what about the cigars, huh?"

"I don't have any cigars, Bullets. And Rubin didn't tell me a thing." Sweat began to bead my forehead and my nose. My armpits felt scorched. "Bullets, how the hell can you stand the heat?"

He put his chin over the candle and his face glowed like a crumpled jack-o'-lantern. "Ah," he said, "the heat don't bother me. You shoulda seen my room on Charlotte Street. It coulda been squeezed into the dumbwaiter shaft and I hadda share it with Frimke too. And no windows. So don't start sounding off on the Dungeon. I'll stay here."

I moved towards the door.

"Commissioner, you think you can bring up the radio for an hour?"

"I'll try, Bullets, I'll try." I knocked on the door. "Pebbles, open up. The interview is over." The bolts didn't move. "Pebbles?" I knocked again. "Bullets," I said, "I think you've got yourself a roommate."

"Just keep knocking, Commissioner. The stooge is probably asleep."

I knocked five more times, and after groaning to myself, I came back to the pen. "Sit down, Commissioner. I'll play you a little pinochle. You wanna play auction or twelve card? But you'll have to throw me some credit. Uncle pinched all my pockets before he threw me in here." Bullets put one arm

160

inside the pen and removed a deck of cards. "My closet. You know." He offered me a cigar. We smoked and played cards. Rubin kept buying flushes and roundhouses, and I lost two dollars and seven cents in less than twenty minutes.

We both heard the bolts shoot back. Bullets scooped up the cards and the money, and tossed our cigars into his water cup. Then he hid behind the pen. The door opened. I recognized Mama's bosom right away. Bullets began moaning. "Oh, Mama, Mama." I strode through the door. Mama stared at my drenched armpits. Then she called into the Dungeon. "Don't worry, Arnold. I've already talked to Uncle. We'll have you out in a few days." She stepped out and bolted the door. I expected her to stare me down, but instead, she smiled to herself. Her cardigan was partway unbuttoned. She wasn't wearing her brassiere. "You must have been ferocious with him. Oh, Nick, I never expected that you would turn out to be such a holy terror."

What could I tell her? I didn't intend giving Bullets and Rubin away. "Mama, I'm only doing my job. Where's Pebbles? I thought I was locked in for good."

"I sent him on an errand," she said. "Nick, take off your shirt. It's drenched. I'll wash it and iron it for you." I tried to resist, but Mama persisted. I felt a little embarrassed standing in front of her with my scrawny chest showing. "Now the hat," she said, holding out her hand.

"No, Mama," I said. "The hat stays on."

She sat down and beckoned me over to the bench. I sat at the other end, guiding my knees warily. My buttocks felt damp against the hard wood.

"Nick," she said, "you don't know what a blight the Home has become for me." Mama, I wanted to say, tell it to the Rabbi. Maybe she was going to coax me into joining the cook's school for spies? "All my plans have been thwarted. Nate keeps putting restrictions on me. Billingsgate abuses the boys. I have to stand by and watch them being underfed. All for the sake of austerity." She stared at the tuft of hair surrounding my navel. I pulled down my undershirt. "And if it weren't for the boys I wouldn't have any companionship whatsoever." I wondered if Bullets was listening? What would he be thinking? Commissioner, tell her she's running out of toilet paper. Mama leaned back and now her breasts bunched together and I could see both of her nipples. Shadrach appeared suddenly and stared shamelessly at Mama's boobs. Mama sat up and her nipples were now directly under my nose. "Shad," I said, "who gave you permission to come up here?"

Shadrach scampered under the bench. I could still see his rumpled snout and the flattened top of his head. Mama leaned back again. I became a little dizzy and lowered my head a trifle. Mama kept talking. "If only there were someone here who could rally the boys and make Uncle see his mistakes. He's let his two ogres assume more and more command." I lowered my head a little more. My nose grazed Mama's left nipple. She brought one arm unassumingly around my head and stroked the back of my ear. I descended all the way and suckled her nipples with a vengeance. First the left one and then the right. They rose instantly and her breasts swelled. Her skirt was already pulled over her knees. She drew my head against her chest. I could hear my heart drum. "Oh, Nick," she said. I refused to relinquish my hold. For Benny and the Indian, I said to myself. Her hands rode along my back. My knees knocked uncontrollably. "Oh, Nick," she said. "Nick. Nick. Nick."

Mama. Shadrach closed one eye.

12

I could see myself getting sucked in more and more. I was already the keeper of the radio, the Commander of D Company and the overseer of the rest of the Home, Shadrach's master and Bullets' confidant, Uncle's protector and the Rabbi's secret disciple, and now, along with the other bargains, I had acquired a mistress! I began imposing all sorts of penances on myself—I would scrub my back with tar every time I was in the shower—but I suppose I secretly enjoyed cuckolding the Rabbi. I wanted to tumble all his theories and principles, and bring a little anarchy to his own doorstep. But somehow, Mama was never a willing accomplice. She refused even to discuss the Rabbi. And while we did battle on her sagging cot, I thought of the Rabbi sitting on his toilet seat behind Mama's wall, and was immediately saddened.

There were no other avenues of comfort. The boys were becoming crotchety, the Jailers were beginning to ignore my orders, the cook decreased my quota of coffee and tea, and Shadrach at times refused to accompany me on my patrols and would either sport with the other bulldogs or wait for me on the porch. And so, almost every day, after Captain Midnight, I would find myself with the Rabbi in his room. Trying to compound my shame, I confessed to him that I had never believed in God, not even as a little boy, that I did believe in devils though, and in all sorts of demonic powers. "I still do, Rabbi. Even now. If anyone wanted to organize a witch hunt, I'd be the first to join. I mean it." I expected the Rabbi to flex his jaw and call me a relic of the Dark Ages. But he sat quietly on his toilet seat and said, "Nick, who can believe in God today? Only lunatics! But devils? That's another story. The devils are in charge of the world. Who else could bring about so much madness in such an organized way?"

"Rabbi," I said, "wait. My beliefs are one thing, but you. . . ."

"I know," he said, "I know. An anomaly, a freak of nature. A rabbi who doesn't believe in God. Why do you think there was such a scandal in the Bronx? And the Rabbinical Council put me in a box and shipped me up here. Now the bugs and the cracks in the wall have the pleasure of hearing my philosophies."

Still determined to punish myself, I sat with both eyes half shut and listened to the Rabbi. His favorite target was Mama. "She eliminates all choice," the Rabbi would say. "Mama believes in a mechanistic universe. Give her an act and she will find you a bundle of motives. She can talk for hours about compulsions and complexes. Anything can be defined and explained. Even the worst horrors. Morality doesn't count. Good and evil become outdated terms. 'I'm not responsible,' the murderer shouts. 'Blame it on my complexes.' And Mama would support him. After all, how can you resist a neurotic drive? Matches burns his mother alive, Bullets breaks arms and noses right and left, and Mama records everything in her case histories. She could follow a motive through the most intricate twists and turns, on land, sea, or air. Brilliant, wonderful, but Nick, after all the twists and turns, trace back the motive as far as you want, someone has to be responsible. Somewhere a choice had to be made. I'm sure Mama could do a wonderful job on Hitler and the German High Command, but I would prefer to strangle them all with their own neuroses. Here is where Benny would come in handy. One bomb. One. . . ." The Rabbi often fell asleep in the middle of his discourses, and I would cover his legs with a blanket and make sure that his behind was secured to the toilet seat. Then I would tiptoe out of the room and close the door gently behind me.

But there was no way of escaping. No matter how hard I tried to muffle my moves, Mama would be waiting for me next door, her nipples already bared for action. And like a good little soldier I would bow my head halfway and march in. Whenever her cot proved unmanageable, Mama spread two blankets on the floor and I ended up staring at the dented tops of her twin cabinets. It was Mama who introduced me to the beguiling arts of female contraception. When I came to her the second time with my Trojan intact, Mama told me to take off "the glove." Then she shook her head. "Really, Nick," she said. "This is the twentieth century, you know." And she removed a plastic box from one of the cabinets. The box sprang open magically and she showed me its contents. "Silly," she said, "haven't you ever heard of a *diaphragm?*"

"Mama," I said, pouting affectedly for her, "where I come from women never wore diaphragms." Actually the plastic box intrigued me. And while I dutifully massaged her chest, Mama often told me about pessaries and potency pills

165

and other wonders of twentieth-century science. "Men," Mama would say proudly, "are becoming less and less necessary. Do you know that under the right conditions sperm can be stored for centuries? And pretty soon ways will be found to produce it artificially. Even sexual contact is becoming archaic. Certain stimulants can probably produce the same effects. Can't you see the advertisements in the *Ladies Home Journal?* Chemically induced orgasm. Satisfaction guaranteed. Every time. Oh, Nick, I'm only teasing you, really. But if men insist on killing themselves off in their wars, women will have to find some way to defend themselves. And when men finally become defunct, it will be their own fault, you know. We'll put the last few survivors in a cage and display them at the Bronx Zoo. *Homo masculanus*, the unnecessary sex."

In the midst of molding her belly button, I envisioned the Rabbi on his bowl, and jumping up suddenly, I said, "Mama, I have to go."

I was determined to do something for the Rabbi, and about two weeks after Rubin left for Fort Dix, I decided to petition Uncle in the Rabbi's behalf. There was a huge bulletin board outside Uncle's door. The legend on top of the board read: "Modern Maccabees. Friends and Graduates of Blattenburg Now Serving with the United Nations." I stared at the snapshots of servicemen tacked to the board. Hirschel Bloom was playing volleyball with two other sailors. Norman Kissel, who seemed about seven feet tall, dwarfed his jeep and the discarded seaplane on the landing field behind him. Bruce Genzelman had turned a palm leaf into a skullcap, and standing in his underpants and in a pair of combat boots, he was balancing himself on a toboggan. His snapshot was signed: "To Uncle, from my new home, the Sundown Kid." I eventually came upon a snapshot near the bottom of the board.

The soldier wore a webbed helmet and a blue scarf, and had obviously taken great pains to appear ferocious. His bayonet was poised under his chin. I didn't even bother reading the tag under the snapshot. Howie Rosenthal. In the infantry. I looked at the snapshot again. His receding chin and rodentlike eyes were unmistakable. I knocked on Uncle's door.

Uncle was sitting behind his desk. Only one of the sconces flanking him was lit. I expected Uncle to be a little annoyed at my intrusion, but he actually seemed pleased to see me. His eyes crinkled softly. "Nick," he said, extending his hand, "how is the keeper of the fort? I've been receiving excellent reports. From Mama, and from the boys themselves." I started to remove my hat. "No, no, Nick. No formalities, please. The hat is quite imposing, you know. It's amazing how a costume can give one stature at times. If materials weren't so scarce today, I would outfit the entire staff. Yes. Nick, how do you think I would look in a campaign hat, eh?"

"Would you like to try it on, Uncle?"

"No, no. I would rather leave it all a little undefined. But one day I will surprise all of you. Yes."

"Uncle," I said, "the soldier on the bulletin board. With the blue scarf. Rosenthal...."

His jowls slackened for a moment, then they wagged vigorously. "Oh, yes, yes. Corporal Rosenthal. The war hero. The War Department has been sending him around. He'll be here in a few days. I think they're trying to do a little extra recruiting. He visits all the Jewish homes and orphanages."

"A war hero?"

"Yes. The last American serviceman to leave Luzon alive. I think he's in line for the D.S.C. It's all in the letter they sent me. There was even a story about his platoon in the *News of the Week*. Killed over a hundred Japs. Something like that. I don't go in for these high-pressure tactics, but I'm sure the

167

boys would enjoy meeting him. Would you like to head the welcoming committee, Nick?"

"No, Uncle. I mean . . . I was just a little curious. But that's not why I'm here. I came over because of the Rabbi."

Uncle's face hardened immediately. "The Rabbi?"

"Uncle, I don't see why classes have to be suspended with the Rabbi around. I thought he might take over my teaching duties."

"I'm sorry, Nick, but I prefer to keep the Rabbi where he is. In his private limbo on the third floor. Let him work out his manifestos on his toilet seat. Nick, I appreciate your concern for him, and believe me, I'm not trying to be cruel. But the Rabbi has been a great disappointment. For all of us. I had hoped he would avail himself if he were given a second chance. That's why I brought him up here. His record, you know, is far from exemplary. He was deprived of his congregation."

"I know," I said. "The Rabbi told me. It was because of his politics."

Uncle smiled to himself; his lips curled in an ugly way. "The Rabbi," he said, "must include a great deal in his politics."

"I don't understand, Uncle. The Rabbi told me that he was an anarchist, and that—"

"Nick, there is an anarchist on every corner in the Bronx. I assure you that no one would have been troubled by the Rabbi's theories? Nick, the Rabbi is an anachronism. There is no place for him in our time. His anarchies and petty insurrections went out the window years ago. Nick, if we broke down all order, we would be at the mercy of the roaches and the ants. There wouldn't be anyone around to put together the Rabbi's toilet seat. Nick, I'm not trying to sell you something. Order is not a sacred thing. But what would happen at the Home if the Rabbi instituted his anarchies? Sure. The

168

boys would lock me in the Dungeon and hang the Jailers from the roof, and maybe Mama would become the mistress of their little pack. But how long would it last? If they didn't impose some order on themselves, they wouldn't even be able to grow a carrot. And either the pack would fall apart by itself or it would be broken up by others. And then where would the boys be? They would be far worse off than before. Foolishness. No, Nick, the Rabbi wasn't chased out of his synagogue because of any philosophies. I don't enjoy tattling on my staff, but I can see that the Rabbi has been taking advantage of you. Nick, he raped a twelve-year-old girl. The beadle's daughter at the synagogue. In his own office. He was supposed to be preparing her for her *bas mitzvah*. You know, confirmation. Could the synagogue prosecute its own Rabbi? So they agreed to banish him and send him up here. In my charge. The Rabbi is a delinquent. No better than the boys."

"Uncle," I said, "if this is just a rumor, it's a pretty rotten thing to spread around. And if it's a lie. . . ."

"Nick, I don't blame you for becoming angry. I expect you to defend the Rabbi. And I'm sorry I was forced to tell you. But Nick, it's no lie. The girl was in a terrible state. She had to be sent away for six months." Rabbi. Rape. God, when will the stories end? Maybe if I search deep enough, I could find my own monstrosities. Did I murder my mother when I was two? "No, Nick, the Rabbi stays upstairs. We'll all be better off. I grant that the Home has impurities, but with the Rabbi's method of cleansing, the good is wiped away along with the bad. I'm not in the market for the Rabbi's insurrections. Nick, I know. Benny and a few of the others can take care of themselves, but where would Boris be without the Home? Or Larry? Lost." Uncle relaxed his jowls, and his eyes began to crinkle again. "Boris. Do you think it was the boys who named him Wolfman? Nick, he carried the name with him from the Bronx. Why Wolfman? Because his mother took him for walks only late at night when there was no one around. She kept him locked up during the day. She didn't want her Boris contaminated by any contact with the *goyim*. She was a fanatic, an hysterical witch. And she managed to communicate her own fright to him. And what could he learn from her? A few Yiddish swear words and melodies. She sang to him at night. That was the only way he could fall asleep. And when the Wolfman sat near the window and tried to repeat the words that he heard from the street, his mother would pull his hair and lock him in the closet. Only golems and the devils in the street spoke English. Nick, who knows now what was wrong with her? Maybe Mama would have been able to diagnose her case. But whatever the reason, she ruined the boy. *Boy?* Mama knows he's older than Benny and the rest, but I never told anyone how old he actually is. Nick, Boris is thirty-five. A man with a boy's mind. And when his mother died, they were ready to put him in an institution. But I knew his problems. For ten years we both lived in the same house. Boris lived with his mother and I lived with mine. And I brought him up here with me. At least at the Home he would be with Jewish boys. And I would be able to look after his needs."

"Uncle," I said, "I don't want to pry, but I went over the Wolfman's records with Mama. . . ."

"I know, I locked him in the Dungeon for a day. Nick, I had to. Boris kept masturbating in front of everybody. In the classroom, on the lawn, everywhere. Nick, believe me, I don't have any bugbears on the subject of masturbation. You won't find me giving lectures about blindness and the loss of vital fluids. Boys play with themselves, what can you do? But in front of everybody! And a day in the Dungeon cured him of the habit. Nick, I'll make a bargain with you. I still refuse to recall the Rabbi to active duty, but for your sake, he can have a few odd jobs. Matches will be thirteen in a few weeks, and I am planning a *bar mitzvah* celebration for him. I will let the Rabbi officiate, and I will allow him one sermon for the occasion. But the sermon has to be approved first by me. I want to see the actual text. Nick, are my terms acceptable?"

"Yes, Uncle, but there's something else. Not about the Rabbi. My boys. How long are you going to keep them in the barrack?"

"Nick, that is entirely up to them. If Benny behaves and I'm convinced that the boys have no more surprises for me, then I will lift the embargo."

"Uncle, what about the radio? The boys are becoming restless. I'd like to restore their radio privileges."

"I don't think that would be wise, Nick. Not yet. But we can tickle their palates. We'll let them have the radio for today. But after that they will have to earn the right to the radio by their actions. Nick, if my terms are no longer acceptable, let me know. I don't want you to go around thinking that Uncle is an autocrat. I make my mistakes too. Uncle is willing to learn."

"It sounds pretty fair to me, Uncle. I'll bring them the radio now. Thanks. I'm sure they'll appreciate it. Goodbye."

I met Shadrach on the porch. He was busy battling with a spider. We both went behind the house to the shed where the radio was kept. I loaded the radio onto Pebbleby's cart. Shadrach raised one paw disdainfully and supervised the hauling. I finally managed to trundle the radio across the lawn.

I could hear the two Jailers shouting. They both sounded drunk. I left the cart near the door and entered the barrack. Shadrach followed me inside. The Marine's two bulldogs were holding the boys at bay behind the gate. One of the commodes was completely smashed. The Marine balanced himself on the other commode; a metal flask danced in his pocket. Three of

171

the cots were turned over. Billingsgate was wearing a candle holder on his head. He had the Wolfman trapped between two of the overturned cots and kept prodding the Wolfman's knees with his broken stick. The Marine sang to himself: "Oh, we're gonna dance on the ceiling, we're gonna dance on the wall...." He saw my campaign hat and saluted me immediately. Billingsgate kept prodding the Wolfman's knees. "You heard him, cowboy, dance. Come on. Dance for us."

"Benja," the Wolfman said. Benny moved towards the gate, and the two bulldogs drew together and growled. *"Benja."*

"Bill," I said. "Leave him alone."

The Jailer didn't bother turning around. "Come on, cowboy, show the Commander a few tricks. Show him what a dummy can do."

"Billingsgate."

"Aw, Commander, I'm just trying to provide a little entertainment for the boys." He knocked off the Wolfman's skullcap. *"Kepele,"* the Wolfman said, and tried to retrieve the skullcap. The Jailer kicked it towards the shower stall and pinched the Wolfman's behind. "Hallelujah! Praise the Lawd! A real live rump steak. Commander, you want me to fry you a piece?"

"Billingsgate, keep your *fucking* hands off him."

The boys stared at me. Billingsgate turned around. His eyes narrowed mercilessly. "What'd you say, Commander?" He saw Shadrach behind me. Shadrach poised his fangs, and Billingsgate lowered his stick resignedly. "That ain't no way to talk to a man, Commander, no sir. Maybe I work for Uncle and you, but you don't own mah soul. That's mah property."

The Marine jumped off the commode; he was still saluting me.

"Take your two dogs," I said, "and get out."

The Marine recalled his two bulldogs. Shadrach glared

172

at them contemptuously; they both skulked out of the barrack. Billingsgate paused near the door. "We gonna catch you some time without your bull, Mister, then you gonna be the one who's doing all the dancing. You believe it."

"Get out. And don't come back here again unless you want Shadrach to have a feast."

Billingsgate slammed the door. Notte came out from behind the gate. "Wow, Commander, you told him, you told him. Hey, Benny, the Screw's all right." Then he inspected the damaged commode. "I know my rights and privileges. Uncle better make the Jailers pay for it. Nobody's gonna crap around with D Company's johns and get away with it. Nobody."

Benny stared at me sheepishly. I could tell that he didn't intend using Notte as a middleman this time. He continued to stare at me. What was he going to say? Thanks, Screw, for helping the Wolfman. I turned my head away from him. I didn't want his thanks. I suppose I was annoyed with myself for having tried so desperately to court his favor, and now my resentment fixed itself on him. No, I didn't want his thanks.

"Boys," I said, "let's start cleaning up the barrack. Oh, I forgot. The radio is outside."

"The radio," Notte said, uncomprehendingly. "Outside?"

"Yes, Uncle is restoring your privileges for one day. And you'd better make good use of it, because I don't know when you'll be seeing it again."

"Benny," Notte said, "did you hear? The radio, the radio. Hey, what time is it? Is it too late for Captain Midnight? Indian, come on."

Notte and the Indian brought the radio into the barrack. Notte was scowling. "Some joke. Bastards. Who the hell bombarded the set?" The roof of the radio had been decapitated; the speaker was caved in.

"Notte, the radio wasn't that way when I brought it over. The Jailers must have...."

"Commander," Notte said, still scowling, "the outlet is behind your bed." Notte and the Indian carried the radio behind the gate. They sat the radio on my commode, and then Notte plugged it in. The Indian stood over the dials. "Wait," Notte said, "let the Wolfman work it. We need a little luck." He called the Wolfman over to the radio. "Benny, tell him the dial on the left."

"Boris, *der linkeh*," Benny said. The Wolfman turned the dial. The other boys crowded near the gate. The radio screeched horridly. "Turn it off." Notte said. "It's broke. Can't you see?" The Indian turned the radio off.

"Balls," Notte said. "We finally get the set and it don't even work."

The boys moved towards their cots. No one looked at me.

CHAPTER

13

I decided to keep to myself and to shun both Mama and the Rabbi. Seeing one, it seemed to me, linked me to the other. I had heard enough dark secrets. Whatever the Rabbi had done was his own affair, and anyway, I didn't want to condemn him wholesale just on Uncle's word. Somehow, the internal tug-of-war between Mama, Uncle, and the Rabbi seemed a little sordid to me. What had Uncle done to earn his right to be at the Home? Had he strangled a widow, or was he simply a hermaphrodite in disguise? No, I didn't want to know anything more about them, and I quarantined myself inside the barrack. Notte invited me to play blackjack with him and Benny, but I didn't want any partisans or allies, and I refused. I was even a little cold to Shadrach. He would sit near my commode and clamor for attention, but I ignored him most of the time. I let down my guard a little and permitted the Indian to feed him.

I read comic books most of the day or watched the Indian carve additional soldiers for the Wolfman's army. The boys expected some more trouble from the Jailers and took turns guarding the door. "Commander," Notte would say, "you better stick it out here with us. The Jailers are gonna lump your ass with ours." But in a day or two my relationship with the Jailers became normalized. The Marine no longer saluted me, and Billingsgate gave me an occasional sour look, but they did put a new roof on the radio and they repaired D Company's damaged commode. The Marine confessed to me with a shamed face that he had taken two tubes out of the radio. "Don't worry, Commander, we already put 'em back. Me and Bill had a little too much juice, that's all." And so, radio privileges were restored, but even Captain Midnight couldn't hold me very long, and I actually considered delegating Big Notte as the official Deliverer of the Radio.

Mama was the first to seek me out. She caught me while I was carting the radio over to A Company. "Nick," she said suspiciously, "did the Rabbi say anything about me?"

"No, Mama." She could see right away that my "no" was rather noncommittal.

"Nick, whatever was between us is in the past. There was never any real involvement. It was strictly gross satisfaction on both sides. He was the only available male around. I wouldn't have anything to do with Uncle's hatchetmen, and it's hard for a woman to live alone. Nick?"

"Mama," I said, "I have to go," and sensing a need for complete abandon, I steered the cart recklessly over the lawn; the radio almost overturned twice. The boys from A Company gathered near the door of their barrack. I managed to quiet the cart.

The boys talked incessantly about the "sojer" who was going to visit the Home, but even the thought of seeing Howie again failed to excite me. Uncle promised to suspend D Com-

176

pany's confinement for the occasion, and Notte told the other boys excitedly, *"A hundred Japs.* You think Corporal Rosenberg's gonna give us a demonstration?"

"Rosen*thal*," I said. I suppose I could have gained the boys' undying admiration had I told them that I knew the Corporal when he was just plain Howie Rosenthal, and that we had defended George Washington's shithouses together, but I wasn't in the mood to spur their excitement. Notte, however, kept it up: "You think MacArthur got his own kike divisions in the Pacific? I know they got separate boogy battalions, but maybe the President is taking over from Churchill and he's gonna form his own Maccabee units. What do you think, Commander Shitz?"

"I don't know, Notte," I said. "You'll have to ask the Corporal."

On the day Howie was scheduled to arrive, Uncle stationed us outside the barracks. We were supposed to comprise a welcoming committee in full force. The boys became restless immediately. "When's the Corporal gonna show?" After we had waited around for about an hour, we saw a jeep appear near the main gate. Tojo's insidious face was painted on one of the fenders, replete with slanted eyes and yellow complexion. A crippled rising sun with its spokelike rays splintered by a barrage of blunt-nosed Yankee torpedoes was attached to the front bumper and kept scraping the ground. I recognized Howie right away. In addition to his webbed helmet and blue scarf, he wore a paratrooper's jacket, a Sam Browne belt, fatigue pants, and combat boots; a knife was strapped to his left knee. Both sleeves of his jacket were decorated with overseas stripes and black patches. There were several sharpshooter's metals pinned to his pockets; the medals bounced tumultuously as the jeep rode across the lawn. Howie leaned against one of the rear fenders and raised both arms over his head. The boys cheered wildly. I hid behind my campaign hat.

177

We began marching towards the big house. I counted cadence haltingly for my boys. The other boys stared at us; they hadn't seen D Company in almost a month. Notte stared back implacably, trying to keep in step with my crazy calls. "Hep, hup. . . ." The driver halted the jeep in front of the porch. Holding the chin straps of his helmet, Howie leapt from the jeep. He almost stumbled, but he managed to grip the porch rail. The Marine's bulldogs sniffed his boots. The boys surrounded the jeep. Uncle called for order and escorted us up to the classroom. The driver remained in the jeep.

It was Uncle who introduced Howie to us. "Boys," he said, "as most of you already know, our own Rubin is at this very moment in boot camp preparing for his encounter with the Nips. I know everybody at the Home will join me in hoping that Rubin and the Rangers will drive the Nips out of the Philippines and shuffle them off to Tokyo or better still, to the bottom of the Pacific Ocean." The boys applauded politely. "But we have here today a Jewish Commando who has already faced the Nips in the Philippines, who stubbornly and almost superhumanly resisted the Nip attack at Lingayen Gulf, and who was the last American soldier to leave Manila on his own two feet. Boys, Corporal Howie Rosenthal." The boys banged their inkwells and cheered. Howie raised his helmet for them. Then Uncle introduced us individually to Howie. The boys saluted "the Corporal" when their names were called. I pulled down the brim of my hat and grunted a disguised "hello." Both Mama and the Rabbi were absent. Had they gone back to playing Monopoly again upstairs? I stared at Howie's sleeves; one of his patches had been sewn on upside down. He drew a diagram of Luzon on the board, and using his knife as a marker, he told us about the Japanese "five-pronged" attack. "The gooks kept us boxed in on all sides. Aparri. Vigan. Binalonan. Manila. Antimonan. Their Zekes controlled the air, and the fire bombs knocked the crap

178

out of McKinley and Nichols Field. All we had was a few Filipino gunners." I heard the Marine whisper to Billingsgate. "That boy knows his stuff. I was at McKinley in '35. Those Filipinos ain't worth a fart."

Howie shook one of his bulging pockets and pulled out a Japanese bayonet, a hari-kari knife, an empty bullet belt, a hand grenade, a dumdum bullet, and a whole stack of tissue-thin bills that looked like sheets of colored toilet paper, but were actually Japanese propaganda leaflets that had been dropped over Manila. He showed us the bayonet and the hari-kari knife, and told us about the Japanese "peewee" tanks and "midget" subs, about the Japanese atrocities on Filipino women and children, about Tokyo Rose and Axis Sally, about the "banzai" bayonet charges and sniping tactics, and then he read one of the leaflets to us: *"American Soldiers. You are still alive? What a miracle! Do you know what awaits you while you are still in the Philippines? Let me tell you. It is the Japanese forces with the combined support, both moral and material, of the awakened Asiatics—the Manchukuoans, Chinese, Filipinos, Annamese, Thailanders, Burmese, Indians, Malayans, and Indonesians. But this is not all. There is still another thing in store for you. What is this thing? I will again answer you. It is a grave. Your grave. Nobody can say where it exactly is, but it is certain that it does exist somewhere in the Philippines, and you are bound to find it sooner or later; far or near. Today? Tomorrow? Who knows...."*

"*Holy Moly,*" Notte said. "Corporal, take down my name. I'm enlisting tonight. Grave, huh? I'll show 'em what it means to start up with the Phantom." He sought out Big Notte. "Biggy, pack your bags. You're coming with me. Anybody else wanna join the Phantoms?"

Uncle Nate looked on solemnly. "Corporal," he said, "you will find that the boys here are not without courage. With the help of God and our great President, our American

179

boys will bombard the Nazis and the Nips, and if the war should endure, I assure you, my boys will be the first to enlist. Corporal, ninety-seven graduates of the Blattenburg Home for Wayward Jewish Boys are today wearing American uniforms. The Blattenburg Brigade. Did you know Lieutenant Shweikopf, Corporal? He was with the 31st Infantry on Luzon."

"Shweikopf?" Howie said, gripping his partly hidden chin. "I don't think so, Uncle. Shweikopf. No."

"Ah, an extraordinary boy. I am still hoping that one day he will come back and take over for me." He smiled broadly. "I'm sure the boys wouldn't mind having a new C.O. Uncle can't go on forever."

"Don't worry, Uncle," Howie said, "me and the General are gonna make the return trip to the Philippines long before you have to retire. And who knows, maybe I'll be taking a few of your boys back with me." He stared grimly at the Japanese bayonet and shook his fists. "Boys, remember the letters O-H-I-O. O-sock-i Hirohito Into Oblivion." The boys banged their inkwells again, and repeated Howie's war chant. "Uncle, I'm sorry, but I have to go. We're keeping a tight schedule. Rochester is the next stop." He saluted us all once more and then began packing the bayonet, the hari-kari knife, and the bullet belt. He left the dumdum bullet, the grenade, and a few of the leaflets for Uncle. I tried to leave first. While Howie buttoned his pocket, I headed for the door, holding down the brim of my hat. But it didn't work. "Nick," Howie called. "Jesus, Nick." The boys stared at us; even Uncle Nate was a little dumbfounded. Howie put his arm around me. We both walked downstairs.

The jeep followed us across the lawn. The driver kept beeping his horn. "All right," Howie said. "I'm with my buddy, can't you see?" I noticed a pile of hand grenades and dumdum bullets in the back of the jeep. There was also an

180

enormous bundle of propaganda leaflets; the leaflets were printed in several colors. "Jesus," Howie said, "how the heck did you end up in this dump? I've seen some wicked places in my time, but this is the worst. They got a ghost factory here or something. And the owner. *Wowee!* What's his name? Yeah. Uncle, Uncle. It's like a prison camp." Howie saw me staring at him. "What's up?"

"Howie, don't you know who Uncle is? He's Moskowitz's *Uncle Nate.*"

His chin dropped a full inch; even his helmet seemed to sag. He cursed himself and began punching the air. "*Shit,*" he said, "I knew I shoulda sabotaged the show. Here I had a perfect chance to get back at Moskowitz, and I blew it. Jesus. Nick, why the heck didn't you signal to me, huh?" The driver began beeping again. Howie brandished the bayonet and the hari-kari knife. "Cut it out, or I swear I'll brain you." The driver looked glumly in the other direction. The boys had already gathered near the porch. "Jesus. A perfect chance."

"Howie," I said, "how did you ever end up on Luzon?"

"Ah, it was a mistake. I was supposed to be with the Air Corps band, but they screwed up my orders. But don't worry. I was an ammo bearer. I never fired a shot. All I did was load up bullet belts, and stab centipedes with my bayonet. I had a regular racket for a while. We were brewing potato juice at the compound, and smuggling whole tankfuls into the huts. And now the War Department is sending me around to all these wacky orphanages and state farms. For once I fell into a deal, instead of a pile of *dreck.* Don't worry, this boy is looking out for himself. I ain't going back to the Philippines, not me. The USA is fine. That's all the territory I ever wanna see again."

"But what happened? I thought you were with a carnival in Philadelphia?"

"Yeah, yeah," he said. "First they took all my jack and

181

then they let me be a glorified pinboy. Philly stinks. It's good for niggers and rich Jews. Everybody else gets nosed out. I stayed with the carnival for half a year and after my money ran out I joined up. And believe me, even wearing a GI monkey suit was better than handling all that carnival crap. I ain't sorry. Not one bit."

"Howie, my tobacco pouch is in the barrack. Do you want me to roll a few cigarettes for you? You can take them on the ride to Rochester."

"Na," he said, slapping the overhanging pockets of his paratrooper's jacket. "I'm addicted to Chesterfields now. That's the only weed I can smoke. But thanks, kid." He stooped over and laced his left boot. "Lousy uniform. I stole something from everybody. The Rangers, the Air Corps, even the WACs. Here, you want my scarf? I can get you a red one, too. From the Rangers."

I wound Howie's scarf around my neck. Howie knotted it for me. "There," he said, "that's official." Then he saluted me. The driver didn't bother beeping. This time he drove around us. "I better get in, Nick, before the screwball runs us over. We ain't really going up to Rochester. That was just for Uncle. We're heading back to the city. Me and the screwball are gonna make a tour of all the canteens tonight. My uniform gets me in anywhere. And the screwball likes to tag along." He climbed aboard the jeep. "Take care, Nick. And keep a tight asshole." He waved to the boys and then the driver took off.

I walked slowly back to the barrack. My boys came rushing in about a minute later. Several boys from B Company were with them too. They all saw me wearing the scarf. Shadrach was sleeping under my bed. I sat down, and poising my knees coolly, I began rubbing Shadrach's neck. "Head Commander," Notte said diplomatically, "could you tell us about the Corporal?" I could feel the boys press close to the gate. I kept rubbing Shadrach's neck. "Could you, Head Commander?" Would Uncle now make me an honorary Maccabee? Commander Lipshitz, the intimate of bulldogs and war heroes. Would I be able to reform Matches and rout the Jailers? The new knight of the realm. With prophylactic weapons and a blue scarf. "Head Commander?" I waited a little while longer before I looked up.

⌐ CHAPTER ¬

14

The cult of Head Commander Shitz was short-lived. Rubin came back to the Home the day after Howie's visit, and immediately resumed command. No one had seen him wearing a uniform. He brought back only his ditty bag. Not even Uncle seemed to know what had happened to Rubin at boot camp. The boys had their own theories. "I'll bet they found out he's a quiff," Notte said. "They don't throw guys outa the Army just for nothin'. Or maybe the Rube couldn't make it without his bulldog."

I discarded all the rights and privileges that had accrued during my tenure as head Screw, and learned to accept my demoted status. I kept the campaign hat and my blue scarf under my bed, put on my skullcap, and returned Shadrach and the radio to Rubin. Actually, I wasn't very disturbed by my restored anonymity. Notte tried to bolster my courage and still called me *Head Commander* every now and then,

184

and the other boys left me alone. Why should I have cared? Bullets would put on his screaming exhibitions again and would probably be released from the Dungeon in a few days, and Rubin would undoubtedly keep the Jailers in check. But things didn't work out quite that way. The Marine began to oppress the boys during their drills in the basement, and Billingsgate, with his broken stick brought out of retirement, now inspected every barrack. And Rubin seemed to sanction their moves.

Pebbleby was immediately suspicious. He no longer trusted the cook's sandwiches. "I'm telling you, Commander, Rubin's a devil now. And the cook is in league with him. They're trying to poison us all out. I'm sticking to onions and radishes." He also had a message for me from the Rabbi. "Commander, the Rabbi wants to know if his toilet seat is keeping you away. When are you coming up for a visit?"

"Tell him," I said, "tell him that I've been busy, but I expect to have some free time soon." The Janitor kept looking at me expectantly. "That's all," I said. "That's all."

When the Jailer began plaguing the Wolfman again, I went up to see Rubin. Shadrach growled as I approached the door. Rubin had obviously indoctrinated him thoroughly. I ignored the growls. Rubin was sitting on his cot. He didn't ask me to come in.

"Rubin," I said, "I'd like to talk to you."

"So talk," he said, without looking up. He opened the ditty bag. A Luger fell out. He pressed the end of the barrel against his forehead and pulled the trigger twice. Then he smiled quizzically. "Don't worry. It ain't loaded. I once saw Paul Lukas playing Russian roulette at the RKO."

"Where did you get the gun?"

"One of the supply sergeants sold it to me. It's only a prop. Feel." I hefted the Luger for him. "See. It's wood. The Rangers use 'em sometime in training."

185

"Rubin," I said, "I wish you'd tell the Jailers to ease up on my boys."

"Ease up?" he said, aiming the Luger at my chest. "No, no. I'm forming a special company. The Junior Rangers. And we gotta keep up the pressure. A few of the runts are gonna have to go. Farbovich and the Wolfman. There ain't no room for skanks in my Rangers."

I put one foot over the door sill. Rubin pulled the trigger. "Stay out," he said. "You can talk plenty from where you are."

"Rubin."

"And I ain't got much time to organize the company. The real Rangers are gonna be calling me back soon." Now he placed the barrel of the Luger against his nose. He didn't look at me. "I'm on special furlough. I may be here a coupla weeks, or maybe a month. That depends. The Rangers gotta send my credentials to Washington. The President has to approve the new recruits in all the special forces. And this time Bill's gonna be taking over for me. So don't get your balls in an uproar. Nobody's gonna be needing you."

I left him with the Luger still against his nose. I didn't bother trying to analyze Rubin's motives. I was much more concerned about Benny. I knew that he would retaliate in some way against the Jailers. But with Matches in the middle, all of Benny's schemes and bombs and three-pronged attacks would come to nothing, and maybe next time Billingsgate wouldn't be satisfied merely with smashing Benny's face. And there seemed to be no way for me to set Benny straight without first informing on Matches, and so, all my alternatives were equally distasteful. I would end up being an informer or a fink no matter what I did. I cursed Uncle for having forced me into his intrigues. And settling for a diminutive role, I decided to sit tight for a little while and await Rubin's next move.

I found the Rabbi waiting for me when I came back to the barrack. The boys were making a great fuss over him. The Wolfman somersaulted crazily between the cots and sang over and over again, "*Shah shtill, der Rebbe gait tantzen balt*," and Notte kept saying, "*Rebbe, Rebbe*, tell us a riddle." Even Benny seemed involved with the Rabbi; I actually saw him smile.

"A riddle, *Rebbe*, a riddle."

The Rabbi turned around. He saw me for the first time. His chin was covered with stubble. His face was drained and his eyes were a little bloodshot. The puny beard seemed to make his appearance a little less incongruous. It wasn't merely a question of respectability. The stubble had a magical effect: I'm sure the Rabbi could have now wrestled with angels or demons and still come out on top.

"A riddle?" he said, palming his chin. "In my face you can find all the riddles you want. The crags, the lines. A contour map of the entire universe. A hundred mysteries in every pore. How many secrets are locked between my nose and my chin, only God knows. Why should you explore the planets? I have in myself all the worlds you will ever need." Then he bowed to each of the boys and excused himself. "I have business with your Commander." I followed him outside. We both walked behind the barrack. The Rabbi's gullet rose. "Nick," he said, "I know. I should have told you the whole story about Mama and me. But I was ashamed. So I railed against her instead. That's the way the Rabbi works. He runs backward all the time. I spoke to Mama myself yesterday. A war conference. What, Nick, do you think it bothers me that you've made a claim to her cot? Nick, you're welcome to her. All the way! No one says you have to visit the Rabbi. It's not a written law. But I'm tired of being the only protagonist in all my plays. The sound of my own voice is beginning to sicken me. Nick." He removed the Seabee cap from his pocket and covered his head, pulling the bill over his eyes. His hands were trembling. He kept wagging his jaw. "It wasn't Mama, no. It was Nate. Nate turned you against me. That much I know. Nick. . . ."

"All right, Uncle told me that you raped a twelve-year-old-girl. Rabbi, you don't have to explain anything to me. I don't think I believed him, anyway. Rabbi, I want to go back inside."

He gripped my jacket and tugged my elbows fiercely. "He told you about *Faigele?* Golem!" Now he released my elbows and dropped his stubbly chin onto his chest. "Fannie. The beadle's daughter. Uncle missed his calling. He should have worked for the district attorney. Nick, what could I do? I was a driven man."

"Rabbi, no confessions, please. Leave me out of it. I don't want to be your secret sharer. Goodbye."

"*Nick.* One thing. She wasn't twelve, she was fourteen. My Faigele. All the Yeshiva boys and the local *nudniks* saw the color of her underpants long before the Rabbi. She was the private property of the Jewish Scorpions and the Skulls. And did Uncle tell you about the *bas mitzvah?* The religious training was her own idea. But it's also true that I could have avoided the whole thing. Jacob wrestled with his angels, and Fannie Ishkowitz only wanted to wrestle with me! And don't think I didn't teach her the *haftarah.* She knew her prayers by heart. But she recited them with her underpants on my table. Nick, were you ever in love?"

"No," I said haltingly. "No, Rabbi. I don't think so."

"That French midget, Stendhal. He's right. It's madness. Not even the devils could have invented it. After all, a devil has a little bit of humanity in him, too. No, it must have been somebody who hated all of us. An absolute ghoul. My whole congregation became matchmakers. Everybody wanted to fix up the Rabbi. And you should have seen the dowagers they

188

brought around. Nick, all I had to do was snap my fingers once and I could have been a man of property. I was offered half of Simpson Street. Nick, they were ready to give me the deed to the synagogue. What wouldn't they have done for their *Rebbe*. But no, the crazy Rabbi was fixed on Faigele. I preferred her underpants in my pocket than the deeds to a hundred synagogues. But Uncle's right. Legally it was still a rape. And when the congregation found out, they claimed that I was using the synagogue for a whorehouse. And Faigele. Who knows. After a session with the Scorpions or the Skulls, somebody knocked her up. And the Rabbi was up the creek! It was Uncle who bailed me out. How he found out about my case, only God knows. And I know I should recriminate myself. But Nick. Who can afford to tell lies? I wrote to Faigele seven times. Honest, I was ready to smuggle her up here, or run off with her to Hoboken. But she never answered my letters. Now you know what kind of person I am. A hopeless case! What can I do? That's my nature. Show me a pretty behind and I'm cooked! That's why it's better that I stay upstairs in my hole. The Rabbi in retreat!" Next he smiled shrewdly. I waited for him to stroke his chin. "Uncle," he said, "Uncle is restoring me to life. At least for a little while. He's allowing me to write a sermon for Matches' *bar mitzvah*. It's a tradition with Nate. As soon as a boy reaches thirteen, Uncle moves in with his *bar mitzvahs*. And what is it? A glass of cherry wine and a piece of stale cake. How could I teach Matches the *haftarah?* He has trouble enough with English. He can't memorize a word." Rabbi, I wanted to say, maybe you should get Faigele to teach him the prayers? But I could see easily enough that he wasn't in any mood to be diddled. And for some reason the stubble on his chin moved me in a curious way. Was the beard going to be some sort of sacrifice? Or was the Rabbi just a little out of his mind? "And Nick, Nate wants to proofread my sermon. He has to approve every word. That's the only way. But better a censored sermon than nothing. Let him take out whatever he wants. The Rabbi will find a way to strike back. Nick, say goodbye to the boys for me. I don't feel like going inside. They'll expect stories and riddles, and I'm already emptied out."

"Rabbi," I said, "I'll be up to see you. Soon."

"Fine." He raised the bill of his cap. His eyes seemed a little less bloodshot, but his cheeks were entirely drawn in. "Fine." He walked towards the house. I could hear him talking to himself. His shoulders sank gradually, and for a minute I thought he was going to shrink into the ground.

My teaching duties were restored the next day, and I decided to hit the boys with a flurry of activities. I held inter-Company spelling bees and even contemplated asking Uncle to outline for me a short course in Zionism, which I intended to teach along with American history. Of course, Bullets began putting on a show for us, but I learned to ignore his practiced screams. After the second day of classes I met the cook in the hall. He winked to me secretly and we both walked over to the landing. "Nick, I just wanted to tell you to keep on the lookout. I'm expecting a little trouble from your boys again. Benny is building up an arsenal of bombs. He's gonna be on the warpath again any day." I thanked him for the information, and then I went over to the barrack.

Pebbleby was in the midst of delivering his sandwiches. He seemed even more nervous than usual. The boys showed no signs of wanting to taunt him. They ignored him completely. He handed me a crumpled piece of paper and began whispering to me. "Bullets left it under his door. It's a note. I thought it was meant for the Rabbi. But the Rabbi says no. It's for you." I looked at the note. The writing was perfectly legible. The note read: "Commissioner. The show is over. The screams were for real. Charlotte Street don't mean nothing to the Rube no more. Get me out of the box. B."

190

"Commander," Pebbleby said. "My time is up." He left me a salami sandwich and a pear with a mottled skin. "Good-bye," I said absently. I tried to recall Bullets' screams. Matches was playing cards with Benny and Notte. I glared at him, but he was too busy uncovering his queens to notice my looks. Notte began complaining. "He always ends up with all the whores." Benny hunched his crooked shoulder. I wondered where he was hiding his bombs?

I found Uncle outside his office. He was adding a few photographs to his bulletin board. Modern Maccabees. I was amazed at my own coolness. "Uncle," I said, "I'd like to speak to you. Inside." He pursed his lips grimly and moved his thumb over the head of a tack. The tack refused to budge. "Stubborn board." I pressed it in for him. There were deep marks on both my thumbs. I followed him into his office. I decided to be absolutely merciless. Uncle had his own hordes of half truths, and now I would bolster an army of lies. "Uncle," I said, without even biting my lip. "Benny knows all about Matches."

"All about Matches?" he said calmly. He even managed a smile. "Nick, are you dealing in mysteries?"

"Uncle," I said again. "Before Rubin left, he told me all about the setup here. About the cook's school for spies." I was ready to turn the screw all the way in. "I'm pretty sure Benny knows that Matches is spying for you."

Uncle's face remained impassive. Nick, I told myself, I think you stepped into Howie's classic pile of shit. Then Uncle finally broke. "Nick, what do you think we should do?" I hoped he was having conniptions behind his masklike exterior.

I leaned one elbow on his desk. "Well, Uncle, Matches is useless now in D Company. It may even harm you having him there. Maybe you ought to work a switch."

"Switch?" His brows knit for a moment. "Yes, yes. An

excellent tactic. A switch. Whom do you suggest that we bring into your Company?"

"Bullets," I said point-blank. "That way, Uncle, the boys won't suspect a thing." Then I added the clincher. "Later you can bring in another spy. Or train one. But Bullets will throw them completely off. His time in the Dungeon is almost ended, isn't it, Uncle?"

"Yes," Uncle said. He was no longer smiling. "Nick, you've proved your mettle again. Take Matches out and bring Bullets in. Perfect. That's beyond Rubin's scope. Absolutely." He actually shook my hand. "Nick, do you push the pawns? *Chess*."

"No, Uncle."

"That's a pity. I'm sure you could learn to drive my pieces off the board in no time. You would be a formidable opponent." Uncle walked me over to the door. "Nick, I will expedite your plan as soon as possible. Goodbye."

I stood outside Uncle's room for a few moments. Matches. Japped. No other way. Save the bombs and the boys. I heard the porch door slam. Rubin was behind the door with Shadrach. I passed them both without saying hello.

CHAPTER

15

Mama took charge of the *bar mitzvah* arrangements. And now she would be in the barrack for days at a time. She was supposed to be rehearsing Matches' *bar mitzvah* speech, but she constantly brought him over to my side of the barrack, and even my commode wasn't much of a sanctuary. And so, in order to avoid any direct confrontation with Mama, I began playing cards with Notte, and promptly lost three dollars in the first day of playing. Notte would display my nickels and dimes on his shelf and wink every time one of the other boys passed his bunk, but the nickels and dimes didn't bother me, as long as they kept Mama out of reach. Matches, however, wasn't very keen on the whole deal. He would have balked at the *bar mitzvah* speech and the other arrangements, he told all of us, but Uncle had promised to lift D Company's embargo for the day. And, he said, he was going to sell his ass to give us all a free day, and he agreed to submit himself to Mama. Notte immediately refused Matches' terms. "Listen," he said, "you don't gotta suck around for our sakes. You don't want the *bar mitzvah*, then it's off. Period." Matches looked around guiltily. "No, Notte. I'll go through with it." And once, while Matches was with Mama on my bed, Notte removed a stack of dimes from his shelf, and after sucking his lip portentously, he said, "Maybe we oughta get the creep something. You think Uncle could order a pen from the city?" He began bunching his nickels along the edges of the shelf. "Can you get a Parker for ninety cents?" I watched the nickels form a row of battlements. "I'll try, Notte. I'll try."

For some reason the classroom wasn't solemn enough for Uncle, and so he crowded the four Companies, the three bull-dogs, and the rest of us into his office and held the ceremony there. Matches, of course, stood in front of Uncle's desk. He wore a skullcap with an embroidered peak, and an enormous prayer shawl was draped neatly over his shoulders. About forty paper cups were assembled on the desk. Each cup was half-filled with plum colored wine. Some halvah in the shape of an enormous gold brick was stationed near one end of the desk. Uncle initiated the ceremony. He wore a red tie for the occasion. A paper flower with a fluted stem, which had obviously been tailor-made for Uncle by the girls from the crippleage in England, was attached to his lapel. Both sconces were working.

"Men, boys, and Mama," Uncle said, making sure that we noticed his red tie. "Why should I waste time with formalities? You all know why we are gathered here. One of our own is being initiated into manhood. According to Jewish custom and law, Matches is now formally a *mensch*. In the years to come, who knows what the President will be asking of him and the rest of you who are a little younger and a little

194

older? Who can say, with the world the way it is? Surrounded by enemies. Enclosed. We will need all the strength that we can summon for our purposes. We will go forth together and fight the fascists in Rome, in Berlin, in Tokyo, and in the other capitals of the world." I began to wonder how many cups of wine Uncle had drunk before we all arrived. "And we will free each and every Jew held captive by Hitler and his agents in Poland, in Hungary, in France, in Austria, in Holland, in Greece, in Russia, in North Africa. . . ." All this from one *bar mitzvah* and forty cups of wine? "But for now, remember, that with manhood comes a grave responsibility. A need to give up part of one's private identity, and to become a member of the world at large. A need. . . ."

The Janitor had already closed one eye. The Jailers were winking to one another. Shadrach, I think, broke wind. Uncle finally came back to Matches. "And to celebrate the occasion, now that Matches is fully fledged, I am taking him out of D Company, and moving him into A. After all, a man can no longer stay with boys." Matches looked at Uncle first, and then at me. I could tell. He knew right away that he had been sold out. "I'm sure he will be worthy of the confidence and trust that Uncle has invested in him. Matches, your speech." Matches' brows burrowed downward towards his cheeks. He stared darkly at all of us. Mama moved closer to the desk and began cuing him, but Matches ignored her efforts. His shoulders began to lump under the prayer shawl. "Speech," he said, "speech." Notte whispered to me. "Whatsamatter, did Uncle forget about the fountain pen?" I waved him off. "Uncle," Matches said, "Ma-ma, Ru-bin, Com. . . ."

"Commander Lipshitz," Mama said.

"Mandershitz, fel-low Mac-ca-bees and others, we are . . . we are . . . and thankful for all . . . Uncle . . . I accept . . . I accept. . . ."

"Matches," Mama said, "start again." Then she turned to

Uncle and me. "You know. His first speech. He's a little nervous." Uncle drove an ant away from the halvah. His jaw seemed grimly set, but his eyes, however, were still crinkling. Matches started again.

"I accept . . . I accept. . . ."

"Boys," Uncle said summarily, "let's sample the wine." Notte handed me a cup. "What the hell is wrong with the creep? Don't he know it when Uncle throws him a good deal? A Company. Raisins for breakfast and Captain Midnight on Wednesdays and Fridays. What a life." I sipped the wine. It tasted surprisingly sweet. Matches stood under one of the sconces. The prayer shawl reached his knees. Uncle began slicing the halvah. I felt someone pinch my ribs. It was the Rabbi. His entire chin was now covered with stubble. "Nick," he said, "are you enjoying the show?" Some halvah was already entangled in his fledgling beard. "Wait until the fireworks start." Uncle summoned him.

"Rabbi, the sermon." He glared at Mama. "I hope we will have at least one small success."

The Rabbi cleared his throat noisily. Then he toasted Matches with his cup and said, "Boys, your Uncle Nate is right. Jews are being roasted and flayed all over the world. And why stop with the Jews? The massacre doesn't begin and end there. Madness is a universal principle. Whoever is out of favor has to pay the price. All majorities, all parties in power create their own master race. Let the Jews capture Arabia, and the Arabs would be out of luck."

"*Rabbi*," Uncle said coldly, raising one brow. "This was not in the text. If you are considering switching sermons, forget it. Rosencrantz, how many more times do you think I will allow you a second chance?"

The Rabbi excused himself ceremoniously, saluting us with his skullcap. "Only a preface, Uncle, that's all. Now the business begins. Boys, don't think for a minute that the holo-

196

causts in Europe today are something new. There were terrible goings on in Europe for hundreds and hundreds of years before Hitler's goose-steppers arrived on stage. When were the Jews ever safe? And where? Holed up in their stinking ghettos, in their little Jewish sections, they were always easy prey for bandits, or the nearest scapegoat for any untoward events among the Gentiles. Let a little Gentile girl die in the street, and right away there were blood accusations. Search the ghetto! Everybody knows that the Jews thrive on Christian blood. Whenever there was too much rain or too little, whenever the crops failed, or the winter was hard, the blame usually found its way to the ghetto doorsteps. No, the Nazis are not unique. They have had all of recorded history to guide them. Whenever something goes wrong, sniff out the nearest Jew. And once, who knows how many hundreds of years ago, when the ghetto of Prague was being threatened, and the bandits were preparing to feast on Jewish flesh, Rabbi Loeb, the chancellor of the ghetto, said, 'Enough. For once we will fight fire with fire.' But whom did he have at his side? A few old men with prayer shawls. All the young men of the ghetto had already been conscripted, and were having their brains bashed in for their besotted emperor in one of his hundred year wars. And so Rabbi Loeb found for himself another kind of army. He heaped together some clay and dust, and with his fingers he shaped out a clay figure. He whispered the Holy Name while he worked, and the figure began to stir. Then he blew life into its nose and both ears, and the first *golem* was born. And even before Rabbi Loeb gave the golem his orders, the golem chased the bandits and slaughtered them like flies. And then, when the golem went after all the Gentiles in Prague, Rabbi Loeb recalled him, and blew into the golem's nose for the second time. Now the golem became a clay figure again, and Rabbi Loeb stored him in the attic of the synagogue. Who knows how many Gentiles the golem would have slaughtered,

197

if the Rabbi had let him run free? No, the Rabbi figured, better a few pogroms than a complete bloodbath. Here, boys, you have a moralist of the first order. After all, the Gentiles were human too! And soon the golem was forgotten. Cobwebs formed over his head, and the dust clogged his eyelids and his nose. They say that even now the golem sits in the same attic, waiting for someone to whisper the Holy Name. And who knows what will happen when the golem is given life for the second time? The Talmudists will tell you that the golem will destroy every Nazi and Gentile in Europe. And it is only a question of time before the deliverer opens the doors of the ghettos and frees every Jew. But my views have a different bent. I say that the golem will attack Gentile and Jew without discrimination. He has lost the Holy Name. This time the golem is in other hands."

The sconce's tipped shadow broke over Uncle's face, but I could still see his frown. "Rabbi."

The Rabbi shrugged one shoulder. "Uncle," he said, "a little coda, that's all. The sermon is ended. Boys, do you know what I will do the minute Uncle sends me back to my toilet seat. I will fashion my own golem. Not out of clay, but out of *dreck*."

"Rabbi, *silence!*"

The Jailers gripped the Rabbi's arms. "And boys, my golem will never hear the Holy Name. And God help Uncle and all the rest." The Jailers dragged the Rabbi out of the room. I heard Shadrach growl. "Uncle," the Rabbi shouted, before the door closed on him, "I'm ready for the Dungeon." Uncle moved in immediately and restored order. Mama distributed halvah for him, and Rubin, Shadrach, and the cook kept the boys away from the desk.

"Boys," Uncle said, "I am sorry that you had to witness such an outburst, but calm yourselves. The Rabbi will apologize personally to all of you. I will see to it myself. I also have

198

some good news. I am ending Bullets' stay in the Dungeon. He will be released tonight." The boys in A Company cheered mildly. "And since D Company is now short one man, I am giving Bullets to them." Benny stared slantily at me, Uncle, and Rubin. I'm sure he was suspicious of Uncle's shuttle. Matches remained under the sconce. I heard Notte whisper to the wall. "One creep goes out, and now a bigger creep comes in." He charged towards the desk. "Uncle, I protest. We don't need Bullets in D Company."

The cook pushed Notte back against the wall. I stepped between them. "Watch it," I said. "Watch it." The cook smiled waspishly. The smile wasn't for Notte; I'm sure it was meant for me. Benny and the Indian surrounded the cook. Uncle intervened.

"Commander, march your Company back to the barrack. Now."

My boys assembled behind me. Matches lagged for a moment, and then he joined the line. Uncle cautioned him indirectly.

"Matches remains here. Commander, Pebbles will bring his belongings over to A Company."

I marched the boys out of Uncle's office. We all heard Matches whimper. I didn't turn around, but I could feel Benny's eyes gouging the back of my skull.

We found Pebbleby emptying Matches' locker. I saw him pack a wormy soap dish, two pairs of frayed socks, a faded undershirt, a rusty belt buckle, and a Gene Autry button into a paper shopping bag. The boys surrounded Matches' cot. "Not my fault," Pebbleby said, folding the shopping bag hurriedly. "Not my fault." Then he left.

Bullets showed up just after dark. One of his eyebrows was split, and both his cheeks were puffed out. He carried his own belongings. Notte sneered at him, but Bullets seemed to welcome the boys' ill looks. "Remember," he said matter-of-factly, without waiting for any further provocation, "I can take on all five of you at the same time. And that goes for the Commissioner too." I didn't bother acknowledging his challenge. "So stay away from me, all of you, and we'll all be in good shape." He unpacked a jar of Barbasol and a shaving brush and stored them unceremoniously inside Matches' locker. The Wolfman cavorted in front of the cot. "Keep the booby away from me. This ain't no circus." Larry Farbovich led the Wolfman away from the cot.

Notte slapped his sides and complained to all of us. "Is he gonna have his own private crappot too? Benny, tell him, who invited him here? We don't need no creeps."

Bullets opened the jar of Barbasol and began lathering his face with the brush. We all stared at him with a little wonder. Benny, of course, shaved the Wolfman's chin every other morning, and worked on Notte's sideburns once a week, but none of the boys ever used Barbasol or had his own shaving brush. Bullets paused and waved the brush at Benny. "Don't get any funny ideas, Spick. I could chew off half your head with one bite."

Notte persisted. "He's gotta be initiated. That's the law of the Company. He can't be admitted without an initiation."

"Initiation?" Bullets said, the shaving cream forming stalactites under his chin. "Initiation?"

"Yeah," Notte said, pressing him. "That's the law. You gotta make a confession. You gotta tell us the worst thing you ever did in your life. That's it. The initiation."

"Dick you," Bullets said. He kept lathering his face. Notte had obviously captured his interest.

"Dick who?" Notte said, ruffling his nose affectedly, and expecting a little sympathy from the rest of us. "No, man. *Dick you.* That's the law. Article four of Uncle's rules of conduct. Either the initiation, or out you go. We ain't got nothin' to do with it. There ain't no other way."

200

"Yeah, well, if there's gonna be any initiation, then we all gotta go through it together. No single deals. You want me to spread my cheeks for you, then you all gotta do some spreading for me. The Commissioner too. No exceptions."

Notte flailed his arms excitedly. "A Company confession, wowee! We'll clog all the johns at the Home. Benny, are you with us? It's gotta be everybody or nobody." Benny frowned ferociously, but he didn't say no. And anyway, Notte took the frown as an affirmative sign. "Commander?"

What could I do? "Okay," I said, shrugging one shoulder at a time. We all gathered around Matches' cot.

"I'm the referee," Notte said. "Whatever the Phantom says, it gotta go. No goosing, no gas bombs, no silent farts, and no phony confessions. Whoever breaks the laws, he gotta pay. Bullets?"

Bullets stared at us and began to fidget uncontrollably. Then he raised his split eyebrow, and smiling omnisciently, he said, "Fellas, I gotta tell the truth. I jerk off with my left hand."

Notte reprimanded him immediately. "You heard what I said. No wisecracks and phony confessions. It's gotta be legit. I'm imposing penalties, Bullets, I mean it. You're gonna end up sleeping in the shower. Now, come on, *confess*."

Bullets walked over to the shower stall. "Ain't anybody got a weed? Ever since the Rube dropped my cigar quota, I been getting terrible cramps."

"No," Notte said. "No stimulants. You gotta—"

"All right, all right, I *futzed* my sister Frimke, you satisfied?"

"That's legit," Notte said. "That's legit."

I stared at both of them. "Futzed?"

"Jesus," Bullets said, coming back to the cot. "Don't you know the English language? *Screwed*. Frimke. I futzed her. Ten times. Maybe eleven. What more do you want?

201

We lived in the same room. Frimke was fourteen, and I was eleven. Last year. I saw all the holes she had in her pants from playing stinky pinky with Heshie Bookbinder. But she wouldn't go down for Heshie. Not Frimke. Heshie's nineteen, and he takes all the hot boxes and the boogy trade over to the lots behind the park. But Frimke wouldn't go. He hadda dry hump her on the roof." The boys edged closer to Bullets; even the Wolfman perked one ear. "It gets cold in the winter, see, and sometimes when it snowed or rained hard, Frimke asked me to move into her bed. We wrestled, and crap like that, and once she pretended she was sleeping and I futzed her. And . . . hey, that's enough. Now it's your turn, Spick."

"Uh, uh," Notte said. "I'm calling the turns, Bullets. The Keeper goes."

Larry shrank away from the cot. "I never did nothin' wrong. Never."

"Get back here," Bullets said, "before I break your arm."

Larry hid behind me. I wasn't in the mood to incur Bullets' wrath, but I couldn't just give Larry up to him; and so, pretending that I was some sort of sanctuary, I said, "Let him work up a little sweat. He'll go last."

"Then it's gotta be the Spick. No more decoys."

We all turned to Benny. Without flinching or hesitating or looking away he said, "When I was riding the boxes on the B & O, I let this old guy play with me. I didn't go for it, but I liked him, so I let him. His name was Matty and he came from Idaho." Then he put his hands in his pockets and leaned against the wall. None of us tried to pry him. Bullets smiled, but whatever he had to say, he kept it to himself. And Notte didn't even bother announcing the legitimacy of Benny's confession. "Next case," he said. "The Wolfman. Benny, tell him in kike. He gotta confess."

"Boris," Benny said. "A *sohd. Zug uns.* . . ."

202

"*Sohd?*" the Wolfman said. "*Benja, ich hub a kleine petzele. Ven vil er vaxen?*"

"So?" Notte said, "Tell us the story."

Benny frowned again. "Ah, he wants to know when his peanut's gonna grow?"

Bullets laughed outrageously and clamped the Wolfman's thighs. "I take it back," he finally said. "The booby's all right. Spick, tell him it's something that everybody wants to know."

"Tell him yourself," Benny said, and brushing past Bullets and me, he crossed the barrack and stood between the commodes.

Larry began mumbling to himself. "I got something. . . ." He walked over dutifully to Notte and Bullets. "Notte, lemme go. I got something now. To confess."

"Who's stopping you?" Notte said. "Go."

"You remember, before the Commander came here, Mama stayed with us. . . ."

"Yeah, yeah."

"Well, once her nightgown was open and I saw her tits." He showed with his hands. "Both. The nipples too."

Notte's cheeks crumpled unsympathetically. "That's it? Mama's tits? What's the big deal? I saw her bombs every night when she was with the Company. We all did." Me too, I wanted to say, me too. "Even the Indian. And he couldn't tell a tit from a nutshell." The Indian seemed to endorse Notte's analogies: he smiled goofily and plucked two imaginary nipples from Larry's behind. "Keeper," Notte said. "Uncle has you pegged. You're a hopeless case." Larry retreated to his own cot. The Wolfman joined him.

Bullets now pointed to me. Notte shrugged resignedly. "Commander, there's nothin' I can do. Your turn gotta come up some time. And we can't allow no special favors, Commander or not. It's gotta be a full confesson."

What was I supposed to confess? I wanted to go the whole hog for the boys, but how? Then I stared at the rumpled canvas stretched across Matches' cot. The cot was a little lopsided. Matches. Would he have told the boys how his mother was set on fire, or would he have simply announced: 'I'm a spy.' I could almost hear him hissing out the word. Spy. And should I have told them now that their Commander, in his own way, was a spy among them? "Boys," I said, "my name isn't Lipshitz. It's Lapucci. And I'm Italian, not a Jew." I expected locked jaws and broken looks, but nothing happened.

"Balls," Notte said. "We knew that the first day you were here. Benny can spot ginzoes a mile away. And Uncle's always pulling off stunts like that. Last year he tried to pass off a carpenter for a general. Commander, you're gonna have to do better than that."

I could feel my pores clog. Lipshitz. Why hadn't I suspected all along that I would end up being the butt of Uncle's ruse? Lipshitz. I searched savagely for an available target. "Boys," I said stickily, "I futzed Mama. Futzed her. Me." This time I got my response. Notte's jaw hung. Bullets almost tripped over the cot. Even Benny seemed a little startled, and Larry was completely overwhelmed. "He futzed Mama."

I walked behind the gate. "Futzed." The Wolfman paired his armies, but the other boys assembled near the gate. Ashamed. Dirty secret. Mama. I wanted to disband my ill-earned veneration. I wanted to comb my memory and expose some dark and terrible thing about myself. Futzed. I was even willing to fantasize for the boys. With my identity restored, I felt a little released. No more Lipshitz. Nick Lapucci, torturer of beetles, cats, dogs. Murdered his own father. Consummated certain mysteries with his mother. Golem. Sprung from a petrified forest of shit. Nourished in dung. Golem. Boys, I was going to say, boys. . . .

The Rabbi stood under the door, the jambs imprisoning

his shoulders. The two Jailers were behind him, and one of the bulldogs. The Rabbi's eyes seemed slightly glazed, and his chin pointed crookedly. Billingsgate nudged the Rabbi's shoulder. "Boys," the Rabbi said, looking dully at the floor. "I am grievously sorry for my criminal behavior this afternoon." Had Uncle prepared a speech for him, or had he allowed the Rabbi to choose his own words? "It will not happen again."

"Rabbi," I said, "come in."

Billingsgate spoke for him. "Sorry, Commander. The Rabbi can't break his schedule. He's making the rounds."

The Rabbi managed a tremulous smile, breaking the jagged pattern of his beard. "I should hire myself out to Walt Disney. I could seduce Snow White for him or be the corrupter of the Seven Dwarfs." The Rabbi didn't need the Jailers' nudges: he left of his own accord.

The boys returned to their cots. I stayed behind the gate.

{꒐ **CHAPTER** ꒑

16

In all matters concerning D Company, Commander Lipshitz was defunct. I was now *Il Duce* for the boys. And I took
to wearing Crazy's hat again inside the barrack. Of course, the
Company was still divided into two opposing camps—Bullets
challenged the other boys on the hour—but I still managed to
keep the peace. "Behave," I said, tilting the hat. "I'll throw you
all out on your asses. I mean it." But the real trouble came
from outside the barrack.

Uncle would visit A Company occasionally or examine at
random one of the bulldog's snouts, but after Matches' *bar
mitzvah* and Bullet's release, he withdrew inside his office and
not only abandoned the kennels and the Companies, but even
left his garden untended. Uncle still showed up for reveille,
but Rubin now ruled the Home. He had Pebbles pluck the
weeds in Uncle's garden and scrub the kennel walls; he ordered the cook to prepare extra sandwiches for the boys who

performed best in the Marine's bayonet drills; and although he didn't actually restore my boys to active duty, he did allow them to participate in his special 'Ranger Preparation' drills. "Everybody's gotta be ready," he said. "Even the screwballs and the fuck-ups." He also delegated full authority to the Jailers in policing the Companies and conducting the drills. The Jailers soon became bolder and bolder. Somehow, Billingsgate secured a new drillmaster's stick. A wolf's head was embossed on both sides of its metal grip; the Jailer would dig the grip into the pit of a boy's stomach, and then say, "Mold that tummy, Applepie, before I spill your guts into the street." And often Benny or the Indian would return to the barrack clutching their stomachs, and would vomit into the commodes. With Uncle practically inaccessible, I tried to reason with Rubin. "Tough titty," he told me. "I can't allow no exceptions. Bill's putting 'em all through the mill. And whoever can't take it, gotta drop out." The boys never complained or asked me to intercede for them, and Notte even joked about Rubin's Ranger drills. "Call me the Phantom Ranger," he said. "The Phantom Ranger." But I could see the terror collect in their eyes every time the Marine marched them over to Uncle's cellar. I was never allowed inside during the drills.

And then, about a week after Bullets' transfer, the drills finally took their toll. The boys had been gone for over an hour. I thought that Rubin might have sent them into the fields behind the house for special maneuvers, and so, I decided to leave the barrack and look for them. But I heard the Marine count cadence even from the door, and I saw the boys marching towards the barrack, their shoulders bobbing irregularly. The Wolfman was missing. The Marine deposited my Company in front of the barrack, and smiling broadly, he said, "You got yourself a spirited bunch, Commander. That's a fact." The boys filed past me and swarmed around Benny's cot. The Marine went back to the house.

"What happened?" I said.

"Balls," Notte said. "The war is on."

"Well? Where's the Wolfman? What happened?"

Notte glanced at Benny. Benny nodded his head.

"Balls," Notte said again. "You know the way the Jailer was giving it to us. With the stick. In the belly and up the ass. Well, today he makes the rounds and he gives me, and Benny, and the Indian a poke, and then he tells Larry to kneel down and kiss the wolf on his stick, which is the same like asking somebody to kiss his ass. And the Indian, I figure, says to himself: There is a limit to the shit I am going to take. And he jumps the Jailer with his knife. Right, Indian?"

The Indian wagged his head.

"Okay, the Jailer drops his shoulder and knocks down the knife. And now me and Benny join the act, but like dopes we left the bombs in the barrack. And the Marine picks us up and piles us in the corner." Notte thrust his head next to Bullets', and facing him nose to nose, he said: "*Creep.*" Then he drew back petulantly and signaled to the rest of us. "I told you he was a creep. All his talk about taking on the whole Company. He didn't even make a move."

I think I heard Bullets hiss. The other boys backed away. I stepped in front of Bullets and stared uneasily at Notte. Was Bullets really fond of carving his initials over the hearts of his enemies? Instinctively, my left hand groped over my chest. "Nuts," Bullets said, and I was immediately relieved. "I ain't going inside that box for nobody. You take care of your ass, and I'll take care of mine. You tell 'em, Kimo Sahbee." He left us and walked over to his cot.

Notte now strutted halfway across the barrack, and he didn't come back until he was convinced that we had all noticed him. Then, aiming his buttocks in Bullets' direction, he said, "That's when Rubin came in. He didn't say one word

208

about the knife. He just told the Jailer to take the Wolfman up to the Dungeon."

"Why the Wolfman?"

"Rubin says it's a Company punishment. The Wolfman's gotta be the goat. He's gotta suffer for all of us."

I sat down on the Wolfman's cot. Pebbleby walked in. "Commander," he said, "Mama wants to see the Keeper. Larry. Therapy. A private session. That's what she told me to tell you."

Uncle needs another spy. Larry. How would Mama wheedle him? Would she offer him one of her nipples and tell him that it was all for the good of the boys? All the anger I could summon immediately fastened on Pebbles.

"No," I said. "Tell her she can't have the Keeper. Tell her to try me. Tell her. . . ." The boys stared at me. Pebbleby stumbled backwards. He excused himself and left.

Larry collected the Wolfman's soldiers and stacked them on his own cot. Bullets twisted the hairs on his shaving brush and glared at all of us. The glare was incidental: I think we were all beginning to suspect that Bullets was harmless. Notte, Benny, and the Indian remained near the Wolfman's cot. Notte's narrow shoulders were working rapidly. "Duce," he said. "I don't give two shits if you hear us or not. We're springing the Wolfman. You can warn Uncle if you want. But it ain't gonna do him no good. No more raids. This is the real thing." Bullets ignored the shaving brush and glanced at his knees. I'm sure he wanted to join the conspiracy.

"No smoke screens or distilled farts. The real thing."

What could I tell them? The Jailers were already mobilized. The boys would be chopped down before they reached the second floor. Or maybe Rubin would allow them to reach the Dungeon, and then collect them all in Uncle's box. Fallen Maccabees. I watched their faces; their earnestness startled

209

me. I'm sure they would have been willing to ravage the Home and fling all of us from the roof in order to redeem the Wolfman. "Wait," I said. "I'll bring the Wolfman back."

I had no specific plan. I only knew that I would have to sidestep Rubin and his Jailers. And so, with some anticipation and a little dread, I boarded Uncle's porch. I didn't know what to expect. Uncle's bulletin board now hung crookedly from one miserable hook, and the snapshots of the Jewish soldiers, sailors, and marines were all smudged, and a few of them had been turned upside down. Howie's snapshot was missing. I knocked on Uncle's door. No one seemed to stir inside the room. I knocked again, and then, after counting solemnly to ten, I entered the room. Uncle's desk was cluttered with paper cups and lumps of halvah. Each lump of halvah had already been overtaken by its own army of ants. The wine in the cups had turned sour. Uncle sat behind the desk staring blankly at the ceiling, his elbows rigid. "Boys," he said. "Uncle is in earnest. Free the Companies. Discharge the dogs."

I approached the desk. The ants ignored me, but the odor of the rotting wine stung my nose. I gripped Uncle's shoulders and stirred him gently. His eyes cleared. "Uncle," I said, "Uncle." I tried to store up a little malice, but the ants, and the cups, and Uncle's flattened looks had already disarmed me.

"Nick," he said, and I could feel his shoulders revive. I watched him collect himself. His eyes began crinkling after a little while. He scolded himself for the filth on his desk, and we both collected the cups and the lumps of halvah, and dropped them into one of the bottom drawers. With the desk cleared, I could feel the malice return and finally take charge. "Uncle," I said. "Rubin put the Wolfman in the Dungeon. I want him out. Now, and no excuses or delays."

210

"Boris in the dungeon?" Uncle said, his eyes now crinkling tentatively. "What was the occasion?"

"I don't know. Billingsgate was working my boys over with his stick, and they bolted. What the hell do you expect? Uncle, you're not going to have a Home left if Rubin keeps up his crazy Ranger drills."

Uncle's lips pursed distinctly. "Nick," he said. "Under the circumstances, I fully approve Rubin's measures. He was setting an example. He couldn't punish the whole Company, so he selected Boris. No, we can't have any revolts in the middle of a drill. Boris stays in the Dungeon."

"Uncle, you know that Boris won't be able to survive in the Dungeon alone for more than a day."

"I'll send Benny up to keep him company," Uncle said, without smiling.

"Uncle," I said, "no more. I'm fed up with your rules and procedures. I don't give a damn if Rubin was following orders or not. I want Boris out. Uncle."

Uncle paused and clasped his hands. Was he going to placate me? I stared him down, and this time he screwed up one eye and said, "Nick, I respect your loyalty to the boys. It's commendable. I'll speak to Rubin. He's reasonable. I might be able to get him to curtail Boris' confinement. Three or four days at the most. But Nick, from now on, no more exemptions. Your boys will have to go along with the rest."

I'm sure I would have been able to bargain further with Uncle, and perhaps, with a little more measured resistance, I might have been able to persuade him to free the Wolfman on the spot, but I just wasn't in a bargaining mood.

"Uncle, tell me. Rubin was supposed to have been a holy terror before he came to the Home. The scourge of the East Bronx. How come he couldn't make it in the Army? And don't give me any crap about the Rangers and the Special Forces. He couldn't even get through two weeks in boot camp. Was he too tough for the other recruits? Did he break up his barrack? Or maybe it was the other way around. Maybe he'd be lost anywhere away from the Home. Maybe he couldn't sleep in a strange bed with other men. I'm no hero, Uncle. But I think I would have had a better chance than Rubin to make it through boot camp. What happened to him here at the Home? I don't think he was ever a tough guy, Uncle. Sure, Rubin raided all the fruit stands on Jennings Street, but what the hell does that mean? He was just a frightened kid from a little ghetto in the Bronx, and you knew it all along. And what did you do, Uncle? You saved him from reform school, and took him out of one ghetto and brought him into another. You crippled him, Uncle, that's what you did. Crippled him. You kept him in your lousy Dungeon for thirteen days and let him think he was the toughest kid in the world. And what happened? The other kids who were here with him left, and Rubin stayed on. And maybe in the Army he found out for the first time that he wasn't so tough. And it scared the living hell out of him. And now he's taking his revenge."

Uncle's eyes were no longer crinkling. But he still managed a broken smile. "Nick," he said. "My congratulations. I should give you my chair. First Rubin's job, and now mine. But you'll have to convert. A Jew in spirit is not enough. We'll ask the Rabbi to instruct you. Of course, it will have to be done legally. Lapucci is out. And then there's still the question of circumcision. I'm told it makes coition less pleasurable. I wouldn't know. But men have made greater sacrifices. Nick, it will take a month. No longer. I'll have you appointed provisional director of the Home. I'll stay on. In another capacity. Then, if you want, you can dismiss the Jailers."

"Uncle," I said. "Your Home stinks. And it's not on account of the Jailers."

He was no longer listening to me. "Lapucci out. Lipshitz legally in. And what will we do with Rubin? Rangers. Stay here. Keeper of the dogs. Rubin."

I left Uncle there behind his desk and walked out of the room. Mama was waiting for me in the hall. "I thought it was you," she said. Mama was wearing one of Pebbleby's denim work shirts. I could see her boobs swell beneath Pebbleby's pockets. She smiled guardedly. "I've finally trapped you, Nick. There's no getting away. Why didn't you send Larry over to me?" She thrust her nipples against my chest. I pushed her away. Her chest throbbed under the shirt. "Mama. Leave off Larry. One spy is enough. What's the procedure, Mama? First you probe them and then you turn them into spies. Why don't you recruit me, Mama? Maybe me and Matches have the same syndrome. Try me, Mama. It ought to be easy."

Mama stood against the bulletin board, the smudged snapshots kissing her shoulders and her behind. She was crying. "Nick," she said. "Uncle was going to disband the counseling program. He was going to send me back to the city. I had no choice. I told him no more, no more. . . ."

"Mama, no sad songs. I don't give a damn how Uncle pressed you. You had no right to screw around with Matches like that. What did you do, Mama? Did you tell him that if he helped out Uncle, he'd find a way back to his father? Or maybe you used a little cut rate hypnosis on him. Or was it a case of simple bribery. Did you let him touch one of your tits, Mama? Or did you tell him that Uncle would make him an official Jewish Commando?"

"Nick," she said, "Nick. . . ."

I walked outside. A Company was holding maneuvers on the lawn. Big Notte was drilling the other boys. The Marine's dogs were frolicking near the porch and were smelling each other's behinds. The Marine juggled a flask. Billingsgate was polishing his new stick. The boys kept performing like brittle

213

jumping jacks. Matches was with them. He watched me cross the lawn. His eyes seemed to beckon to me. I knew no way of redeeming him. And I turned away ashamedly and entered the barrack.

"Where's the Wolfman?" Notte said, looking up gloomily. He and Benny were sitting on the commodes.

"Notte," I said, "guard the door," and then I sat down next to Benny. Notte stood near the door and watched the boys in A Company drill. He was a little puzzled. "What's up, Duce?" Then the Indian walked over, and they both began aping Big Notte.

I began to fidget: the rim of the commode kept pinching my behind. Benny sat placidly. I raised one buttock. "Benny," I said, whispering, "I'm with you. Count me in. Maybe I can't help you make your bombs, but I can still throw them. And if you don't trust me, it's all right. I'm still going to help you. Even if I have to free the Wolfman all by myself."

I shouldn't have tried to anticipate Benny's reaction. I assumed that he would either call over Notte and confer with him, or else he would reject me and my terms outright. Instead, he sat on the commode with his chin jutting stonily. Once or twice I thought I saw a smile almost break through his drawn lips. In the end, he asked me to roll a cigarette for him. Nick, I told myself, you're in, you're in.

214

17

Of course, Notte would have preferred leaving Bullets out of the plot. But it would have been too much of a nuisance conspiring behind his back, so Notte finally agreed to give him a marginal role. He would become our portable arsenal and carry all the extra bombs, but under no circumstances would he be allowed to toss any of them. After a little initial reluctance, Bullets gave in to Notte's terms. "What if I'm attacked?"

"That's your problem, creep. Just save the bombs."

"Notte," I said. "Where the hell are Benny's bombs?"

Notte strolled behind the gate and stood triumphantly in front of my commode. "We figured the Jailers would never search your crapper, Duce." He reached into the commode and pulled out two dented tin cans with twisted plugs. "Benny made seventeen. And each one has the farting power of a two ton elephant. Even a gas mask wouldn't do any good. Not against a fertilized birchbark bomb. Benny brewed the whole thing." Then he plunged one arm gingerly into the commode and restored the bombs. "Duce, they don't have a chance."

Benny walked back and forth irritably. "Screwball," he said. "We haven't tested them yet. So shut up."

Notte smiled wackily. "Benny, lemme sample one on the Jailers." He danced around the commode like an inspired gnome, his shoulder blades hopping. Then he sat on the commode, his tiny behind hugging the knotty board. His dance had diminished him, and he sat now with his belly heaving erratically, already spent.

Benny took over. "It's gotta be tonight. Boris can't be alone in the dark."

Notte immediately revived. "What about Matches?" I could feel my heart pound. "Benny, you promised you'd let him in if you made a move. I can sneak over to A Company in a minute. We can't leave out the little creep."

Matches. Mama. Here we go 'round the loop again. "No," I said. "It's too risky. *No.*" Notte drew closer to Benny. "No." Mustn't tell. "Rubin's already on the alert. And if the Jailers or the cook catch you outside the barrack, even Benny's bombs won't do any good."

Notte ignored my pleas, and kept petitioning Benny. "A promise is a promise. That's what they call integrity, Duce. Benny, is Matches in or not?"

"He's in," Benny said calmly, without trying to hinder my status in the Company but the boys' hardened faces were undebatable. Benny's decision was inviolable. Wolfman. Matches. How long would Rubin keep Boris in Uncle's box? And what would happen to the rest of us? "He's a spy," I shouted. "A spy. Matches. He's a spy. Working for Uncle. That's why you never had a chance last time. Mama recruited

216

him. And the cook trained him." I felt released, unburdened, and terribly ashamed.

Notte spoke first. "Don't believe him, Benny. You saw the way Matches went after the Jailers in the cellar. He ain't no spy. He's with us." Then Notte turned on me. "You're the spy," he said, his eyes brimming with hate. "You." And he began pummeling my chest with his tiny, wrinkled fists. He was crying, and he licked his tears unashamedly. I welcomed the blows, but I barely felt them. His fists grazed my chest like paper balls. Benny's army. Phantoms.

"*Notte*," Benny said, and Notte immediately recalled his fists.

"Commander?"

"Benny, it's true. If Notte runs over to A, Rubin will be down on you in a minute."

Benny leaned one elbow against the gate. I sat on my bed and began rolling cigarettes for the Company. The tobacco dribbled wastefully, and the cigarettes crumbled in my hands.

"Notte," Benny said. "Matches is out."

I left the injured cigarettes on my bed. I had to get out of the barrack. "Boys," I said. "I'm going to recruit the Rabbi. Larry, give out the smokes. I'll be back soon." I passed Notte's cot. He pulled back his gnomelike face and glared at me fiercely. I managed to steady my knees and walk out the door.

The Rabbi had abandoned his toilet seat. He now sat on a little bench near his door. The threads of a spider's web were entangled in the ragged tufts of his beard. A lumpy blanket was spread over his knees.

"Rabbi?" I said.

He looked up and smiled obliquely behind his beard. "Nick. *Shalom*. They say that Turgenev did his best work while he was in exile. Why not Rosencrantz? A bible for anarchists and petty revolutionists. I'll send a copy to Roose-

217

velt. I'll prove to him that anarchy is still an important principle. Let him keep social security, but the Army and the Navy will have to go."

"Rabbi?" I said. "Boris is in the Dungeon."

"I know. Pebbles told me. Nick, we will have to petition Uncle. That's the only way."

I leaned over the bench. "No petitions, Rabbi. Uncle can talk us all under the table. Me and the boys are storming the Dungeon. First we'll use Benny's bombs and then we'll present petitions. Rabbi, are you in with us?"

The Rabbi rumpled the blanket and uncovered one knee. He mumbled behind his beard.

"What, Rabbi, what?"

"Nick, what can the bombs do against the bulldogs and the Jailers? At the Home the Rabbi is persona non grata, I know. A phantom. He doesn't even exist. But maybe Uncle will listen. Nick, I give you my personal guarantee. Boris will—"

"Rabbi, no embellishments, please. I'm destroying the Dungeon. Are you with us or not? We don't expect you to throw any bombs, Rabbi. Just a little support."

The Rabbi clasped his thighs and rocked the bench; the lumpy blanket rode his one knee like a collapsed tent. "Nick, your Rabbi had a hero once. Trotsky. But he landed like a fallen star in Mexico, and his whole international movement became dust and prattle. And while we all waited for the revolutions to come, the Master ended up with an axe in his head. No, Nick. The Rabbi will stay here. The only traveling he will do is between the bench and his toilet seat. Mama's right. I'm a case. Good for nothing. Talk. Nick, even if I petitioned my knees, they still wouldn't move. I'm cursed with my own inertia. Nick, all my revolutions bloom and rot in my mind. That's as far as they go."

"Goodbye, Rabbi."

218

"*Nick.* What will I do if Uncle decides to chase me out of my room? Where will I have to go? Better a congregation of bulldogs, goons, and delinquents, than nothing at all. And if I should provoke Uncle now, I'll lose the toilet seat and everything else. Who wants a corrupted rabbi? Rosencrantz the renegade. Nick."

"Rabbi, goodbye."

Even from the stairway I could see the blanket riding the Rabbi's knee. I banged into the railing. I groaned, but it wasn't because of the pain. Revolutions. Bombs. Our whole scheme seemed insane. We needed Crazy on our side. I resurrected Crazy and envisioned him battling the Jailers and the bulldogs, spilling blood for the Wolfman's sake. What ever happened to Frannie Faye?

Rubin and the Jailers were sitting on the porch. Shadrach was with them. Billingsgate maneuvered his left leg capably, and I tripped and landed in Rubin's lap. Shadrach eyed me sadly for a moment and then growled. Billingsgate chuckled to himself and slapped his knees. "Rubin," he said, "looks like you got yourself a little ol' sugar baby." I stood up, trying to flex my knees gracefully. Billingsgate tripped me again. This time I tumbled over Shadrach and caught my nose in the mesh of the screen door.

"Leave him alone," Rubin said.

I shambled down the porch stairs, my arms flailing miserably. Billingsgate called after me. "Hey, Commander, Commander. Tell your boys the Wolfman sends his regards." Turning halfway, I saw him slap the neck of his stick against his palm. "Only it's in kike, and Benny boy will have to do a little translating. Rubin, what's the word? *Meshugah.* Stiff. Batzo. Commander, the peanut brain is climbing the walls. He don't go for Uncle's cage. Tell Benny boy. We already got a welcoming committee for him in case he's thinking about springing the stoop."

219

I wanted to charge up the steps and batter the Jailers, but I sniffled instead and walked over to the barrack. Billingsgate kept shouting. "Hey, Commander, get this. Uncle's thinking of hiring out the Wolfman. For the county freak show." His rumbling laugh seemed to shake the lawn. I hurled imaginary bombs at all of them. Shadrach, too. My shadow toppled over the door of the barrack. I raised one shoulder and already felt transformed. I entered the barrack a completely potted and fully bloomed insurrectionist.

Thick bales of smoke rose behind the door. The boys were sitting on the Wolfman's cot. All of them had cigarettes in their mouths. Larry Farbovich looked a little green. Benny was holding my tobacco pouch.

"Where's the *Rebbe?*" Notte said crossly, the tip of his cigarette curling towards his nose.

"The Rabbi has his own problems," I said, charging through the smoke. I heard the Keeper cough.

"*Jesus Christ.* Benny, take it away from him. Do you want him to choke up his lungs?" The Keeper smoked defiantly and stifled his cough.

"Notte," I said. "Bring out the bombs. We're moving now. The bastards are assembled on the porch."

"*Screw,*" Notte said, his cigarette contorting like an eel with an electric eye. "Nobody moves without Benny's okay. The bombs stay in the crapper."

Benny dangled the pouch. The Wolfman's cot sagged nervously and seemed ready to cave in.

"Benny. I just saw the Jailer. The Wolfman's cracking up. How long do you think he can last upstairs? I know. They're expecting us to make a move. But if I sneak a few bombs inside the porch, I think I can smoke all of them out. And then. . . ." The boys glared at me.

"Benny," Notte said. "Don't trust him. He's a fink. He'll

220

take the bombs and use 'em on us. He's one of Uncle's jocks. *Him.*"

I marched behind the gate. "What the hell do I have to do to prove to you that I'm on your side."

"Turn to shit," Notte said simply. "Turn to shit."

I stayed behind the gate. Bullets funneled his hands over his mouth and blew smoke rings with enormous wiggling bodies across the barrack. I watched the smoke rings float easily over the cots. Benny turned his back. His narrow shoulders and wrinkled skullcap seemed to censure me. I was going to demand back my tobacco pouch. I think I fell asleep.

Pebbles and the Rabbi were standing under the door. I noticed them first. The Rabbi was wearing his Seabee cap and a denim jacket. The sleeves barely reached his elbows. Pebbles was carrying two boxes and a duffel bag. The Rabbi knocked shyly on one of the lopsided jambs. The boys turned around.

"Two recruits," the Rabbi said. "We came to join the revolution." His eyes seemed a bit foggy, and the edge of his beard hooked unevenly. Pebbles remained close to the Rabbi. "Nick, how could I abandon you and the boys? The Rabbi donates his toilet seat to the Home. His place is here. What can Uncle do to me? I'm already dispossessed. Pebbles, my fortifier. Please."

The Janitor reached into the duffel bag and removed a dented watering can and a mug with a broken handle. He tipped the can and a colorless, bubbly liquid poured noisily into the mug. "*Shalom,*" the Rabbi said, and drank from the mug. "You think Benny is the only chemist here? Distilled potato juice with a little pepper and corn starch. Pebbles' own mixture. Manufactured in Uncle's kitchen. Better than rye. A hundred times over. How else could I overcome my natural inertia?" He drank again, and this time some of the potato

221

juice dripped down his chin and clotted his beard. "Boys, the revolution."

Notte frowned at the Rabbi and the mug. "There ain't gonna be no revolution. The Commander queered everything. He's been jocking for Uncle since he came here and now he's trying to cover it up by putting the finger on Matches. And the little creep ain't even around to defend himself."

"What?" the Rabbi said, the mug shaking in his hand.

"The Commander says Matches is Uncle's personal pigeon. *Rebbe*, if you wanna let him put the blinder on you that's your business, but I know Matches ain't no spy."

"Notte," the Rabbi said. "It's the truth. Matches. He is." The Rabbi gripped the mug with both hands and held it near his chest like a chalice. "A spy."

"Rabbi," I said. "You knew it all the time? And you told the boys about the Maccabees and let them storm the Dungeon. Rabbi, they never had a chance. And you knew it."

The Rabbi pounded his chest with the mug. "I told you before. Expect nothing from this rabbi. He's the lowest of the low. Notte, save your accusations. I'm the fink here." The potato juice splashed over his denim jacket. Pebbleby loosened the Rabbi's fingers and took the mug away from him. "Mama told me all about the little school she and Dobrilubov were running together. After all, at one time I had a little power over her." The Rabbi tried to wink, but his lashes caught, and the eye refused to open. "Notte, don't be upset. We're all spies of a sort. But most of us usually end up betraying ourselves. Notte. . . ."

"Benny," Notte said. "Throw 'em all out. The *Rebbe*, the Commander, and the Janitor. One bomb, Benny, and I'll bring back the Wolfman myself."

"Notte, the Rabbi came to redeem himself. Why shouldn't he be his own deliverer? Who else would be willing to undertake the job? Notte, I came to help. Don't deny me now." The Rabbi's jagged face formed a patchwork of broken lines in the dim light of the barrack. His huge, fleshless hands seemed to retract. "*Notte.*"

Notte's glare gradually softened, and he stared at the Rabbi pityingly. "*Rebbe*, it ain't just a speech? *Matches?* The little Jap. We'll save a bomb for him. The Phantom don't forget."

"Notte. The boy can't be blamed. Mama worked on him for half a year. She wound him through a whole world of persecutions and complexes. I'm familiar with her procedure. She convinced him that by working for Uncle he would actually be protecting the other boys. *'Eliot, you know that the boys all have your own malady. They're set on destroying themselves. Let's help them. Let's make sure that they don't damage their minds and their young bodies. Let's—'* "

"*Duce*," Notte said, turning to me, "you can have the bombs now. All you want. I'm with you, Duce. I'm ready to go."

"Go?" the Rabbi said, "where?"

"Me and the Duce are attacking the porch."

"Idiots," the Rabbi said, the lines on his face now converging erratically and forming irregular bands. "The Jailers will skin you alive. And what can Benny's bombs do against the bulldogs? They have ironclad noses. No, today is out of the question. None of us will ever reach the Dungeon. And Boris will rot inside." The Rabbi raised one hand. "Tomorrow. Tomorrow we will attack. And we won't stop with Boris. A tremor is not enough. We need an earthquake. If we allow Uncle to keep control, we'll all end up as his victims. And there will be no other opportunities for us to break Uncle's yoke. No, first we will free Boris and then we will take over the Home." The Rabbi pointed to the duffel bag and the two boxes. "Pebbles has already raided the kitchen. We have enough food for a month."

Notte stared suspiciously at the Janitor. "I don't trust the creep. How do you know he ain't a counterspy? Maybe he's jocking for Uncle in reverse?"

"Notte. Pebbles is with us. Do you think he enjoys his servitude under Uncle? *No.* And Notte, who has the time to answer your accusations? We have a revolution on our hands. Boys, when we start something, who knows where it will end? That's the trouble. One bomb can shatter the universe, if it is thrown in the right direction. What will happen when we take over the Home? Only God knows. Uncle will call in the Rangers and the National Guard, and we will all end up in Sing Sing. Boys, we have to reform Uncle. That's the only way. We need a manifesto. A declaration of aims. No more skullcaps. No more war scares. No more drills. No more stinking sandwiches. Mama, Rubin, the goons, and the bulldogs will all have to go. Each Company will have its own autonomy. We will regulate ourselves. No more reveille. No more Dungeon. We will accept nothing less than a total reformation."

"*Rebbe*," Notte said. "How do you know Uncle's gonna accept your manifesto?"

"Uncle's not a dope. And what choice will he have? We'll already be in power."

Larry began coughing again. "*Rebbe*," he said dimly, his eyes choked with smoke. "*Rebbe.* When are we gonna take over?"

"Tomorrow," the Rabbi said. "Tomorrow. Tomorrow."

18

Larry threw up in the middle of the night. The Rabbi cooked some dried leaves in the pot that Benny had used to prepare the bombs, and then fed them to the Keeper. The leaves had a magical effect. The Keeper clutched one of the Wolfman's wooden troops and immediately fell into a deep sleep. The Rabbi kept the rest of us awake.

"Tell me," he said. "What was Kropotkin—a revolutionist? No, he was a maker of maps. And Bronstein, that little Ukranian Yid. *My Trotsky*. What would have been my fate with him? He despised anarchists. I would have upset his architecture." I was ready to plug the Rabbi's mouth with Notte's wrinkled skullcap, but that would never have put an end to his polemics. "His inspired geometry. Was the Master interested in people? Only in forces. What was history to him? A *parallelogram*. Lev Davidovich, the Rabbi is interested in thirty Jewish boys from the East Bronx. Let history take care of itself. Pebbles, please. Some potato juice." And then the Rabbi began working on his manifesto. But in a few minutes his chin was already somewhere in his lap. "Notte," the Rabbi said dreamily, "wake me at five. . . ."

Notte finally blew out the candles. His worn heels rocked the floorboards. Bullets slept with Benny, and the Rabbi was assigned the Wolfman's cot. Notte huddled over him, and covered the Rabbi's legs with his own blanket. Pebbles was supposed to sleep with me. The mattress creaked under us. The bed began to pitch. I decided to sleep on my commode. Its bumpy rim kept me awake for a little while.

I could see the lumpy outlines of the boys' cots. Benny's candle revived for a moment. A wisp of smoke rose over the cots and seemed to kiss the shoulders and backsides of the boys. Omens. A benevolent sign. The smoke ignored the Rabbi, and I became gloomy again. I contemplated abandoning the Rabbi, the boys, and the Home. What could I do? Where would I go? Lipshitz-Lapucci. I decided to stick with the boys. The Janitor talked in his sleep. "Rabbi's gonna put in a few grievances for me," he said, the mattress rocking under him. "No more food deliveries. No more. . . ." I think I dreamed of Father Finnocchino's dwarfs.

Notte woke me. "It's after seven," he said. "The Rabbi's cracking up." The commode loomed behind me. I had ended up sleeping on the floor. The Rabbi martialed us with shouts and curses. "Dummies. I say five and he wakes me at seven. This is the way to start a revolution? Pack, pack." I wore Crazy's hat over my skullcap. We inspected our bombs and then assembled near the door. Notte left first. "All clear," he said. "All clear." The Indian followed him. Then Larry, Benny, Pebbles, Bullets, and me. The Rabbi was last. We all waited behind the barrack. "Remember," the Rabbi said. "As soon as Rubin blows the *shofar*, get on your guard."

226

We heard the porch door slam. The Rabbi's ears perked instantly. "Notte," he said, "find out." Notte leaned his head expertly over the edge of the barrack. "It's the Marine," he said. "The bulls are with him." We froze against the barrack wall.

"*Rebbe*, do you think the dogs will sniff us out?"

The Rabbi held up one finger brazenly. "No. The wind is with us. But with those cockeyed dogs, you can never tell."

"Oh, oh," Notte said. "*Rubin*. He's got the horn, *Rebbe*. He's lifting it."

Rubin's bleats rocked the barrack. The Rabbi calmed us down. "Let him blow. Let him blow."

The Marine began counting cadence. Notte reported back to us. "A Company's coming out. Matches. Jap, Jap. Rubin's bringing over B and C. Denny Spitzer is limping."

"Notte," the Rabbi said. "Just the essentials, please. Where's Uncle? And Mama? And the other goon? And Shadrach? We don't make a move before Shadrach shows up."

"Shad's with Rubin, *Rebbe*. Now Mama's coming out. With Uncle. But the Jailer ain't around. *Rebbe*, Uncle don't look so good. He's holding on to Mama's arm. He keeps stopping, *Rebbe*. *Rebbe*, you think Uncle just had a stroke?"

"Not yet, Notte. Wait. When he sees us, then he'll have his stroke. Notte, reveille will be over in a minute. Where's the goon?"

I could see Notte's back tense. "*Rebbe*, he's coming out. The Jailer. He's smoking a cigarette. The stick is in his pocket. It keeps jumping. He's walking behind Mama and Uncle. He touched Mama's tush. Uncle didn't see."

The Rabbi steadied his shoulders against the wall and sucked in some air. Then he put on his skullcap, arranging its blocklike roof: the pompon defied the wind. "Boys," he said, "it's time. Notte, lead the charge. To the porch. To the porch." He raised his head skyward. "*Shma Yisroel*. Now."

Like a band of demented sprites, we charged across the lawn. The bombs kept juggling in my pockets. I almost lost Crazy's hat. The Rabbi cautioned us. "Don't look back." I heard the bulldogs bark. Uncle groaned.

The Indian reached the porch first. Then Notte and Benny. The Janitor's bouncing duffel bag blinded my view. He had dropped one of the boxes. I tripped over the box and lost Crazy's hat. I saw the Rabbi reach the porch, and then I crawled after the hat.

"Nick," the Rabbi shouted. "Nick." His face was behind the screen; the wire pocked his cheeks. "Nick, give them the business. A bomb, a bomb." The boys clustered around the Rabbi. My arms were numb. I managed to remove one of the bombs. Notte kept motioning to me. "Duce, pull out the plug. The plug. That's the only way to release the stink."

I removed the twisted plug and then tossed the tin can. Nothing happened. "A dud," Notte cried, "a dud." Benny's shoulders sank behind the screen. I saw the Rabbi rock his head.

"The dog, Nick, the dog."

I turned around and stared at Shadrach's snout. Rubin and the Jailers were running towards us. The other two bull-dogs were behind them. Uncle was sitting on the ground. Mama kept fanning him. The boys in the other Companies broke ranks. Their skullcaps glared and bobbed in the morning sun and formed crooked constellations. Shadrach performed for Rubin and the boys: he growled with great clamor and circled me twice. "Hold him, Shad," Rubin said. "Hold him." I put on Crazy's hat and pulled the brim over one eye. Shad-rach withdrew his snout and stared at me: the hat transfixed him in some strange way. Maybe he thought I had been made the head Screw again. His sense of allegiance was obviously all fouled up. He looked once at Rubin and then at me, and then howled shamelessly. I heard the tin can hiss. A burst of

228

green smoke shot over my head. Rubin and the Jailers retreated. "God," I said, squeezing my nose. Notte and the Indian helped me onto the porch. We watched the smoke invade
the lawn. Notte hugged the screen.

"Boys," the Rabbi said, "barricade the doors. Front and
back. Who knows when they will become immune to the
stink?"

"Rabbi," I said, pointing to the ceiling. "The Wolfman,
the Wolfman."

The Rabbi's pinched cheeks wore a pained look. "Nick,"
he said, tilting his enormous jaw. "Take Benny. Go."

We ran up the stairs, Benny and I, the banisters trembling
in our wake. We ripped at the bolts and forced open the Dungeon door. "Boris," I said, "Boris." The Wolfman was sitting
in Uncle's box, his knees near his chin. The screened walls of
the pen cast speckled shadows on the Wolfman's hunched
body. He was playing with one of his shoes. His skullcap was
stuffed under his belt, and his frazzled hair clung to his ears.
The pen was locked. "Maybe Pebbles has the key." We
dragged the pen out of the Dungeon. The light from the stairway probed the furrows under the Wolfman's eyes and exposed the welts on his arms. *Bill's work.* We stared into the
pen. There was a hornlike turd in the Wolfman's shoe. The
floor of the pen was littered with wads of urine-soaked paper.
The Wolfman looked at us and then clapped his hands furiously and tried to force some sort of crazy rhythm from them.
I was sure he was invoking the genie of the Dungeon, and I
expected toads or bats to fly out of his hands. Instead, he sang
for us:

> *Potsche, potsche kichelach*
> *Gott vet koifen shichelach*

We carried the pen down the stairs. Notte met us on the second floor.

229

"Uncle's in the classroom."

I looked at him.

"*Rebbe*, I mean, *Rebbe*."

Notte helped us bring the pen into the classroom. The bombs were scattered on the desks. The Rabbi, the Indian, and the Keeper stood near the window. Their backs were pressed together.

"Where's Bullets and Pebbles?"

"They're guarding the doors."

The Rabbi turned around. He saw the Wolfman in Uncle's box. "Nick, tell me, who can be a rabbi in these times? Should I cherish my God when all the evidence in front of me not only denies his existence but also his name. Let the Cabalists find holiness in every act. Who knows? Maybe Boris in his cage is working out God's will in a cockeyed way. But why should I even bother maligning God's name. Let him exist or not exist, he's already out of the picture. None of us deserves a God. The whole tribe stinks. After all, the evil in this world didn't come from another planet. Hitler roasts Jews today, maybe tomorrow the Arabs will be out of fashion. Nick, what can I do? I still believe in all the mysteries. I should have been a conjurer, not a rabbi." The Rabbi smiled grimly, like a sinister jack-of-spades. "Nick, I'm cracking up. The war is on and the Rabbi needs his soliloquies. Benny. Notte, *somebody*, please, take Boris out of the cage."

"Rabbi," I said, "it's locked. Maybe Pebbles has the key."

The Rabbi sent Notte after the key. Then he approached the pen. "Boris. Don't worry. You'll have company soon. Uncle will find a cage for all of us."

The Keeper raised his hands. "Uncle's under the window."

The Indian grabbed a bomb.

"Wait, wait," the Rabbi said, and we all collected near

230

the window. Uncle stood near the porch. Mama and the two Jailers supported him. Rubin was behind them, leaning on his knees. Shadrach was with them. The other Companies were still on the lawn. I noticed Matches among them. A few of the boys were tossing their skullcaps. The Marine's two bulldogs held them all at bay. Shadrach saw Crazy's hat and began howling again. Lumps formed on his thick, armored coat, and his enormous snout dragged along the ground. Uncle shouted up at us.

"It's his fault. Him with the hat. Not Benny, not the Rabbi, *him*. That imposter, that fraud." I moved away from the window. "Him. Do you think I couldn't have dealt with Benny's uprisings and the Rabbi's complaints? That bastard upset the balance. Boys, listen to me. Your Commander, Lipshitz, is a total fraud. He's a *goy*, a *goy*, a guinea spy. He doesn't belong here. He never did. His name is Lapucci, not Lipshitz. Nick. Nick. I befriended him, I took him in, and how did he repay me? With thistles and thorns. He betrayed me. All of us. Benny, Bullets, Rabbi, Notte, Farbovich, for God's sake, give him up. Yes, that goy can afford to ruin us. What does it mean to him? He'll crawl back inside his own hellhole. But Rabbi, boys, where will you go without the Home? Guinea goy. Nazi. Come downstairs. Rabbi. Boys."

I heard Notte shout from the ground floor. "Screw, Uncle, screw."

Uncle now petitioned the Rabbi. "Rosencrantz, I charge you. Cause all the mischief you want, stay with the goy, but first bring down the boys. Rabbi, do you know what will happen when I make my report to the Rabbinical Council? You will be grounded permanently. No more pulpits, Rabbi. Maybe the Japs can use an extra preacher. Rabbi, remember. You've lost your immunity. The Army knows what to do with unfrocked rabbis. You'll be loading cannons and shoveling

231

shit. Rabbi. . . ." Uncle's voice gave. He coughed fitfully. The Jailers released Uncle's arms and smiled to themselves. The sun bleached their faces. Shadrach kept howling.

"Rabbi," I said guiltily. "Now's the time. The manifesto, Rabbi."

"Nick," the Rabbi said, patting the pockets of his denim jacket. "I left it in the barrack."

I approached the window tentatively. "Rabbi, say something. Answer his charges."

The Rabbi leaned his head out of the window. The wind lashed his skullcap and hurled it skyward. We watched the skullcap spin frantically and then pause suddenly in midair, its pompon still wiggling, and plunge to the ground near Uncle's feet. The Rabbi clutched his head with one hand, and then began to sing: *"Yisgadal v'yiskadash shma rabbo. . . ."*

Benny noticed my puzzled looks.

"It's *Kaddish*," he said. "The prayer for the dead."

The Rabbi's shoulders began to hop. Benny and the Keeper enforced the Rabbi's melody, their shoulders bobbing in rhythm to his words. Even the Indian sang. I took off Crazy's hat, and bracing my skullcap against the wind, I began to sing with the Rabbi and the boys. My shoulders responded automatically. Shadrach stopped howling. He stared at my skullcap for a moment and then growled at the Rabbi and me; somehow, he must have understood that he had been duped. Uncle heard the Rabbi's prayer and revived immediately. I saw him shake his fists. "Maniacs."

The Rabbi paused in the middle of his prayer and shouted down to Uncle. "Nathanson, I say *Kaddish* for every lost soul in this world. I mourn for the living and for the dead. I mourn especially for you. You are a walking dead man."

"Shut him up," Uncle said. "Shut him up."

"Nathanson, you wanted to build your own Jerusalem in the wilderness, and you imported your little Jewish pioneers

232

for that purpose. Delinquents from the Bronx. You wanted a new tribe of Judah, away from the Gentiles. A little separate Jewish estate. But you controlled your fantasies and obeyed the laws. You couldn't keep your pioneers with you forever. You knew it. Yes, the incompetents, the stragglers, the morons, the weak ones stayed on, and the others you shipped back to the Gentiles. But you didn't have to worry. They were already incorruptible. Sainted Jewish knights. Safe even among the Gentiles. You. . . ."

Uncle's knuckles gleamed in the sun. "Rabbi, Sing Sing, Rabbi. You and the goy. The boys I'll deal with in my own way."

The Indian was becoming restless: he wanted to fling his bombs. I turned around. The Wolfman held a turd in his hand. I had forgotten to put a few of his soldiers in the Rabbi's duffel bag. Notte was behind the pen. "*Rebbe*," he said, "the Janitor can't open the box. Rubin has the only key."

The Rabbi saw the turd. "Boris. Are you making us an offering? We could all use a little *dreck*. Farbovich, stay near the cage. Keep him company. Nick, we have to give Uncle a little credit." He pointed to the turd. "Would they allow this in a state hospital? Boris, play."

I heard the Marine's bulldogs bark. Matches had broken away from his Company and was running across the lawn. His skullcap bobbed and flared. Notte approached the window. "Bastard," he said, "bastard." Matches dodged between the Jailers and tumbled in front of the porch. "Benny," he said, "lemme through." He was crying. "I belong upstairs." Mama was behind him. Her elbow grazed his skullcap. "Lemme." He searched the window for some welcoming sign. What could I do? Wave to him and tell him to come up? The boys would have used their bombs on me. Ashamed, I turned my head away. The Rabbi followed suit.

Notte didn't wait for Benny's approval. He arched his

233

back and called down to Matches. "Join the Japanese Army." His shoulder blades bristled fiercely. "Lousy screw. Nip. Jap. Suck Mama's left tit. Jap. Jap. Jap. Jap." Matches recoiled. Notte's words cleaved to him, and he crawled towards the porch, his elbows tucked under him. He looked up once. Was he staring at the Rabbi or at me? "Jap. Jap."

"Enough, Notte," I said. "Enough." We all looked down again. Matches had disappeared. "Where'd he go?" the Indian asked. Notte threw a bomb. It exploded in midair, and the green smoke sent Uncle's party scurrying back across the lawn. The Rabbi closed the window. The Keeper was already coughing. "Balls," Notte said. The smoke cleared slowly. One of the bulldogs had become asphyxiated. He lay on the ground, his legs and belly writhing. Was it Shadrach? I couldn't tell. Notte saluted himself. "Victim number one." Benny watched the dog. I scanned the lawn. Matches was still missing. "Maybe the bomb got the Jap too," Notte said. "*Rebbe, Rebbe,* if all the bombs operate like this one, we'll be in business for months. *Rebbe,* for months."

"*Rabbi.*" We all turned around. The Janitor stood near the door. He was balancing six apples against his chest. "Bullets. The back door. Gone. He left the barricade."

"I knew it," Notte said. "Once a creep, always a creep. I knew we couldn't trust him. I'll bet he's in the Bronx by now. Futzing his sister. *Bullets.*" Somehow, I couldn't begrudge Bullets his escape. I hoped he would make it back to Charlotte Street. Who knows? Maybe I saw my own lot bound up in some way with his. Bullets and me. Notte motioned to the Indian. "Downstairs. Guard the back door."

The Indian rebelled. "I ain't no sentry," he said, squinting casually with one eye. "Send somebody else."

"Wait, wait," the Rabbi said. "Where's the fire? Farbovich, watch the window. Let me know if they make a move."

Pebbles passed out the apples.

"Rabbi," Notte said. "We ain't gonna be able to keep up no revolution on this diet. We were better off under Uncle's whip."

"Notte, wait until the storm quiets down. Then we'll raid the kitchen. It will be bacon and eggs for all of us."

We sat and munched the apples. The Indian began sniffing. "Something's spooky. I don't like it." He walked over to the door. "Smoke," he said. "I smell smoke." Notte and I ran into the hall. We saw the smoke rise leisurely from the ground floor and spill through the banister rails. "Matches," Notte said. "Revenge. He set us on fire." We ran back to the classroom. "Rabbi, we're on fire. Matches did it."

The smoke groped through the hallway, bumping the walls, and finally reached our room.

"Boys," the Rabbi said. "We'll have to abandon ship. The revolution is over."

Benny remained near the window. "I'm staying here."

"Me too," Notte said. "Me too. I ain't tasting the Jailer's stick no more. Not Notte." The Indian, of course, stuck with them. The Keeper clutched the Rabbi's denim jacket. Pebbles had already run out the door.

The Wolfman gripped the walls of the pen. "Benja, Benja," he said. "*Hais.*"

"Benny," the Rabbi said. "Are you going to leave him here in the box to choke and die? Benny, the hell with causes and revolutions. Boys, believe me, we'll all survive the Jailers. Let's go."

Benny scowled, but he moved away from the window. The Indian and I lifted the pen. The Keeper tried to shoo away the smoke. "Balls," Notte said. The Rabbi groaned.

ᵈᵈ CHAPTER ᵈᵈ

19

We all escaped. We even managed to drag down the pen before the porch collapsed. Notte still had his bombs, but the Rabbi stared at our blackened faces, and surrendered us without a fight. Rubin had already organized a fire brigade, and the boys from the other Companies, still a little daffy from the green smoke, shuttled across the lawn with pails of rusty water. Uncle sat near one of the kennels, only vaguely aware of Rubin's labors. He knew the house was lost. The other conspirators were confined in A Company's barrack, but Uncle had the Marine march me past the kennels and over to the Rabbi's car. I wasn't even allowed to say goodbye to the Rabbi and my boys. "Get in," the Marine said. "If Uncle'd let me have my way, I'd shove you back into the fire." I had no possessions: only Crazy's hat. And while the house burned, the Marine chauffeured me to the Blattenburg station. "Cock," he said, shunting me out of the car. "If you ever show up here again, I'll kill you myself." And then he drove off, the Rabbi's makeshift fenders rattling.

The tiny, sandbagged fort still stood near the deserted station, its ack-ack gun intact. I managed to flag down a train, and after some minor rerouting, during which an ex-air-raid warden lectured me on the crucial differences between a blackout and a brownout, I landed in New York, in the middle of a blackout. I stayed that night at the McBurney Y, sharing a room with three sailors from Dallas. The next day I found a small apartment on 116th Street near Riverside Drive. I still had my father's annuity. And anyway, I took a part-time job in the book store across the street. Sitting on a rickety stool five mornings a week, I guarded the cash register, an open book propped slyly on one knee. I went through all of Dickens that way in less than a month. Somehow, I survived the winter.

In the spring I became a little restless. I began writing letters to Notte, Benny, and the Rabbi. I mailed all the letters in care of the Blattenburg Home, but neither the Rabbi nor the boys ever wrote back. I suspected that Uncle Nate had pocketed my letters, but what could I do? Skipping work one morning, I decided to tour the East Bronx and look for Bullets. I hailed a cab on Broadway. It took us an hour and a half to locate Charlotte Street. "Who ever goes here?" the cabby wanted to know. "Pissing gas like water during wartime." The fare was three dollars and seventy-five cents. The cabby flicked my five dollar bill. "Who can pick up a fare here? I'm going back to civilization." I told him to keep the change.

There was nothing very special about the rows of rusty fire escapes on Charlotte Street, except for the fact that the fire escapes themselves served as parlors, toilets, and playpens.

237

A little girl on my side of the street leaned against the rail and peed down from the third floor, her pearlike buttocks gleaming under her raised skirt. The women on the fire escapes below didn't seem to mind. *"Pishekeh,"* one of them chanted, and then went back to her business. Several boys congregated outside a candy store near the fire escapes. None of the boys wore skullcaps. One of them was smoking a cigarette; he couldn't have been more than ten. Another Notte. I searched their faces for a wink or a smile, for one redeeming sign. "Bucharevsky," I said, approaching the candy store. "Does anyone know where Bullets lives?" The boys ignored me. "He has a sister. Frimke. Tell him Commander Lipshitz is looking for him. *Bullets.*" The boy with the cigarette went inside the candy store. He brought out a man with a mangled ear.

"Meyer," the boy said. "I think he's a downtown shill. One of Solotaroff's boys. What do you say?"

The man allowed me one dismal look. "Take a walk," he said. "Take a walk."

I obliged him immediately.

I didn't go on any more excursions. In fact, I roosted in my apartment most of the time. No one paid much attention to the air-raid drills that summer. We were expecting other kinds of trouble. Everybody talked about the big race riot in Detroit. There had already been some minor skirmishes in Harlem, and Kelly, the skinny paraplegic who ran the kiosk on 116th Street, had one theme: "The black bastards are gonna raid Morningside Heights, you'll see. A white ass won't be worth a cent in this neighborhood." I believed him. Then, on the last day of July, the trouble came. A policeman shot a Negro soldier, and that night Negro rioters looted half of Harlem. I slept through the holocaust, but the next morning Mayor La Guardia announced over the radio that citizens in

238

the areas surrounding Harlem should remain calm: there had been no race riot. "Just hoodlums," the Mayor said. "Hoodlums." I ran downstairs for a paper. Kelly's kiosk was closed. But I saw him sitting inside, behind his boarded window.

"Nick," he said, "are the jigs in the street?"

"Kelly, there's nobody around. The riot's over. The Mayor was just on the radio. He says it was all the work of hoodlums."

"My ass," Kelly said. "Don't tell me. It was a revolution. I heard it all last night. Sitting here. Like the end of the world. Nick, the jigs have taken over. It was a phony broadcast. The jigs made him do it. Nick, for Chris' sake, stay off the street."

I left Kelly inside the kiosk. I started walking towards 125th Street. Revolution. I was frightened, and intrigued. I didn't want to go back to my rooms. Revolution. I paused at 125th Street: it seemed like a magical border line. The stores on the other side of the street had been raided and looted, their windows smashed. An uprooted barber's chair sat in the gutter, near a plate of broken glass. Rolls of toilet paper were piled on the chair. Only one of the stores had been spared. A tiny laundry. The words "Colored Man Only" were scrawled on a cardboard sign in the window. I crossed the street. A Negro soldier inside a bar near Old Broadway hailed me. "Hey," he said. "You. You." The bar was unusually dark. I saw myself being victimized a hundred times over. Was the soldier one of the raiders? Was he the head of a band? There was a sign in the window. Same words. "Colored Man Only." But the window had still been smashed. *You. You.* I went inside.

The soldier bought me a drink. His name was McKenna. I told him mine. "I was with the Nigger 92nd," he said. "Trained in Georgia. Took us down by bus. Don't train no black troops up here. Don't give a damn. Had our own Nigger

Army. But shit, man. You think they let us see any action? We laundry soldiers, that's all. Just came back from the ETO. Dover. In England. Had our own Nigger canteen. Don't tell me no bull about the Red Cross. Motherjumpers. How come they make black and white service clubs? I ask Chaplain. He say, 'Boy, the President is doin' his best. He take care of us. You see.' Chaplain, all he good for is suckin' white ass. Nick, you a Marine?"

"No," I said. "*No*. I was never in the service."

"Good. The Old Man say Japs subhuman. Nips. Yellow-bellies. But what he say about us when he with the other brass? Blackbellies. Nigras. Okay, Japs are motherjumpers, but don't tell me nothin' about yellow. Skin is skin. When a black soldier need blood, he gotta go to the Nigger blood bank. They don't allow him no white blood. Too precious. Shit, man. You ever give yoh blood, Nick?"

"No," I said. "I'm a little anemic."

"Good. You save that stuff, hear? You get a little healthier. Maybe you eat some black meat. Then you take yoh ass down Nigger blood bank."

He bought me another drink. I became a little bolder and asked him about the riots.

"Shit, man," he said, his eyes darkening. "You one of them travelin' dicks?" I assured him that I wasn't. "You know Detroit. They breakin' black ass everywhere. In the Army. Out the Army. Overseas. Everywhere. And we gonna do a little assbreakin' sometime too. But this was local, man. Local." I could tell. He was still a little suspicious. "I had nothin' to do with it, man. I been sitting here all this time. This was nothin'. You know, man. Spot attacks. Tickled the Yid pawnbrokers, that's all. Next time we gonna organize. You see. We gonna work up a Nigger division. I give you my card, man. Nobody touch you. You all right." He turned around abruptly.

240

"House, House, where the john? I gotta leak." I watched him shuffle towards the rear, his head bobbing lightly. Then I left the bar and walked up Old Broadway.

There was a dumpy synagogue in the middle of the block. The stores flanking the synagogue had been looted—the words "Ikey Kikey Jew" were smeared across one awning—but the synagogue itself had not been touched. The enameled windows, the crooked signboard, the pockmarked door, the brassy ornaments, and the one dinky Star of David were all intact. A man wearing a blocklike skullcap and a black caftan stood on the steps of the synagogue. The caftan hugged his bony knees and rode his shoulders like a spook's shroud. He was smoking a cigarette. He looked up, and I noticed his wild, ungroomed beard. Our eyes met. *Rabbi*. Rabbi Rosencrantz. We embraced each other in the middle of the street. The Rabbi blew his nose. We were both crying.

I didn't waste any time on preliminaries. "*Rebbe*," I said. "How are the boys?"

He looked at me dully, his beard raking the buttons on his caftan.

"Rabbi . . . Benny? Notte? The Wolfman?"

"Oh," the Rabbi said. "Oh." I could see his jaw flex under his beard. "Nick, who knows? Like Arabs. They're scattered all over the land. Notte is in one reform school. Benny is in another. The Wolfman they put away."

"Put away?" I said, already aware of the Rabbi's intent. *Boris. Boris.* I remembered him behind the screen. Uncle's box. Clap hands. *Potsche, potsche kichelach.*

"An institution," the Rabbi said, checking my reverie. "Could I fight the courts? Who would listen to me?"

"What happened to the Home?"

The Rabbi sucked his cigarette. "Home? Nick, they wouldn't allow Uncle money for another house. And how

241

could he manage from the barracks? A few inspectors came. From Albany. And they took the boys away. Two days later Uncle dropped dead. Thrombosis they said. Who knows." My fault. My fault.

"Nick, don't put all the blame on our little putsch. What we did we had to do. And Nick, maybe we lost the war, but the revolution was still a success. All right, the Home was destroyed in the process, but what can you do? Nick, after you left, Uncle told me, 'Rabbi, pack your belongings. I'm shipping you out.' But talk is talk. He let me stay on. And the boys? He locked them up for a day, and then he merged them with B Company. Notte, the Wolfman. The whole troupe. And Uncle banished Rubin's drills right away. It's true, he kept on the goons. And the Jailer used his stick on occasions, but it was better than before. Nick, what's the use of talking? How long did the reformation last? Two weeks. The inspectors came right after you left. And then, no more Home."

"Rabbi," I said. "What happened to Mama?"

"Mama? She took off with the Jailer. Bill."

"And the Janitor?"

"Pebbles? Would I leave him stranded? I brought him back with me. I forged a few documents and made up my own recommendations, and I ended up here. In Harlem. The last outpost of the Jews. And Pebbles is now the janitor of the synagogue. It was written into my contract. Otherwise I would never have accepted the job." The Rabbi curtsied, holding the hem of his caftan. "Nick, look at me. No more a revolutionist. The Rabbi has retreated into orthodoxy."

"Rabbi," I said. "The synagogue. Is it for black Jews?"

He smiled politely, trying to control the cigarette. "No, no. That's downtown. Near Lenox. They have their own jurisdiction. But don't worry, I have Seventh Day Adventists

242

and Abyssinian Baptists up here for my sermons. And occasionally a Holy Roller. They all come in wearing skullcaps. The Rabbi hasn't lost his form." He winked at the shattered glass in the street, the pouch under his left eye wrinkling superbly. "Why do you think we were spared? The synagogue has already become a shrine."

The Rabbi's cigarette burned unevenly; his beard was cluttered with ashes. "*Rebbe*, since when do you smoke?"

"Nervousness," the Rabbi said. "Nervousness. I need something in my mouth. Oral satisfaction. Mama knows. And besides, it goes well with my uniform."

One of the enameled windows behind us opened with a squeak. Someone called to the Rabbi. "*Rosencrantz. Rosencrantz.*" The cigarette hopped in the Rabbi's mouth.

"Nick, it's the president of the synagogue. He was stranded here last night. He's still afraid to come out. What can I do? They made me the watchman. I'm on the day and night shift. But I can't complain. My president has a daughter, tits galore. And a bankbook to go with the boobs. But I think the Rabbi has lost his appetite." He blocked the edges of his skullcap with his palm. "Nick, come around again. Any time. I'm always here. *Shalom*, Nick. I have to go."

"*Shalom.*" He was already on the top step. "*Rebbe?*"

He turned around. Under the glint cast off by the dinky star of David, the Rabbi's beard seemed slightly ravaged.

"*Rebbe*, Rubin, *Rebbe*. What happened to Rubin?"

He paused. "Rubin? Who knows. He was still in one of the barracks when I left." And then the Rabbi was gone.

I stayed outside the synagogue for a little while, making promises to myself. Somehow, I would get in touch with the boys. I would scour every reform school in the country. There was a broken coffee pot in the street. Probably left by one of the raiders. Not worthy enough to be taken as booty. Its snout was missing, but its loosely hinged lid and old fashioned body reminded me a little of a tabernacle. I wondered what it contained. I picked up the pot. The lid came off. Only coffee grounds and bits of glass. I put the pot on the steps of the synagogue. And then I left Old Broadway and walked home.

❧ ABOUT THE AUTHOR ❧

Jerome Charyn is twenty-seven years old and the author of the critically praised novel ONCE UPON A DROSHKY. *Mr. Charyn lives in New York and has published short stories in* COMMENTARY *and* MADEMOISELLE. *He is currently at work on a play and his third novel.*